One Soft, Snowy Night

"Aurora."

He kissed her. It was a long kiss, filled with smoldering passion, and she shuddered with emotion as he brushed his fingertips across her cheek. Then his lips traveled slowly downward to her neck, lingering on her collarbone. Her eyes closed and Aurora gave herself up to the exquisite sensations that swept through her body until they reached the center of her passion. As she bent her head back, a small moan escaped her.

Aurora raised her lips to his. Again their bodies melted together as they kissed passionately.

"I must have you," he whispered . . .

D1424497

KATHRYN ATWOOD

Aurora

JOVE BOOKS, NEW YORK

AURORA

A Jove Book / published by arrangement with
the author

PRINTING HISTORY
Jove edition / October 1987

ISBN: 0-515-09260-6

Jove Books are published by The Berkley Publishing Group,
200 Madison Avenue, New York, NY 10016.
The name ''JOVE'' and the ''J'' logo
are trademarks belonging to Jove Publications, Inc.

PRINTED IN THE UNITED STATES OF AMERICA

10 9 8 7 6 5 4 3 2 1

To Madge,

who remembers the story
of a silver seal,
and who made the challenge
that led to it and much more

Lovely kind, and kindly loving,
Such a mind were worth the moving;
Truly fair, and fairly true.
Where are all these but in you?

Nicholas Breton,
An Odd Conceit

I would like to thank Ms. Lindsey Fulcher,
librarian at the Museum of London,
for her kind help.

PART I

1582

1

In the partial darkness of the cavernous room the girl sat, her back propped against one of the slimy stone walls, her legs drawn up tightly in front of her, her bent arms and head resting across her knees.

She appeared as though she were asleep, but she was listening dully to the muffled noises she heard from day to day. She should have been accustomed to them by now.

From across the room, she heard the rustlings of the others as they shifted positions on their straw pallets, the handfuls of rank straw which passed as beds. The straw was never swept from the noisome room. It stank of urine, sweat, and feces, and of blood drawn by vermin from the young inhabitants.

She heard other sounds, too. Some of her companions snored in their sleep; others muttered fitfully, their words indistinct. One of the boys, she didn't know where or who he was, cried every night. She didn't know if he ever slept. The others, long accustomed to him, slept as best they could. Another boy and a girl next to him shrieked, their high-pitched voices piercingly sharp.

The girl ground the heels of her hands against her ears to stop the horrible sounds. Still, the screaming ripped through her brain. She dropped her hands. It was no use; it never was.

When the shallow light through the high window died into the darkness of night, she often heard a girl's soft laughter and a boy's low voice, too distant for her to catch the words.

Then there were more rustlings, strange sounds she couldn't identify, liquid cries and moans which made her breath catch and her face burn.

From the greyness around her, a skeletal hand snaked out, grabbing her ankle. She slapped at it, and the fingers withdrew. Every day, every night, she had to defend herself in some manner. The first time, she'd been terrified, and had screamed and kicked until the hand retreated. She knew now that she didn't have to go to that extreme, that she had only to slap or to push the hand away.

There were other sounds as well: The rasping breath of several of the room's inhabitants, a rattle welling up wetly from their lungs; the dry coughing that lasted for hours; the delirious mumblings of fevered minds. She also heard the disturbing sounds the rats made as they wandered through the room, hunting through straw, clothing, and sleeping bodies. Occasionally someone cried out, having been bitten by one of the rodents. Sometimes, she heard a sharp squeal from a rat, no doubt pinned down by one of the boys, its head smashed with a cup.

It was a nightmare existence, a terrible dream from which she prayed she would wake before too late, before she became one of these feeble, mindless things that crawled and stumbled through the fetid straw.

Tonight, as always, she prayed for her release—through death, if need be. Tonight—or was it day? She was unable to tell because the small patch of sky which showed through the window far above was a deep grey—it could either be dawn or dusk.

By listening intently to the noises around her, she had almost missed a new sound. Someone was walking down the corridor outside the room, and then she heard voices, male voices. For a moment hope sprang up inside her, but she quickly forced it away. Often she had heard these sounds when they meant nothing more than a meal. And yet . . .

The unfamiliar noises stopped outside the room. She had heard two voices this time instead of the usual offkey whistling of the jailer. Would the men pass by the door and continue on their way?

She held her breath.

A key scraped in the lock, and then the great wooden door, some five inches thick and banded with metal strips to give it even more strength, swung open with a faint groan of its unoiled hinges.

2

The girl stood up, as did several other children near her. She rubbed her eyes, then peered through the gloom to see who was there. She saw one man entering the room, while another stood outside in the hall. The second man held a torch, and some of its flickering light spilled into the room, momentarily blinding her in its intensity. She looked away, blinked, and then glanced at the man who had entered.

She could see only a silhouette, so she took a few halting steps forward. The closer she came, the more details she saw. He was tall and lean and seemed to be dressed in the fine clothes of a nobleman. Around her, the others scrambled to their feet, or sat, if they were too weak to do otherwise. All stared at the unexpected visitors.

"More light, you fool!" the first man called. The jailer hurried into the room and held aloft the blazing torch. The harsh light cast deep shadows into the corners, while the rats squeaked and scurried into crevices.

"I thought these children were to be trained," the man said as he stared at the virtual prisoners. Somewhere a girl coughed.

"Some be." The jailer offered a casual shrug as he scratched his side. "Others not be. It not be up to me to decide."

"None of them look as if they've been outside this cell since they arrived." The jailer had no opinion to give, so the man turned his attention to the children. "Form a line," he commanded harshly. The girl wondered if he always spoke thus, or if his voice reflected his horror at what he had found.

Without hesitation, the children obeyed, for this man's voice was the voice of authority. The girl brushed flakes of filthy straw from her soiled dress and matted hair, and pushed into the back line. There were many children, and the room was narrow, so they formed two rough lines.

One of her companions, a dark-haired girl with eyes as black as midnight and who slept not far from her, was arranging her ragged petticoat and tattered blue skirt around her scrawny hips. The girl realized it was the other's soft moans of pleasure she had heard earlier. Embarrassed, she glanced away.

The well-spoken man coolly surveyed the circle of silent children gathered before him. They ranged in age from two to seventeen, and all wore the remains of well-worn and ill-patched blue livery. Most were the sons and daughters of vagrants, debtors, and criminals; others were orphans, abandoned at birth or later in life, with no other place to go.

The boys and girls lived and slept together in the damp and reeking cell, for there was no room for separate accommodations. No effort was made to educate them, or to take care of them; they existed in conditions generally unfit for animals, despite the officials' boastful claim that this institution existed to help the children of London's unfortunates by training them in various trades.

The girl stared at the man, whose bland expression had not changed since they had crowded before him. If he were appalled by the unkempt hair infested with lice, the soiled and tattered clothes which scarcely covered them, the dirty faces, listless eyes, and racking coughs, he gave no sign. The children might as well have been cattle being appraised for the market.

An icy hand seemed to clamp her insides, and she sucked her breath in sharply. What manner of man was he to be so unmoved?

Perhaps he had seen too much despair in his life to be outwardly affected.

The jailer made a sharp motion, and the girl glanced his way. She had seen him before. He was more than a head shorter than the visitor and stout in stomach and body. His nose was flattened across the bridge, as if broken more than once, and a grizzled beard littered with crumbs edged his

doughy face. The condition of his clothing fared little better
than that of the young inmates, and he smelled of stale beer
and sweat.

While the stranger continued to survey the children, the
jailer kept shooting glances at him, as if he expected him to
disappear suddenly in a puff of smoke. Stepping closer to the
visitor, he held the flickering torch higher so that more light
spread throughout the room. His pallid face broke into a
ragged smile showing broken teeth.

"I'll tell ye what I know of each 'un, milord," he said, his
tone wheedling, his words practiced from prior experience.
When the man made no reply, the jailer continued. "That
'un," he pointed a long finger to the small girl who sucked
her thumb in the front line, "is scarce above ten winters. 'Er
father sold 'er for a crown, 'e did, and then bought 'imself
sour wine and puked 'imself to death. The skinny one next to
'er 'as not been 'ere long, milord; and not goin' to be long,
for she's coughin' up blood now.

"The boy behind sold 'is sister to the worst brothel in
London, after 'e got tired of usin' 'er 'imself, and then what
'e don't but end up in 'ere, milord, and 'e's a rare 'andful,
too. I've 'ad to beat 'im back several times, but o' late 'e
moves around little, and usually just sits, pissin' on 'imself. I
think there be something wrong with 'is 'ead. There's others,
milord, far more others that I've not mentioned. Of course,
milord, it all depends on what yer wantin' the child fer." The
jailer winked lewdly and made a sound like a rusty chuckle
which exploded into a wet cough.

The stranger turned his cold expression onto the jailer, who
promptly subsided and ducked his head, unable to meet the
man's stabbing look. The stranger looked away in disgust.

The jailer glanced back at the children, and after putting
the torch into a metal bracket alongside the doorway, grabbed
a girl from the front row and hauled her to the front.

"What do ye think? She be pretty once she be plumped
up." The jailer pinched one of her hollowed cheeks. Then his
hand slid down her flat chest to her hip and lingered on her
backside. She did not move. She was a particular favorite of
his, and he had often visited her. Sometimes he brought her
an extra crust of stale bread. Each time after the jailer left, the
poor child wept.

The man appraised her. She was about twelve, and her face was pale from lack of sunlight, and her eyes were clouded from pain. But there was something in them that he couldn't identify. An illness, or madness. He shook his head, and the sick girl was thrust back into the line while the jailer made another selection. This child was no more than six years of age, and she whimpered piteously as the jailer grabbed her skinny forearm.

"No."

The single crisp word was sufficient for the jailer. He returned the little girl to the others and stared up and down the line, tapping his foot as he considered the alternatives. The pickings would be more varied in the months to come as the increasingly colder weather drove the homeless children off the streets and into the prison and other institutions like Bridewell. At the moment the good selections were slim.

"Would ye be wantin' a boy?" the jailer asked hopefully. "I've several here—"

"No. I have no need of a boy."

"Ye be a 'ard one to please, milord. The others come in and pick 'em right off, boy or girl, mostly it don't matter. Sometimes they don't even leave, but use them right 'ere." He made a wet sound with his lips. "I done it meself a few times." He chuckled again. "Ah, here be one."

"No," the stranger said again, his tone equally firm. "I want to see the girl in back. The one standing all the way to the left. You *do* know which side is left, do you not?"

The jailer shot a broken smile at his visitor—surely the man was joking. Then he plunged into the lines of children. He returned, bringing the girl forward into the circle of light.

She blinked, but as she realized that the stranger was staring at her, she dropped her gaze to the filthy floor. Her face grew warm, as it had when she heard the strange cries of the girl and boy in the night. But she wondered what he wanted, and feeling no fear at that moment, she raised her eyes to meet his.

The man saw before him a girl who could have been anywhere from fourteen to eighteen. He could not be at all certain in this poor light, and God knew she might even be younger; there were plenty of *those* here.

The girl was tall for her age, almost as tall as some of the boys, and while her slender body was far too thin, it hinted at the promise of womanhood and showed that until recently she had led a healthy life. Her hair, unwashed, uncombed, and no doubt lice-ridden, seemed to be a dark reddish blond, and her green-blue eyes were fringed with black lashes. Her face was gaunt from hunger, but he saw the traces of its normal heart shape.

Her expression was fearful, but for now he could do nothing about that.

"This is the one."

"Ah, a good choice, milord," the jailer said in an oozing voice. "She be a fairly recent arrival and be in the pink yet." He reached forward to tweak her breast, but his hand was knocked away by the man.

"Don't touch her," the stranger said coldly, and the jailer retreated.

Before the girl could protest or even express surprise at having been selected—selected for what? she wondered uneasily—she was dragged outside the cell into the dingy corridor by the dirty jailer, and the cell door was slammed with great finality behind her. She glanced back at it, thinking of the others who stood and waited and despaired, and tears filled her eyes.

The visitor tossed the jailer a small leather bag. The jingle of its contents made the grizzled man grin. He released her arm reluctantly, and she cradled it with her hand, slowly rubbing the bruises he had left.

"Thank ye, milord. Good luck with yer new purchase. I'm sure ye'll get much out o' 'er, too." He cackled, and the girl felt sick. She was only too glad to be rid of the creature at last.

The tall man ignored the jailer and took hold of the girl's arm. He was firm, though not unkind, as he led her through the grim darkened corridors of Bridewell. The man appeared to know precisely where they were, though she felt the place was a maze. Finally, they reached an outer chamber furnished with a few crude benches. She remembered seeing this room once before. It was large, and looked like the entrance to the royal palace that Bridewell had once been. The only occupant was a man sitting on a bench, and he bore a striking resemblance to the beadle who had brought her to this horrible place.

The girl shuddered and turned away. Her benefactor removed his short cloak of fur and swung it around her shoulders. Before she could thank him, he led her outside into the pale grey coldness of the November afternoon.

The girl closed her eyes in the winter light, so piercingly bright after the dim cell; then she opened them gradually, willing them to adjust. She rubbed them, blinked again, and found she could see better. She breathed the fresh air deeply, her lungs long accustomed to the staleness of the cell. A dank mist was rising from the Thames a few yards away, and she shivered, despite the cloak.

Her benefactor waited for a moment, allowing her to get her bearings, and then without another word he escorted her to a well-muscled bay whose reins were held by a small, unwashed boy. The man tossed a silver coin to the urchin, who caught it eagerly and stepped aside. Taking the reins, the man swung easily into the saddle and then reached down for the girl, pulling her up in front of him.

In that brief moment when the man was not holding her, she had sufficient time in which to flee. Yet curiously she did not consider that alternative. After all, had not this man rescued her from prison? She owed him something; she could at least remain with him to learn why he had selected her. When she was settled before him, he flicked the reins, nudged the horse, and they rode away from the dismal prison.

3

The man's arms clasped the girl loosely, impersonally, almost as if she were a sack òf grain. Yet she sensed the strength of his arms, and knew they maintained a firm enough hold to prevent her from sliding off the horse if she were so inclined to escape.

Escape. She almost laughed aloud. Escape . . . to where . . . from whom? She had no place to run, no one to whom she could turn. No one except this strange and silent man who had brought such a change in her fortune.

The girl was still bewildered by this sudden shift in her life. Could it have been less than half an hour ago that she had been in prison with no hope of ever leaving? She shivered, despite the protection of the cloak, and looked around.

As the couple left the prison, they followed the course of the Fleet River northward, then crossed the Fleet Bridge toward Ludgate Hill. The girl didn't recognize this part of London, but she reminded herself that in the short time she'd been here she hadn't seen much of the town.

She had come with her cousins to London only a few short months before. Yet it seemed far longer—more like a year in that prison. She had arrived in mid-August, and now it was November; those months were gone from her life forever. At this thought, she felt tearful, and she sternly told herself not to be a child. After all, had she not stopped being a child four years ago?

Four years ago come spring, her mother had been struck by

a terrible fever one day as she went about her chores in their country cottage; by nightfall, before an herbswoman could be fetched, her mother was dead. The girl had fallen prey to the fever, too, but being younger and stronger, she had survived. When she had recovered, she saw her mother buried, the cottage sold for what money she could get, and then she went to live with her aunt.

Her aunt, a woman nearly two decades older than her late sister, lived some distance from the girl's beloved home. The girl had known her only from her mother's conversation and thus was somewhat hesitant to go to her, but the aunt proved most welcoming to her young relative.

The girl cheerfully helped with the chores that the aunt could no longer do, while the older woman spun tales of marvelous days and deeds to her eager young listener. It was a good, quiet life; her aunt began to educate her, saying that every girl should know as much as every boy.

Yet the aunt had a frail constitution, and often spent her days in a sickbed, and the girl found she had much work to do. She didn't complain because she was becoming very fond of her aunt, and so she did all she could to help the woman through her numerous illnesses. But the following summer, the woman developed a chest cough that could not be shaken, and as the days passed, the woman's strength waned, until she finally died one morning before dawn.

The girl then went to live with a great-aunt and great-uncle, who lived on the outskirts of her aunt's village. From the beginning, the girl did not like them and her great-aunt made it plain that she viewed her penniless relative as little better than a free servant. Gone were the pleasant evenings and wonderful stories she had known with her aunt; her evenings now were devoted to mending the clothes of the household, to fetching whatever her great-aunt and great-uncle desired.

The great-uncle was also unkind, and when he felt that she had responded to one of his orders too slowly, he would slap or pinch her, admonishing her to be quick about her duties. But she minded that far less than what was to come.

One night, under the cover of darkness, her great-uncle sneaked into her tiny room in the airless attic, waking her after she had fallen into an exhausted sleep. Then he sat upon the edge of her bed and talked about how much he would like to have had a pretty little girl like her, and wouldn't she let him be her father? And weren't fathers allowed to give their little daughters kisses?

The girl fought off the man's advances; finally, exhausted and defeated, he returned to his own cold bed. That morning, long before the couple rose at dawn, the girl left. She knew she had cousins in a neighboring village, and she knew that she would find a home with them.

The girl had been right, for although her cousins had numerous children, ranging in age from a newborn to thirteen, her good-natured relatives welcomed another hardy worker for their small farm.

It was a tiring life, particularly during the spring and summer when crops had to be planted, but she enjoyed the fall harvest and the festival that inevitably followed. For the first time in her life, the girl had companions close to her age, and during their free hours, her three oldest cousins ran with her through the wide fields, taught her to swim in the clear creek behind the farmhouse, and gave her riding lessons upon the old half-blind pony.

These three cousins, all male and eager to please, fairly worshiped their young relative, and when she rode the pony she became their queen while they were her nobles. She sent them off to war, and they returned, after many long battles, with fine booty of newly dropped acorns and tiny red apples that tasted as sweet as cherries, delicate grey and white feathers tipped with cornflower blue, all of which they presented most formally to their little virgin queen. She bestowed kisses upon their cheeks as rewards.

For several years this nearly idyllic life continued, and she grew tall and strong and became even lovelier than before, while her cousins grew straight of limb. They vied good-naturedly for attention, and she found that she liked them equally.

In late summer, the mother, two of the boys, and the girl decided to take some of their wares to market in London. The journey had been long by cart, but the girl had enjoyed her first glimpse of the walled town as they came through the village of Hampstead, which looked down into the Thames valley.

The market, too, had proved exciting with all the confusing, yet exhilarating bustle and the varied noises of the hawkers, farm animals, and sightseers. And this market, the girl knew, was quite different from any other in the country.

Within the walls of London, this open-air market crowded more people through its narrow aisles than she'd ever seen in her life. And never before had she seen such a variety of merchandise, from the different types of foodstuffs to the amazing assortment of clothing and household utensils.

The girl's eye was caught by the bright colors of material in one booth, and she stopped to admire the pretty scarves of light cloth that the bald man with the greasy dome claimed to be silk transported all the way from exotic Cathay. He selected a dark green scarf that he claimed complimented her coloring, but she shook her head, knowing the price was too high.

When she turned around, the girl realized she had lost sight of her cousins. She was confident that she would soon find them, but she looked into each stall without any success. For several hours she stood in the same spot, hoping they would pass by, as doubtless they were also searching for her. But they didn't appear, and she left the marketplace, thinking they might be searching elsewhere for her. Wandering through London's narrow streets, she called for her cousins, but no one answered.

At the end of the first day, the girl sold what she had in her basket—a few loaves of bread and a berry pie she had made only the day before—and then the basket itself. She had only a few coins, but she realized she might need them. That night, frightened and alone, she slept in a doorway, huddled under her woolen shawl.

The next morning, she ran to the city gates, only to discover that she didn't know which gate she'd originally come through. She had only the money she'd earned the day before—hardly enough for a meal—and she had no idea of how far away London was from her home. She only knew she couldn't walk there.

Silent tears seeping from her eyes, she continued to wander through dirty byways and streets. A few days later, she noticed a man with a dog following her, and she grew frightened because she had heard terrible stories of what often happened in London. She began to run.

The man and dog stayed behind her. She dodged down alleys and around corners, praying that she had lost him, but each time she glanced back, the man was growing closer. In her haste, she stumbled: in that moment, the dog, a savage-looking cur with matted fur and a thick leather collar, was upon her, seizing her gown in its jaws.

She tried to twist away, but the man grabbed her with steel-hard fingers. She screamed and fought, but he proved too strong; he pulled her, fighting all the way, to a cart where three others of her age meekly sat, watched over by another dog, as fierce as the first. The man roughly pushed the girl into the cart and then slapped the horse upon its thin rump, and the cart rumbled away.

This man, a beadle, then took the children to Bridewell Prison, where London authorities confined orphans and waifs, as one of her cellmates cheerfully informed her.

Her informant paused and grinned, showing a gap where his front teeth should have been, and said he had lived there since the age of three, and that he doubted they would ever leave. He spoke in a nonchalant manner, and she shuddered. From that moment, the girl never doubted his word, for what hope existed of her ever being released? No one knew she was here; no one wanted her; and so here she would stay.

The girl knew that her cousins would search for her as long as they possibly could, but eventually they would have to return home. She cried, thinking they would believe she had run away from them, and the tears fell harder when she realized she would never see them again.

For the duration of her imprisonment, her life had been a constant struggle—she fought daily to eat, to have straw to lie on, and to stave off the advances of the boys.

But now, all of that was changed; as quickly as she was imprisoned, she was set free. Bewildered, she wondered what happiness—or sadness—this new part of her life would bring.

4

In this unfamiliar part of London, the crowded buildings
sprouted up from the unpaved streets like rotting toadstools,
their bases wide and squat, their upper stories narrow. At
certain points, the structures leaned so close to one another
that they almost became one and the light from the sky was
cut off, plunging the street below into an eerie darkness. A
darkness not too dissimilar to the one she'd experienced in
Bridewell, the girl thought with a slight shiver that had
nothing to do with the coldness of the air around her.

As she and the man rode through just such an artificial
tunnel, she stared up at the patch of grey sky and saw with
surprise a snowflake spiraling downward out of the sullen
clouds.

When last she'd seen the sky, it was the hazy blue of
August. She had lost many months of her life, but she
thanked God that it hadn't been more.

More flakes started to fall, until they were swirling around
her. She tasted their coldness upon her lips, felt their feathery
caress upon her eyelids, and then dropped her head to shield
herself. But she could feel the delicate touch of the snow
drifting against her hair and face.

The girl had no idea how long they had been riding, and
could only hazard a guess that it was longer than an hour. Her
companion—her benefactor, she corrected herself—had not
spoken since riding away from the prison with her, and she
wondered what he was thinking.

And she wondered what fate awaited her. But perhaps she shouldn't think about fate. At least not yet. For now she must simply be happy to be released from that terrible prison. As for what would come next . . . she would worry about that later.

The houses and other buildings had grown meaner and closer in the past few minutes, and some of them were little more than hovels. Occasionally the girl would catch a glimpse of someone—a man, she supposed—leaning casually in the darkened recesses of doorways and silently watching their progress. She sensed hungry looks following them.

It was foolhardy, she thought, for a nobleman such as her rescuer—she assumed he was wellborn by the glimpse she'd had of his clothing and manners—to ride through such a vile place. Surely his presence would invite attack of some sort. She waited, scarcely breathing, afraid of what might happen, but nothing did. Few people were out on the streets, and only occasionally did the girl see a small bonfire warming indistinct heaps of rags.

She shivered when she realized how easily she could have been one of those human wrecks. If the beadle had not discovered and pursued her, what would she have done? Where would she have gone? With no money, family, or friends, would she have resorted to the petty crimes that the homeless and hungry were compelled to commit? 'Twas no sense, she told herself, to look back upon a past that might have been.

Scrawny dogs poked through piles of garbage heaped along the streets. Mercifully, the cold weather had frozen the garbage so that it no longer filled the air with its stench. Here and there she saw skinny cats curled up on windowsills as they watched the dogs below, waiting for their rivals to leave.

Few carts rumbled along the slick streets, and the other horsemen they passed did not look up. On this miserable day, only a handful of pedestrians had set about on their errands, and the sense of her being alone with the man intensified.

The girl's eyelids drooped downward as the weariness she had known for months swept over her. She was alone with this man in a cold place, the only sound being her breathing and the muffled clopping of the horse's hooves. She was alone in a world of grimy white, peopled only by cats, dogs, and flickering bonfires.

The girl yawned, feeling the welcome tendrils of sleep curling around her, and her head nodded forward. But at that moment the horse quickened its pace. She sat up, straightened her back, and looked around with interest.

They passed through the city wall at Ludgate to the countryside and proceeded east along the road. The number of dwellings dwindled, and the snow fell more heavily. But even through the veil of white, she could see the landscape.

Gently rolling hills swept off into the distance, with dark stands of trees dotting their crowns. Snow sat like white caps upon the tops of the naked trees, making them look humorous. The girl smiled for the first time in months.

There wasn't much traffic this late in the afternoon, and other than a solitary horseman who passed them riding rapidly toward London, she and the man were the only ones out in the snow.

She felt the man shift as he stared after the wayfarer, as if expecting him to turn and follow. But when the horseman passed into the distance, her benefactor seemed satisfied, and they continued on their way.

In the short time that she had dozed, the wind had started to howl, and it whipped the skeletal branches of the nearby trees as if they were cat-o-nine-tails. At one point, the man was forced to duck to avoid being scraped across the face by a razor-sharp branch.

The remaining light began seeping from the leaden sky until the girl could scarcely see. She didn't know how the horse found its way, but perhaps, like a cat, it could see in the dark. She dozed again, fitfully this time, with her head lolling against the man's shoulder.

She was dreaming about the prison. Once more she found herself in Bridewell, having been promptly returned by the stranger, who did not find her satisfactory. He was handing her over to the leering jailer, who also looked like her great-uncle, and she was crying as though her heart would break, begging the stranger to give her another chance. The man smiled a cruel smile, while the jailer grinned triumphantly, grasped her wrists, and led her, struggling, back into the stinking darkness.

She whimpered and awoke with a start. For a moment, she was confused and, not knowing where she was, began to tremble violently. Slowly, she remembered, and she peered around but could see nothing beyond the white curtain of snow.

"Where are we?" she whispered.

The man did not seem surprised that she spoke. "Still on the original road. You didn't sleep too long, and we shall soon be at our destination."

She nodded, but could think of nothing more to say. She wondered where he was taking her, but the unpleasantness of her dream clung to her, making her too frightened to ask. As they continued riding, the snow stopped, and finally she saw the moon peering through the clouds.

Not long after that, the horse changed direction, and she saw with the help of the faint moonlight that they were traveling up a straight and narrow avenue lined thickly with tall hedges. She could see nothing beyond their snow-covered tops. Gradually the lane widened, and the hedge dropped away. The land sloped upward, and they trotted across a snow-covered heath, its trees silent, white sentinels.

Beyond that lay another road hemmed by hedges, and then they rounded a corner. Directly before them, though still some distance away, an immense house rose out of the flat land. In the dim light, the girl could not see many details, though she noted that the two lower stories were hewn from rough greystone, while the top floor was constructed of dark wood, interlaced with plaster which shone white in the moonlight. The building's many twisted chimneys of brick were etched against the sky, and most of its numerous windows were dark, like the eyes of some watchful beast. She could see candlelight gleaming through a window on the ground floor.

The horse's gait quickened, as if it recognized its home and knew that food and a warm barn would soon be its reward. As they drew closer, the girl could see ivy, its bare vines weaving a thick interlocking bramble across the house's facade. She could also see that the house was not new, but rather of an older age, and built almost like a fortress.

Was this her benefactor's home? she wondered. Surely it

must be, for where else would he take her? Soon, she told herself, she would know.

They rode down into a wide ditch that once had served as a fortification, and then the horse scrambled up onto the slippery ground opposite and headed toward the right side of the house. There, the man stopped the horse in front of a stable, and she smelled the ripe odor of horses and fragrant hay which drifted from it. She could see a light shining from inside and realized that someone had been waiting for them.

The man slid down, his feet sinking into snow that came up to his ankles, then put his hands around her waist and lifted her gently from the horse. She trembled a little at his touch, but whether out of fear or some other emotion, she didn't know.

The man took her arm while he walked the horse inside. He handed the reins to a small tow-headed boy, who grinned at him and peeked shyly at her before stripping off the damp harness. The man watched as the boy industriously rubbed down the horse with dry straw and scooped a handful of oats from a barrel.

Satisfied that his horse was well-cared for, the man drew the girl outside. They walked toward the house, their footsteps muffled in the snow, and when they were within a few feet of the thick wooden door, he stopped and turned to look at her.

"This," he announced, "is your new home."

5

Before the girl could speak, the man rapped once upon the door. The door sound was curiously soft, almost as if he did not want to be heard by anyone other than the inhabitants of the house. The girl wondered at the man's furtiveness. What was it that he needed to hide? Her presence? Or his? Yet they were too far from London for anyone to be near. When he had waited a few minutes, he knocked again, and then, without waiting, he quickly opened the thick timber door.

The girl found herself standing at one end of a hall of some magnitude. Smoke-darkened oak paneled the walls halfway to the ceiling: above the oak, the walls were plastered, their white surfaces molded into intricate geometric designs.

The hall was chilly and quite damp. No welcome fire burned in the great stone fireplace, and the girl shivered, wrapping the cloak around her more tightly. Several long white tapers burned in pewter candlesticks set on small tables, and she decided that it must have been the light from these that she'd seen outside.

Overhead, heavy wooden beams arched more than twenty feet above her head, and as she gazed up into their dark depths, she thought she detected a slight movement. When it did not repeat itself, she shook her head and told herself that she was tired, that her mind was playing fanciful tricks.

At the far end of the hall was a door, and another one lay to the girl's left. Three other doors broke the plainness of the right wall, while beyond the lefthand door an old-fashioned narrow stone staircase wound its way upward.

This cold and sterile entrance was not a welcoming sight, and the girl hoped that the occupants—if there were any—proved friendlier than this forbidding room. Why had the man called this her new home? She could not even begin to fathom the reason. Whatever exhaustion she had felt during the ride had disappeared; she now felt a tingling anticipation.

At that moment, the door on their immediate right swung open, and a man stepped in to greet them. Short, with thick legs and arms of long proportions, this new arrival was stocky to the point of plumpness, and yet he seemed a strong figure.

His wrinkled face was quite tan, doubtless a result of having spent many long days in the country sun. This gave him a wizened look, although he did not seem to be out of his fifties. His grey hair was cut long and lay in haphazard curls across his skull. His beard was grey and brown, and he had thick grey eyebrows. He wore slightly sagging trunk hose of blue broadcloth, a shirt of good and impeccably clean white cloth, and a blue coat. At his side was a long dagger in a fine casing.

"Sir," he said with a soft Kentish accent, bowing, "my mistress waits within. This way, please."

Girl and man followed the manservant through the door. This room was much smaller and warmer than the hall. It was also paneled in golden oak, with similar plaster designs above, but it evoked a far more welcoming atmosphere.

Another door lay to the left as they entered the room, while an immense stone fireplace of the same weathered grey color of the house's exterior took up the remaining space of that narrow wall. Windows divided into panes by stone mullions lined the long outside wall.

The furniture was sparse: a single wooden table, several benches and stools, a low chest with an intricately carved front on which several pieces of Venetian glass were arranged on a Turkish carpet, and a single high-backed chair with a needlepoint cushion which was placed close to the roaring fire.

A large tapestry in somber colors hung on the wall by the door through which they'd come; the subject looked intricate, but the girl decided she would have to wait until daylight to see the details. A tall screen of pale and unfamiliar material stood to one side of the fireplace.

The vast ceiling was so high that its beams, no doubt blackened with age and the smoke of countless fires, were lost in darkness, though the fire cast a cheering yellow light about the room. There was light, too, from several tapers that rested on the table and chest. A woman sat on a stool before the fire, a book open in her hands.

"Thank you, Dickon."

The servant bowed and left without speaking to the girl or man. The man took the girl's arm and brought her closer to the fire. When the door closed, the woman set the book down carefully, wiped her hands on her apron, and then stood up to face her guests. She appeared to be some years older than the girl, perhaps in her mid-twenties or younger. Her dark blond hair was parted in the middle and knotted in the back, with several curls wisping about her high forehead.

Her full skirt of quilted brown opened in the front to reveal a richly brocaded underskirt. The neckline of the matching bodice was low, but a partlet of embroidered linen kept the gown modest. Her long sleeves were decorated from shoulder to wrist with jeweled buttons that caught the light from the fire and candles. She wore low-heeled shoes of leather, and a necklace of gold links glittered about her slender neck. She also wore several cameo rings, as well as simple ones of twisted gold.

She was one of the prettiest women the girl had ever seen, with a face gentle and unlined. It was the expression of a good and virtuous woman, yet her eyes were faintly sad. She smiled at the girl and then glanced at the man.

"This is the one?"

The man dropped into the chair by the fire. He pulled off his fringed gloves and let them fall to the floor. Then he thrust his hands out by the fire. He nodded, a spare movement of his head, and the girl realized he must be extremely weary, as well as half-frozen from the ride. She held out his cloak to him, but he shook his head.

Awkwardly the girl continued to stand, not knowing what was expected of her. The woman smiled again reassuringly, and gestured for her to join them by the fire.

"Welcome to Grey Wood. Come warm yourself, child."

Obediently the girl stepped forward. After laying the cloak across a bench, she spread her cold-stiffened fingers out to the warming flames and discreetly studied the couple.

They sat for a moment longer without speaking. Then the woman rose and, opening the door next to the fireplace, called softly to a servant.

Presently, a teenage girl with waistlength red hair came in carrying a tray on which there were three mugs filled with steaming liquid. The girl had a wide mouth and dimpled cheeks, and while she was hardly a beauty, she had a wholesome, endearing look. Her eyes were big and blue, fringed with dark lashes, and she had a faint sprinkling of freckles across her small nose. She wore a simple gown of blue, with an apron tied about her waist, and blue slippers.

The servant carefully set a mug before each of them and listened quietly as her mistress gave her instructions for bringing a meal. Meanwhile, she sneaked curious glances at the two newcomers, and after bobbing a curtsey, she left.

When they were alone again, the man glanced toward the girl.

"This is Constance Westcott. She is a widow of good reputation, and the owner of this house."

The girl murmured a greeting, unsure if she should curtsey. She wasn't a servant, after all. But she was surprised to learn that the woman owned the house; she had thought it belonged to the man.

"I trust you are hungry, child? Betty, my servant, will be bringing a meal."

"Oh, yes, mistress. I haven't eaten in a while," the girl shyly admitted, realizing she didn't know how long it had been since her last meal—so long ago in that terrible prison.

"Eat what you can, then, child."

"Thank you," the girl said gratefully, her voice barely louder than a whisper. She looked down at her clasped hands. It was odd, the girl thought, that no one had bothered to ask her name. She could offer it, but curiously she felt reluctant. She would wait for them to ask.

The man took a sip from his mug. "I don't think she's had a meal in days," he said, indicating his disgust with a shake of his head. "The place was a virtual hellhole. Filth and vermin, and a jailer who was worse than any of his charges, and no effort made at any provision beyond incarceration.''

"Did you expect differently?" Constance asked, her voice ironic.

The man made no reply as he stared into the flames. He continued to drink and finally drained the mug in one swallow.

"Giles?"

"I'm all right," he said, rousing himself. "Just tired. It's been a long day." He rubbed his face with one hand and looked back to the flames. The girl wondered what demons tortured him so, but before she could pursue that thought, the woman spoke to her again.

"Sit down, please," she told the girl. "You must be exhausted as well."

Promptly, for she was growing tired again, the girl sat down on the bench, arranging her ragged skirt demurely and then folding her hands in her lap. They were trembling ever so slightly, and she didn't know if this was due to fear or to her gnawing hunger. What was going to happen?

6

For a few minutes, the man spoke to the woman, telling her what he had found in the London prison. His melodic inflection proved that he was a well-bred, educated man, but when he spoke of Bridewell, his tone was harsh.

Her stomach rumbled, and eagerly the girl picked up her mug and sniffed the liquid; then she took a cautious sip. It was apple cider flavored with cinnamon—delicious. She drank quickly, draining the mug in a few swallows, and then realized she shouldn't have been so greedy. God knew when she'd get more—her stay in the prison had taught her that much. She looked down guiltily at the empty mug, but she glanced up in time to see Constance smiling at her.

The girl had no sooner set down her mug when Betty entered the room, bearing another tray. The servant set a steaming plate of stew before the man and one before the girl. Its spicy seasonings and rich meat smelled wonderful, and the girl's stomach rumbled. Betty giggled softly, and the girl smiled in response. Dark bread slathered with sweet country butter and another large mug of mulled hot cider completed the meal.

The girl began to eat, realizing the extent of her hunger and the length of time since she had had a decent meal. She forced herself to take her time; after all, she didn't want to get sick, and within a few minutes her hunger pangs subsided a little.

As she tore the delicious bread into smaller pieces and

mopped the stew's rich juices with it, the girl studied her unexpected benefactor, who, having finishing his meal, closed his eyes and leaned his head against the chair.

From where she sat she could see he was well-built, with little fat upon his bones—a man of moderate tastes, which somehow pleased her.

She remembered how tall he had seemed when they stood together in the room; he must stand above average height. She was tall for her age, but even so she'd had to crane her neck to look at him.

His long, finely boned hands testified that he was indeed a nobleman, except that several fingers bore faint scars and callouses—almost as if he'd once been forced to perform heavy labor. His prominent cheekbones slanted attractively in a lean, tanned face, which was almost, but not quite, dominated by a narrow high-bridged nose. And his wintery grey eyes, as he stared into the flames, were unfathomable beneath thick dark brows.

There were tiny lines at the corners of his eyes, fine thin lines as if he had once smiled a great deal—though the girl had not seen him smile. His dark hair, a little longer than the current fashion, was tinged with a few strands of silver, as were his moustache and neatly trimmed beard. His mouth with its thin, straight lips, hinted of disapproval, and she felt that laughing, much like smiling, was alien to him. But that had not always been the case, she corrected herself. She felt that once he had been a merrier soul, but that something had driven the joy from his life.

He looked to be in his early thirties, but the girl couldn't be sure. She sensed, however, that he had had a hard life, and she felt a stab of sympathy for him. What could have happened to make him so somber? She continued her surreptitious study. The man wore a satin doublet covered by a quilted jerkin of identical cut, both fashioned of a somber grey that matched the shade of his eyes. A row of plain gold buttons marched in a straight line down his jerkin, while several buttons decorated his long sleeves. The stiff white ruff around his neck was small and simple, compared with others that the girl had seen. He wore black trunk hose, and his stockings were plain and fastened by cloth garters tied around the upper leg. His shoes were black leather, protected by pantofles, simple overshoes that bore traces of mud and use. On his head was a black broad-brimmed hat. A sword in a scabbard of plain dark velvet hung at his side from a leather belt about his waist, while around his neck was looped a plain silver chain. Earrings set with tiny diamonds glittered in his ears.

When he caught her looking at him, the girl dropped her eyes. She didn't want him to think she had been staring rudely at him—even though she had. Her cheeks flushed with embarrassment. How common he must think her. She shuddered at what he must have thought when he walked into the cell at Bridewell.

The girl began eating the remnants of stew on her plate. Constance beckoned to the man, who reluctantly rose and followed her to the other side of the room. The girl watched with interest as the two stood by the windows.

They were talking about her, the girl thought, and she wondered what they were saying. For some time the man and woman conversed, although the woman talked more than the man. The girl could not make out the words for their voices were low, yet she could see that the young widow was agitated.

About her? the girl wondered. Had the man's arrival—with a girl in rags—been unexpected?

Finally, when the disagreement seemed settled, the man and woman returned to the warmth of the fireplace. Once again the man sat in the chair as if all his movements were calculated, while Constance pulled her stool close to the hearth and stared into the flames. Despite the tension in the room, the girl returned to her meal. Betty had brought in another plate of stew to replace the empty one, as well as more bread and cider; the girl certainly wasn't going to waste this food. She managed to eat two more plates of the rich mixture before her hunger was completely satisfied.

She glanced around as she ate more bread. Her gaze stopped on the screen she had noticed before but hadn't examined closely. It was made of some fine lavender material set within a wooden frame. The cloth was perhaps even silk, she thought. Fanciful pictures of griffins, dragons, and winged horses, as well as other marvelous beasts, were embroidered on it in gold and silver thread. She yearned to study more closely the tapestries and other lovely things in the room.

As her stomach filled, she felt more comfortable than she had been in months, and a certain lassitude crept over her, stealing away her attention. She yawned and then shook her head to stay awake. This wasn't the time or the place for sleep.

The others hadn't spoken while the girl ate, and when she was finished at last, she soaked up the remaining gravy with the last crust of bread and pushed her plate away, emptied her mug, and then wiped her mouth daintily with a linen napkin. She looked at the couple expectantly.

The girl had little doubt that now she would learn the reason why she had been taken from the prison and brought to this house so far outside London. She tried unsuccessfully to quiet the fear at the base of her stomach. She had to know why she had been taken, but she was afraid—afraid of what they planned to do with her.

The man turned his dark gaze on her. "My name is Giles Blacklaw," he said, his tone as somber as his gaze, "and it doesn't matter what your name is—or has been, child—because that is the past, which no longer exists."

She waited, scarcely breathing.

"You must push from your mind all that has happened to you within your short life. That is gone now—all of it—as though a slate had been wiped clean. Do you understand?"

She nodded, although she wasn't sure that she understood.

"From now on your name is Aurora."

The girl blinked in surprise. She had anticipated . . . but not this. She wasn't prepared for it. "Why—" she began.

The man held up his hand before she could say any more. "Why I do this is not important. 'Tis enough for you to know that it is being done. Now, simply listen to me before you ask any questions."

The girl nodded hesitantly. There was nothing else she could do, and her fear had not been lessened by his words.

"As I said when we were outside, this is your new home. This will be where you live, with Constance, from now on. I will visit from time to time, but I will not live here. Do you understand?" The girl nodded again. "Good. After you are finished—if you desire further nourishment—you are to sleep, and in the morning your first lesson will begin.''

''First lesson?''

''Yes.''

''I don't understand.''

''You don't have to just now, Aurora.''

The girl frowned slightly at the use of the unfamiliar name. ''I don't understand. I don't know what lessons you mean, and most of all, I don't know why you rescued me from the prison—although you mustn't think I'm not grateful, because I truly am.''

''Giles!'' Constance said, amazed. ''You haven't told her?''

''There wasn't time.''

''For what?'' the girl asked, becoming more and more bewildered. Her head was beginning to ache, and she felt as though she were being swept from one eddy to another.

''There wasn't time to tell you my reason for taking you from that prison.'' He smiled, and the girl thought the expression was not at all pleasant. ''You see, I plan to turn you into a noblewoman.''

7

Aurora blinked rapidly as she considered his astonishing words. A noblewoman? What did this man mean? How could he accomplish, or pretend to accomplish, such a deed? Was not nobility a matter of proper birth—or perhaps of marriage? Was this not something that only the Queen herself could do, bestowing titles and thus nobility upon those she deemed worthy?

And even if this man could turn her into a noblewoman, why would he want to do so, and, most of all, why her?

"I don't understand," she said bluntly, looking from Blacklaw to Constance.

"At the moment, it isn't necessary that you understand my reasoning, which is very complex, child," Blacklaw replied. "All that you must do is obey me. That is sufficient for you to know."

"No."

"What?" Astonished, he lifted his eyebrows and stared at her. "What did you say?"

In the face of what seemed abrupt anger, Aurora almost lost her nerve and replied meekly that she would obey him, no matter what he said. Almost. But she did not. Instead, she resolutely told herself that she had every right to know his intentions. Lifting her chin with what she thought was defiance, she looked him straight in the eye.

"I beg your pardon, sir, but it *is* proper for me to understand what you mean by turning me into a 'noblewoman'—if such a deed may be accomplished, as I rather doubt. For 'tis my life with which you toy so boldly, and while I am indebted to you for delivering me from that prison, and while you may be supposed to own me because of your purchase of me from Bridewell, I allow that my spirit is not yet dead inside my body. And until such time, I must know.''

Constance chuckled quietly. ''A very pretty speech, Aurora. Very pretty and brave, indeed!'' She glanced at Blacklaw. '' 'Tis obvious the child has spirit, as well as a mind of her own. I think you made a wise selection, Giles.''

He stared at Aurora, and he looked as bewildered as if a dog had begun to preach sermons from the pulpit of St. Paul's Cathedral.

Aurora almost giggled aloud. Blacklaw's eyebrows drew together as he shifted impatiently and drummed his fingertips upon the wooden arm of his chair. It was obvious to Aurora that she irritated him.

''Perhaps, perhaps, child. Well, what you think or what you wish to know is of no consequence at the moment. Soon enough, Aurora,'' he said, before she could open her mouth to protest, ''I guarantee that you will know my purpose. Now, I have overstayed myself and must leave. Good night. Constance. Aurora.'' Abruptly he stood, claimed his cloak, swung it around his shoulders, nodded to the two women, and left.

Aurora stared after him and then looked to the widow for an explanation of his abrupt departure. She felt as if she had won some small part of an extremely confusing struggle, but she couldn't be sure. Suddenly, nothing of this day seemed at all sure to her.

Constance smiled reassuringly. ''I know you are confused, Aurora, and there is much to explain, but not tonight, I think. It is already quite late, and I fear I have been quite remiss in my duties. Aren't you tired after your unusual day?''

Aurora nodded, aware of the exhaustion spreading throughout her body and mind. She was bone-tired—not from the ride from London, because after all it hadn't been that lengthy, but rather from her constant struggle to survive in the past few months. She had had to be alert every minute of her day— whether awake or asleep. She had never been able to sink into a truly deep sleep; she had always been worrying about the next meal or the next problem. But now she thought she could sleep for at least a month.

As if reading her mind, Constance beckoned to her. "I'm sure you want to sleep now. Come with me, if you will."

Constance picked up one of the candles and opened the door through which Betty had earlier entered.

On the opposite side of the door was a small dark hall; directly across it was a door to a room that was clearly the kitchen. Betty sat inside on a stool by a large fireplace, eating her meal.

Aurora smiled at her tentatively, and Betty smiled back, revealing a wide, yet not unattractive, gap between her two front teeth.

Several feet away from the kitchen door was a narrow stone staircase leading up. Aurora realized these weren't the stairs she'd seen earlier and wondered how many staircases there were in the house.

Holding the candle before her and cupping her free hand around the flame so that a draft wouldn't extinguish it, Constance occasionally glanced back as she lead the way upstairs. Once she cautioned Aurora to mind her step, for the footing on the worn stone could be treacherous.

"I shall leave a tour of the house until tomorrow when you are somewhat more rested. In the meantime, I urge you not to wander about, although I rather doubt you'll be so inclined. While Grey Wood doesn't look very large from the outside, Aurora, it is a veritable rabbit warren once you are within its walls. It was built a long time ago, the kitchen being part of the original core. It has been added onto for many centuries, and thus it has grown into a bewildering maze, which can baffle the unwary guest."

Aurora nodded. She wished only to collapse on a bed.

Finally they gained the second floor; its landing opened onto a long narrow gallery. Aurora cast a fleeting glance toward the huge portrait paintings lining the wall. Their stern subjects bore themselves stiffly and formally in their outdated costumes.

These were no doubt ancestors of Constance's family, or rather of her late husband's family. What a shame, Aurora thought, to be widowed so young. And quite unbidden to her mind came the thought that perhaps Giles Blacklaw provided some comfort to the pretty woman. Not a worthy thought, Aurora lectured herself, but then she *was* tired.

A number of small round tables were set in the gallery, and stools were scattered throughout its length, while along one wall stood a chest on which rested several stringed musical instruments. She also saw several chairs with backs of stamped leather and a beautiful ornate mirror of Venetian glass. Aurora tried to note the many details, but she was tired and there was too much to absorb at once.

"We're almost there!" The widow paused at the end of the gallery and turned to the right down another, smaller hallway. They appeared to be in a newer part of the house, for here the ceilings were higher, the halls a little wider, and the ornamentation on the walls and floor fresher and less scarred by the passage of time.

They filed past several closed doors until they finally stopped in front of a door painted green.

"Here we are." Constance opened the door and walked into the dark room. "This will be your room, Aurora. I hope you like it. If you need anything, I am in the room down to the right."

Constance used her candle to light several tapers in pewter candlesticks throughout the room. Then she knelt on the brick hearth and began laying a fire. Aurora thought she should help, but her exhaustion had slowed her limbs, and she didn't know if she could even bend over. In a few minutes when the fire was at last burning brightly, Constance turned and smiled at her.

With as much interest as her tired body would grant, Aurora looked about her room. A large four-poster bed of dark wood took up most of one wall. It looked like a great shallow box raised above the floor and supported by a post at each corner. The tops of the posts were connected by a cornice, and from this hung rich brocade curtains. The curtains facing the room had been pulled back and tied by a cord.

At the head of the bed was the tester, a large panel of intricately carved wood. A silvery-brown fur rug covered the bed, while several pillows had been plumped at its head. An embroidered coverlet in blue, green, and gold was folded neatly at the foot.

A low chest sat at one side of the bed, doubling as a bench. A high casement window with red glass rose some feet above the chest, and Aurora hoped she would be able to open the window. Even in the winter she enjoyed fresh air, and after the confining cell at Bridewell, she craved it more than ever.

A stool by the hearth; a press, or closed cupboard, for clothing; and a flat-topped cupboard on which rested a basin and ewer completed the room's furniture. A tapestry, not much larger than the stool, hung above the fireplace, while on the mantel sat a low bowl filled with dried herbs, whose gentle fragrance Aurora could smell, even from some distance away.

"I have set aside some clothes for you in the press," Constance said briskly after Aurora had expressed her admiration of the room. "Originally these gowns and other garments were mine, and thus, I hope they will not prove too large. You are exceedingly thin right now, and will doubtless fill out once you are fed properly, but if the clothes do not fit now, then 'twill be no problem for us to take them in until we have others ready for you. You do sew, do you not?"

Aurora nodded sleepily. Her mother had stood over her many long hours until she had mastered the skill of small, neat stitches.

"Good. You may bathe in the morning before you break your fast, if you desire. I am sure there are lingering memories of the prison which you wish to scrub off. Of course, there's a pot under the bed for you, and there's fresh water in the ewer. Is there anything you wish tonight, Aurora?"

The girl shook her head. The widow had already given her so much. Her words, she realized, were a little formal, but nonetheless sincere. "I can think of nothing else that I would need further, Dame Westcott. Above all, I thank you for your great kindness in sheltering me, a stranger."

The woman nodded. "We shall see if you thank me upon the morrow," she said enigmatically. "Good night, then, rest easy, and I shall see you in the morning."

8

When the door was closed, Aurora sat down upon the bed quickly, almost as if her legs would no longer support her, and stared unblinking at the flames as they flickered along the wood.

The wavering, ever-changing colors were gradually bewitching her; already she could feel her eyelids drooping. She shook her head and yawned. She mustn't fall asleep sitting up. She stretched slowly, feeling aching bones ease slightly, and looked around the room.

Her new room was beautiful, far more luxurious than she could have ever hoped. And how it differed from the terrible lice-infected straw on which she had slept for months.

She smoothed her hand across the fur rug and pressed down with her fingers. Underneath, it felt almost like a thick feather bed, and she sighed, remembering the beds she'd slept upon so long ago at her mother's home, relics that her mother and grandmother had made. They were lost now, like everything else from her past.

She mustn't think about her past—or her future—at least, not now.

She stood and stripped off her clothing, so dirty and ragged, and dropped it on the floor. What a relief to finally be rid of those rags! Tomorrow she would gladly burn them.

She grimaced as she glanced down at the grey streaks on her body. She would be heartily glad of Constance's offer of a bath in the morning. She couldn't remember the last time she'd washed, and she was in sore need of it.

Naked, she padded across the cold wooden floor and, dipping her hands into the equally cold water, splashed it onto her face and hands.

When she finished with a superficial washing, she dried herself on the embroidered linen towel that was laid to one side and then blew out the candles. She paused to hold out her hands once more to the fire. A chill swept down her spine, and she quickly crossed over to the bed and pulled back the covers.

The linen sheets looked fresh and clean, and with the cold nipping at her heels, she prepared to slide into the bed. She was stopped, though, by a sound outside her door. She paused and listened. There it came again, faintly. She crossed to the door, opened it, and peered out. Something soft touched her bare ankle. Startled, Aurora leaped back.

"Meow."

A tiny black kitten made itself known by an even smaller feline cry, then wound its way between her ankles, rubbing its bony head against her. Aurora laughed, amused that she had been startled by something so incredibly tiny, and then closed the door. She dropped to her knees and stroked the kitten's fur. The triangular face with its long ears lifted toward her, and Aurora stared down into slanting eyes as blue-green as her own.

"You're a beauty," she whispered, as if she feared Constance would hear her, "but so tiny. Are you the runt of the litter?"

The kitten answered by licking the girl's fingers, its little pink rasping tongue tickling her. She giggled and continued to stroke it. Suddenly the kitten flopped onto its side, and for a moment Aurora thought it was stricken. Then she realized it was rolling onto its back and wanted its tummy scratched.

She obliged for several minutes, but when her head began to droop, she stood up, despite the kitten's protests.

"I really have to sleep now," she informed the kitten, who blinked, stood, and stretched lazily.

She didn't remember seeing a mother cat in the house, but the cat and her family could be in any of these rooms.

Apparently the curious kitten had been attracted by the voices of the two women and had come seeking company. Aurora was very grateful for its soft, warm presence on her first night in this house.

She walked back to the bed and turned around to see if the kitten had followed her. When she did not see it, she felt a stab of disappointment, but when something silky brushed suddenly across her feet, she knew where the cat had gone.

She lifted the unprotesting kitten, which was hardly as big as her palm, and set it down on the fur coverlet. Then she slipped into bed, releasing the green cords and letting the heavy curtains drop into place. She crawled under the covers and pulled them up to her chin.

The kitten walked up and down the bed, patiently seeking a comfortable spot in which to sleep. When it finally found one, by Aurora's head on the plump feather pillow, it patiently kneaded the pillow with its tiny claws. Then it turned around several times before finally settling down, tail to nose, with one paw draped across its tail.

Aurora laughed, and gently touched the cool pink nose. The kitten answered with a purr remarkably loud for such a small creature.

One of the bedcurtains did not hang straight, so that she could catch a glimpse of the fire through the crack. As she lay there, with the purring kitten curled next to her, she stared wide-eyed at the fire, and one thought after another tumbled through her excited and confused mind, temporarily banishing sleep. There was so much to think about, but where to begin?

For no reason that she understood, Giles Blacklaw had given her the name Aurora. Why? What did it matter what her name was? Or what her name was not? Certainly, the name was a most unusual one; no one she'd ever known had had that name. So perhaps it would not be so terrible to be known as Aurora from now on.

"Aurora," she said aloud, and then giggled. The kitten mewed softly and licked her ear.

Something else puzzled her. Why hadn't he given his title when he introduced himself, when it was apparent that he was of the nobility? He moved and talked like a nobleman and had the manner of one, yet curiously at the same time he did not.

And why had he chosen her? Why had he come to Bridewell seeking her? Why did he wish to make her a noble-woman? None of this made any sense to her, and she wondered if tomorrow would bring any answers.

Giles Blacklaw had said that tomorrow her lessons were to begin.

Lessons?

Was that why Constance had said that she might not thank her upon the morrow? What would happen then? Aurora would have pondered these puzzling matters, but the kitten's purring lulled her, and her eyelids shut gently. Already she was slipping into a deep slumber.

9

It seemed to the girl that no sooner had she drifted into a dreamless sleep than her sanctuary was invaded by the distant slamming of a door, followed by a thunderous voice calling for someone named Aurora.

She was Aurora.

Abruptly her memory of that name returned, and she sat up, the covers falling to her waist. The kitten stirred, mewed once, and rolled over onto its side, with one tiny paw tucked across its eyes.

Aurora pushed aside one of the bedcurtains and stared at the unfamiliar room as she tried to remember where she was. You're back in the prison, a part of her whispered. This is only a dream, a pleasant one, but nonetheless just a dream, and soon you'll wake up and find yourself in Bridewell.

No, she corrected herself. Wherever she was, it wasn't a dream. It was real, and Bridewell was a nightmare from her past.

Relieved, she yawned and stretched and then pulled the sheet up to her chin as she looked around the room. It couldn't be late because the light filtering through the red glass of the window was the palest shade of rose.

She lay down, making a warm cocoon for herself. The kitten curled into a ball within the crook of her arm and began purring. Her eyelids drooped as sleep began to claim her once more. She couldn't even remember what had awakened her.

There it was again! She opened one eye. Yes, it was

definitely a man. She recognized Giles Blacklaw's voice.
Whatever did he want this early in the morning? She supposed she should get up and find out what he wanted, but why had he arrived so soon? She hadn't had time to bathe or to break her fast.

Yawning, she reluctantly pushed back the covers and swung her feet over the side of the bed, shivering as a blast of cold air curled around her ankles and crept up her bare legs. Giles Blacklaw called her name again, and she rubbed her eyes. She must get ready. Her lessons must be about to begin. She yawned once more. The kitten echoed her yawn, showing its small sharp teeth, and the girl smiled.

During the night, the fire had died and with it had gone the room's heat; she thought it was almost as icy as if she had been outside. Shivering slightly, she went to the press and opened a drawer, inhaling its sweet lavender fragrance.

In the press she found several changes of clothing, all of extremely good material. None of the garments were extravagant, nor did they look as if they had been worn often. She searched through the press until she collected the items she needed.

Quickly she pulled on the black woolen stockings and tied them with garters of ribbon. Already she felt warmer. A white chemise of fine holland embroidered with tiny pink and blue flowers intertwined with delicate leaves slid easily over her body. Had Constance done the needlework? she wondered. It was exceedingly fine, and she hoped she could learn to be half as skillful as the widow. A petticoat of red cloth came next, and she smiled as she laced it up. She had never worn clothes as fine as these. She selected a simple gown of grey velvet and long wide sleeves. She was relieved that the neckline was not fashionably low, as her mother and aunt had taught her always to be modest.

Among the items Aurora found was a small starched ruff of linen, but her fingers fumbled, unaccustomed to the ruff's stiff fittings, and so she put it back. It would have to wait until she could ask Constance for help. She slipped her feet into soft leather slippers, finer than any she had ever seen. She pulled her hair back, then twisted it into a knot, pinned it, and placed a white cap upon her head.

The material of the gown was so soft, she thought, as she

gently fingered a sleeve and traced the line of delicate buttons. The gown was far better than any she had ever worn, and she wished she could see what she looked like.

'Twas vanity that, she informed herself, but still she wished she could. She wondered what Lord Blacklaw would think when he saw her no longer looking like a beggar. She'd best leave *that* thought, she told herself grimly, until she'd had a bath and had rested for a few days more.

After she had tied on an apron, she was satisfied that she was wearing everything she should be wearing, and she started to leave when a piteous meow sounded. The kitten was stranded on the bed, which was far too high for it to jump from. She smiled and picked it up, kissing it on the top of its head.

"How could I ever have forgotten you, little one?" she said softly. The kitten rubbed its head against her thumb, and with a smile she carefully set the little animal in the pocket of her apron.

She found her way downstairs without any false turns, and as she passed the kitchen she saw Betty already at work. She smiled at the other girl, who returned the smile shyly.

Giles Blacklaw was waiting by the fireplace in the warm room downstairs. Constance was standing there too, opposite him, with her arms akimbo, tapping one foot. The woman did not look particularly pleased to see her guest so early in the morning.

"Good day, Lord Blacklaw," Aurora said, dropping a slight curtsey. She lowered her eyes with what she thought was a demure expression, but through her eyelashes she could watch him without his knowing. Today he was attired in black from head to foot, and in these somber clothes he was just as handsome as he had been the previous day—and just as intriguing.

"She has manners enough, I see, Constance," Blacklaw said to the widow, as if the girl was not present. "That will be greatly to our advantage, I think." He was about to speak, when he suddenly stared at her apron. "Your pocket is squirming."

She giggled softly, drew out the kitten, and then set it down. It ambled off toward the kitchen in search of food.

"Ah, that's where she's gone," Constance said. "I didn't see her this morning."

"She was meowing outside my room last night, and so I let her in. May I keep her?"

"Of course, child. What will you call your new little charge?"

"Lucye."

"An unusual name for a cat," Constance said.

"In honor of a girl I knew . . . once long ago." Aurora smiled a secret knowing look.

"Are we finished talking about the cat?"

"Yes, Giles," the widow said. "Now, why have you come bellowing and slamming into the house to rouse us from our sleep?"

"I wanted to start Aurora's lessons."

"It's too early. Why it's hardly past dawn—and what you're doing here at this most unseemly hour I don't know— but she hasn't settled in yet. She needs more time before the lessons begin. They can wait a day, two days, perhaps even longer. She should rest from her ordeal, or she won't prove a very adept student. Besides, she hasn't even had her breakfast this morning, much less bathed the prison dirt from her skin. Come back in a few days or even better, Giles, a week's time." Constance gave him a firm look.

Blacklaw glanced from her to Aurora and then back to the widow. He shrugged casually. Aurora thought that he wanted to disagree with Constance, but strangely he did not.

"Very well, Constance, she shall have her days of rest. But I shall return in a few days, and the lessons will commence then. In the meantime, I trust you will begin educating her in other matters."

"Of course."

Just as he had done the previous night, he nodded abruptly to the women, turned, and left briskly without a further word. Aurora had a feeling that what would doubtless become an ordeal had been put off for at least a few more days.

10

"Giles is a man with but a single purpose," Constance said in response to Aurora's puzzled expression. "I think you will soon discover that. Well, enough of that for now. You are looking much more rested this morning, child, and I confess that you look very fine in those clothes. How do you find the fit?"

" 'Tis excellent. Indeed, I think I could ask for nothing more. The others looked quite fine, too." The girl paused. "I don't know how to say this, but I know that I should thank you and—" She stopped when Constance held up a hand.

"This is not the time," the widow replied, her tone wry. "You have much to do this morning before you thank me. Are you eager for a bath?" Aurora nodded briskly. "Good, I assumed you would wish to bathe, and so Betty has been heating water in the kitchen. You will find a tub there."

As Constance promised, Aurora found a wooden tub waiting on the hearth, set close to the fire to keep the water warm. This tub, she thought, was positively spacious compared to the one she'd bathed in at her mother's home. After months of being in prison, she would have appreciated a tub of the smallest size.

Betty smiled shyly, again showing the gap between her teeth. With a cloth wrapped around her hand, she grasped the handles of an immense iron kettle hanging in the fireplace and tipped it onto its side over the tub. Steam rose from the tub as

45

the hot water met colder water. Betty pointed to a second kettle set over the flames.

"That be done soon, mistress, if you need more." The girl's voice was high-pitched but pleasant, with a soft accent like Dickon's.

"I'll need it later for rinsing, but not right now, Betty."

"Aye."

Aurora looked for the kitten but didn't see it. She wondered if it had gone off somewhere to nap after her meal.

"Here is some soap," Constance said as she walked into the kitchen. She handed the small fragrant bar and a bath sheet to Aurora. "I shall leave you for now, but if you need anything, please ask Betty."

"Thank you."

Betty turned her back as she worked so that Aurora could have some privacy. Aurora quickly slipped off her clothing, folding it neatly across a chest flanking the fireplace. Then she set the soap and bath sheet on the freshly swept hearth and stepped into the tub. When she sat down, her knees were practically pressed against her chest, but she didn't mind. At least she would be able to wash away the dirt and the memories of the past few months.

"Have you seen the little black kitten, Betty? She slept with me last night, and I was wondering where she'd gone."

"Oh, aye, she came in, bellowin' for her meal, like the others. No doubt, she's gone off to tussle with her brothers and sisters."

Aurora smiled and cupped her hands, pouring water on her head and savoring the sluicing sensation as the water trickled down her face. She washed her long hair, massaging her scalp with soapy fingers. She rinsed it as best she could and twisted it on top of her head so that she could wash herself easily. Then she washed her face.

She settled back, her neck against the rim of the tub; and studied the kitchen—its kettles, iron pans, brass pots, and spits, as well as the brewing implements and various dairy vessels. The kitchen contained two fireplaces, both brick and blackened by decades of cooking fires. A large wooden table stood in the center of the room, and to one side was a cabinet with pots hanging above it. Alongside that hung several baskets containing onions and a few withered apples. There were several stools in front of one of the fireplaces, and a smaller table sat next to the brick oven.

Once again, she thought it was the best kitchen she had ever seen. Her mother's kitchen, and her aunt's, had been very small compared to this one. Not for the first time did she think that Constance Westcott must be a very wealthy woman.

She closed her eyes but was roused by a small meow. She sat up and peered over the side of the tub. The black kitten stared up at her.

"There you are, Lucye." The kitten mewed in response, and Aurora smiled.

The water had cooled considerably in the past few minutes, so she scrubbed herself vigorously with the geranium-scented soap. Did Constance grow the flowers that were used to scent her soap? She would have to ask the widow later.

Aurora rose gracefully from the tub, and as she reached across for the bath sheet, several droplets of water sprinkled the kitten. Instantly Lucye howled, shook her head, and streaked from the kitchen, and both Betty and Aurora laughed.

"She'll be back soon. Have no doubt 'bout that, miss."

"I hope so!"

Close to the fire, she kept warm as she briskly rubbed the soft bath sheet across her skin, feeling it tingle in response. She inhaled deeply, smelling the clean scent of her own body. It had been a long time. . . . She wound the sheet tightly around her hair to keep it from dripping as she dressed, and when she had finished, she sat beside the hearth and combed her hair with her fingers to dry it.

It seemed strange to sit without offering to help while Betty emptied the tub, but she knew that the girl would not let her. Aurora didn't know what her position in the house was, but she knew it was not as a servant girl—not when Giles Blacklaw said he wanted to make her a noblewoman. No, she corrected herself. He had said he would train her as one. Was that not different? She didn't know.

"Have you lived at Grey Wood all your life, Betty?" she asked when the tub had been emptied and the hearth swept.

Betty propped the twig broom in the corner by the fireplace and nodded vigorously. "Oh, aye, mistress. Me dad and mum worked here afore me, and my brother Edward is the mistress's groom."

That would be the small boy she had seen the night she arrived with Giles Blacklaw. ''Is Dickon part of your family, too?''

''Aye, he be my uncle.''

''I see. And what of your parents? Do they still work here as well?''

Betty's face took on a mournful expression. ''They be dead these six years now, miss, 'bout the time the master died. It was a mighty fierce fever that took 'em. Took the master and my mistress's little ones, too.''

''Mistress Constance had children?''

''Oh aye, the sweetest little boy and girl what ever lived, and all of two and three, the precious little mites.''

''And they died from the fever?'' The servant nodded. ''How sad!'' Constance had not seemed a woman in mourning, but then, it had been six years since her family died. Aurora shivered and moved closer to the fire. She had lost her own family, too.

Lucye had crept back and was curled at Aurora's feet. She stroked the kitten's back as she watched Betty take bread out of the oven and, with strong, capable hands, arrange the large, steaming loaves on the end of the table.

''What of Lord Blacklaw's family?'' Aurora inquired. ''Are they neighbors of your mistress's?''

''I don't know nuthin' 'bout them, mistress, except that they come from way up north, close to where them barbarians live. The master here and the lord were friends, though.''

Constance's late husband and Giles Blacklaw had been friends. Very interesting, Aurora thought; and thus when the husband died, Blacklaw had simply stepped in to take his place . . .

No, she told herself. That wasn't true, and even it were, it wasn't her business. Why did her curiosity about their relationship persist?

As Betty was wrapping the bread in white muslin to keep it fresh, Constance walked in, her eyes wide as she took in Aurora's fresh, clean appearance. ''Come, let me look at you.''

Aurora gently pushed Lucye's head off her foot. Then she stood and slowly turned around at Constance's bidding, while the widow stared at her—*as if I were a horse going to market,* Aurora thought uneasily.

When Constance spoke again, it was in a musing tone, almost as if to herself. "Yes, I think Giles might just be right about this. But then he always had a good eye." She smiled briskly, as if to change the subject. "Would you like breakfast now?"

"Yes, please, I'm still famished."

"I would think so, after what you've been through." She looked at the servant. "Betty, we'll dine in the other room."

"Very well, mistress."

"Follow me, Aurora."

The two women entered the room where Aurora had taken her first meal at Grey Wood. Bright golden light poured through the tall windows, and Aurora skipped over to look out at what lay beyond.

The sunlight shone on the vast, snowy field before her, making her eyes ache from the brilliance. A line of tall trees lay behind the field, hinting at a nearby woods. Several small buildings, one of which she thought was the stables, lay off to the right.

Through the gaps in the skeletal trees, Aurora glimpsed low hills far off in the distance, and once again she wondered how far Grey Wood was from London. She should have asked Betty. Or she could ask Constance. She didn't think the woman would be reluctant to tell her. After all, there wasn't any reason to be secretive, was there?

She could distinguish few details under the blanket of snow, and she wondered what the grounds would look like in the spring. Perhaps she would be here to see for herself.

Of course she would, one part of her replied scornfully. After all, where else could she go? She was far too indebted to both the man and woman to leave until she had fulfilled her part of their plan.

Aurora turned around to find Constance watching her. She smiled at the widow, who motioned for her to sit at the table. Within minutes Betty entered, bearing a wooden tray laden with dishes. She set the dishes down and then left.

For her first breakfast at Grey Wood, Aurora dined on several slices of fine white bread, unlike anything she had ever tasted before—quite unlike the coarse brown bread to which she was accustomed. The bread was still warm from the oven, and she slathered it with sweet butter and then nibbled at dried pears and raisins in the bowl before her. She washed down the bread with a rich warm ale. Constance ate her own meal in silence, which Aurora welcomed. She wasn't sure she was ready for what the other woman had to say. Finally, she wiped her sticky fingers on the napkin laid before her.

"Are you ready then, Aurora?"

"Ready?" She wasn't sure what the woman meant. Were the lessons to begin? Constance had wanted her to rest for a few days. "I don't understand? Ready for what?"

"To explore Grey Wood."

"Yes. Quite ready." And Aurora smiled, vastly relieved.

11

"Grey Wood is very old," Constance said as she paused outside the small dining room. "I have lived here all my life, and I don't think I've explored all of it fully. Which, of course, presents quite a challenge to an adventurous soul."

"You've lived here all your life?" Aurora asked, suddenly confused. "I thought that Grey Wood was your late husband's estate."

Constance smiled. "It is—or was, for of course, it's mine now. I was Geoffrey's cousin, and we all lived here—a great sprawling family of aunts and uncles and cousins, and connections whose lineage no one seemed to know, much less understand." She paused, remembering other times, long ago. "Of course, I am the only one left now at Grey Wood."

"Betty said something about a fever that swept through the estate."

"Six years ago this Christ's Eve. It was a sad time for us. Dickon—my servant whom you saw last night—was the only one who did not fall ill, God be praised. He nursed us, those he could, and slept not at all during that time. Poor man. He tried to save my husband, and my children, and his own family, but they were taken into God's hands. Blessed be His name."

Constance made the sign of the cross, and for the first time Aurora noticed the gold cross inlaid with pearls that hung around the woman's neck.

"They died, and I survived, as did Betty, and Edward who was a very young child at the time."

"I'm sorry."

Constance's eyes glittered brightly, as if from unshed tears. " 'Tis the past, and I think about it little. I have no doubt that you have your own sorrows. Come, tell me your story, for I've not heard it yet. 'Twas inhospitable of me not to ask before this."

Aurora shrugged; there seemed so little to tell, particularly after she had heard Constance's sad tale. All too well could she imagine the house filled with the dying and the dead, and the single man left on his feet moving among them, doing what little he could to ease their discomfort.

"My mother died four years ago, and I went to live with her sister. But my aunt was sickly, and she too died soon after. From there I went to a great-aunt and great-uncle, but he . . . bothered . . . me with his advances, and so I went to live with cousins. I was with them when we came to London."

"And?" Constance prompted.

"And it was then that I was separated from my companions."

"Poor child. What did you do then?"

"I wandered about the town for a few days—I had only a handful of pennies from the sale of bread I'd brought to market. I knew no one, and I slept wherever I could find a place to lay my head. After some time, I noticed a man with an ugly dog following me. I tried to get away, but he finally caught up with me."

"He took you to Bridewell then?"

"Yes."

"How long were you there?"

"A few months. Though it felt far longer than that." With a shudder, Aurora looked away. The day was too sunny for her to dwell on the memory of those long dark months.

"Well, we must both put away our sorrows. Now I shall show you this splendid house."

"Thank you."

"You're familiar with the kitchen," the widow said as they stepped into the room. Betty was nowhere to be seen, but the delicious odor of newly baked bread lingered in the air. "And, of course, the morning room where we ate breakfast. Beyond the kitchen is a series of storerooms."

The walls of the first storeroom were of grey stone, and rough wooden shelves lined them from floor to ceiling. Various jars and boxes filled the shelves. To one side was a closed door.

"That leads to another storeroom where we keep the larger items, and from there you can go outside, as well as to the cellar, where we keep our butter and milk."

"This is a rather large house for just four people," Aurora said casually.

Constance seemed not to notice anything odd in the other's observation.

"Yes, 'twould be so, except that my household numbers more than four. I have two other servants, Samuel and Peter, who are away now. They have gone to sell some of the cattle, and will be back in a few days. But, even with them, the house these days is too large, too lonely. It is no longer filled with the sounds of running footsteps or laughter."

Aurora's eyes misted slightly. "Perhaps it will be again some day."

Constance smiled sadly. "Perhaps . . . some day."

As the two women retraced their steps through the kitchen and into the morning room, the kitten joined them, daintily following Aurora.

"She seems to like you, child."

"I know, and I'm glad." Aurora wanted to say that the kitten gave her companionship, but she felt a little embarrassed, so she said nothing. They entered the hall Aurora had seen last night when she arrived at Grey Wood. Constance pointed to the doors.

"Those lead to the kitchen and other workrooms. And this," she said, moving across to the barred door, "leads outside."

"Outside?" Aurora asked in a puzzled tone. This didn't make sense. The house had looked much larger from the outside. How could they have reached its other side already? Constance lifted the bar and pushed open the door to show Aurora. She smiled at the girl's delighted expression.

Before them lay a spacious courtyard. Aurora made out the lines of several stone benches under a layer of snow and what looked to be a fountain. Brick paths ran along the perimeter and through the center of the courtyard; in the middle sat a bronze statue.

"It must be wonderful in the spring and summer," Aurora marveled, thinking what a perfect retreat it would be.

"It is. The sun reaches it in late morning and stays until early afternoon. It is my refuge on warm days, and here I grow some of my herbs. I have other gardens in back of the house, as well, but I will show you those later. Perhaps when we have a warm day."

She closed the door, barred it, and then opened the door on the left.

The room beyond was a magnificent great hall, its upper reaches decorated with plaques of the Westcott family's baronial arms. A gallery wrapped around one end, which Constance explained had been where musicians entertained long ago on festive occasions.

"I fear that was well before my time. 'Twas far more common in the youth of Geoffrey's father, although I do remember several occasions when this entire hall was lit with fire and candlelight, and filled with musicians and knights and their ladies."

Several large stone fireplaces, showing little recent use, marked the outside wall of the hall, with tall narrow windows interspersed between them. A seat of highly polished dark wood sat at the base of each window, and the oak floor gleamed from the sunlight that streamed through the windows. Three oversize wooden chairs were pushed together under the musician's gallery, and a few benches lined the walls. A huge table, longer than any Aurora had ever seen, stood neglected in the middle of the room. A single long sword was displayed above the central fireplace.

The two women crossed the great hall, their footsteps echoing hollowly in its immense emptiness. Aurora tried to imagine what the hall must have been like in the days of great entertaining—awash with the light of fires, warm with laughter and good-natured arguments and the sweet tones of music. She shook her head, and the image faded as they went through a door at the far end.

They entered the formal dining room, its floor tiled with blue, green, and gold delft. In one corner sat a stove with its green glazed tiles decorated with the figures of saints. The center tile featured the likeness of a fierce dragon being slain by St. George. In the middle of the large room was an oblong table—dark, weighty, and heavily carved, its four bulbous legs were linked together by stretchers almost at floor level. One massive chair sat at the end, and two long, plain benches were at either side.

Flanking the fireplace were two cupboards consisting of three open shelves, supported in tiers by four posts. The rear posts were plain, but the front pair were heavily carved in the cup and cover shape, resembling a ceremonial chalice. A large number of fine silver and pewter dishes were prominently displayed in both cupboards.

"As you can see, this room is too large for me to dine in alone, which is why I had the smaller table moved into my sitting room."

Aurora nodded and followed Constance to the next room. Looking in, she gasped.

It was aglow in blue, pink, grey, lemon, and salmon. Looking upward, she saw twin rows of small stained glass windows, through which the sunlight painted the room in glorious, delicate hues.

"This was my husband's room. When we were first married, he commissioned the windows from an old monk, who had learned the process from his father. The religious died soon after they were finished."

"They're . . . wonderful," Aurora whispered. She felt as though she were in a church. The glass portrayed scenes of men and women and terrible beasts—stories from the Bible, she assumed.

"Let me show you the rest of the room." Constance led her toward one of the walls, dominated by a fireplace of black stone, unlike the others Aurora had already seen. A clock of brass some two feet high perched on the mantelpiece. "It's German," the woman said, "and was brought back to us by a friend who frequently traveled abroad. Geoffrey was very proud of it."

In front of the fireplace was a massive wooden chair, its wide seat covered in black velvet. A stool with a needlework pad upon it stood nearby. Aurora suspected that Constance and her husband had spent many hours here together. As her eyes grew more accustomed to the softly glowing light, she realized that numerous closets were built into three of the walls. The widow opened one and beckoned to Aurora. Inside, books filled the shelves. Reverently the girl reached out to touch a leather-bound volume, and then pulled her hand back. She didn't want to offend Constance.

"It's all right," Constance said.

Aurora slowly pulled out a thick brown book and opened the vellum cover. The yellowing page was covered in a flowing script in an unfamiliar language. Holding the book as though she were afraid it might crumble, she looked at the other books—North's translation of *Plutarch's Lives*, Lanquet's Chronicle as well as Raphael Holinshed's, Sir Henry Savile's translation of the four books of Tacitus, Thomas Johnson's *Cornucopia*, several Bibles, a volume of Chaucer, the poetry of Lydgate and Skelton, the *Book of Physic*, the *Glass of Health*, and more.

"Do you read?"

"Yes, my lady."

"I'm pleased to hear that, and no doubt Giles will be, too. But, Aurora, there is something I must ask of you immediately."

The girl looked puzzled. "Yes?"

"Don't call me 'my lady.' Please. I want to be your friend, so simply call me Constance."

Aurora nodded, relieved not to have to be so formal with the widow.

"In time, though, you will be able to read these and many more."

She looked up from the book. "When I'm made a noblewoman, that is." She could not keep the irony from her voice.

"Yes." Constance moved away, obviously not wishing to discuss that matter. "My husband had hundreds of volumes in this library. He searched through many lands for them, and when his friends traveled, he would have them bring back books for him. Geoffrey was a very educated man, you see. He spoke five languages and wrote three more, and had many diverse interests." She ran her fingertips lightly across the spines of some of the books. "You will be using some of these volumes when your education begins."

"Do you often read them?"

"When I have the time, which is not often, although I must

confess I wish I had more hours to spend among them. In the winter, there is less for me to do, and often I come here of an evening.''

On one of the walls hung hand-painted maps of the World, of France, and of England and Scotland, and a perpetual almanac in a frame. Aurora returned the book to the closet, closed the door carefully, and then studied the maps for a few minutes.

On a large, heavyset table lay a writing slate, a counterboard and cast of counters, a pair of scales and set of weights, a pair of scissors and a penknife, a whetstone, compasses, a foot-rule, and pens of both bone and steel. A large globe stood on the floor alongside the table. Aurora lightly touched the globe.

The next room was Constance's own closest, and in it were more books—principally prayer books and volumes of poetry and psalms. There was a large collection of trunks and boxes, and glass vessels of various forms and uses, many of enamel or china. Aurora saw trenchers, knives, shears, graters, snuffers, molds, and brushes; in short, all the equipment Constance needed for her many duties.

''Are you tired?'' Constance asked sometime later.

''A little,'' Aurora admitted.

''The first floor took longer than I expected, and we hardly explored at all. We can save the other floors for tomorrow, so, please, lie down if you wish. I know you are tired yet from your ordeal in prison. It's afternoon now, and you don't need to do anything until we have our dinner later.''

''Afternoon already!'' She looked at Constance, astonished. Surely hours had not elapsed since they'd started on the tour of the house.

Constance smiled. ''Time has a strange way here, too, as you have already found.''

''I see that. Yes, I think I'd like to lie down for a while.'' She put a hand over her mouth to cover a yawn. ''I'm more tired than I thought.''

''Too, you weren't allowed to sleep in as late as you doubtless would have liked.'' Aurora nodded, remembering how Giles Blacklaw's shouts had awakened her.

The two women parted at the stairway, and the kitten followed Aurora up to her room. She closed the door behind her and crossed over to the bed, setting the kitten down on it.

The bed had been made, no doubt by Betty, and several gowns Aurora hadn't yet seen had been laid across the press. Once more she yawned, and then she pulled back the coverlet, slipped off her shoes, and crawled into the bed. Lucye began purring loudly, its fluffy head tucked close to hers, and with that lulling sound nearby, Aurora soon fell to sleep.

12

After she left Aurora, Constance returned to her husband's closet and sat in the chair that had been his. She leaned her head back and closed her eyes, inhaling deeply. She could smell so clearly the ink and spicy cinnamon and oiled leather, scents she had come to associate with him, almost as if he were still in the room. Tears stung her eyes, and she pressed her fingers against them.

Showing Aurora the house today had stirred the many ghosts within her, ghosts she had thought long laid to rest.

She missed Geoffrey and her children; no matter what she did, she could not ease that sense of loss. After the death of her family, she had mourned for months and had been unable to function from day to day. Finally, Dickon had taken her by the hand and announced it was time to look forward.

And she had understood. He had mourned his family as much as she had grieved for her own, but she had become a special burden to him, making it difficult for him to do his work. And she had expected him to continue doing his work, even while he himself was bereft. From that day on, Constance had mourned less and less, giving way to bitter and unhappy tears only during the long dark hours of night as she lay alone in her great bed. That bed had not always been lonely. In the six years since Geoffrey's death, there had been two or three men, but none had eased the pain in her heart.

None until Giles Blacklaw. And even then she wasn't sure if he eased the pain so much as intrigued her, making her

momentarily forget her loss. But, as to whether they suited
. . . that she didn't know. She didn't understand him but only
knew that he had been a friend of Geoffrey's and was of
course a friend of her own.

Yet even Constance didn't know what Blacklaw intended
for the girl. She knew he had wanted an aristocratic-looking
girl of around sixteen, and certainly he had found one in this
girl he called Aurora. She seemed well-bred, far better man-
nered than many city people Constance knew. She was also
aware of the girl's fear and wished she could do something to
alleviate it. But she couldn't—at least not until she knew
what Giles intended. And knowing that might cause more
fear, she reflected, and she shivered, wondering what the
months to come would bring.

The next afternoon, after a brief luncheon of cheese and
bread, Constance and Aurora continued their tour of the
house. Once again the kitten accompanied them on Aurora's
heels.

They returned to the entry hall and ascended the narrow
stairs. Aurora was surprised to find that today, like the day
before, she hadn't seen either of the servants since breakfast,
but Constance explained they had work elsewhere in the
house.

"As I said yesterday, Grey Wood is very old. The kitchen
forms the core of the old house, although I think it was
actually an ancient fortress at one time. This used to be a
hilltop, but it's been worn down by the passage of time, and
you can see that it only rises a little now. There is the
remnant of a ditch around it, too, but somewhere along the
way one of my ancestors decided he would make Grey Wood
into a great house, and he began building walls and wings
until we have the monster I live in now.

"My ancestor was extremely eccentric, and not very effi-
cient, I fear, and I think few, if any, of the original rooms
were torn down when he began his renovation. He simply
added onto them. Still, it's an interesting house. Perhaps later
in the day I'll tell you more about its history."

"I would like that very much."

As Aurora followed Constance down a hallway, she realized that this wasn't the gallery that led to her own room,

and, looking around, she saw that she had not been here before.

The widow chuckled. "It can be very confusing, particularly at night, which is why I recommend that you don't wander around by yourself for the first few days until you become better acquainted with the house. I do not have a staff numerous enough to hear your shouts if you should become hopelessly lost within these mazes of rooms."

"Very well. I'll stay with you, if you don't mind, Constance."

"Not at all."

Aurora glanced behind her and saw that Lucye kept falling behind, so she picked up the kitten, and the women continued their tour. The rooms along this wing were bedrooms and had not been empty long, judging by their looks. Aurora thought it sad that no one stayed in these rooms and wondered if the house would ever be filled with people and laughter again. She suspected that these rooms had been occupied by Constance's family when she was a child, or by close friends who came to visit.

Most of the rooms were sparsely furnished, although the furniture was quite fine. The beds were of carved oak, with elaborate curtains closed around them. Some of the chests were inlaid with what Aurora thought was irridescent white stone, but which Constance explained was either mother-of-pearl or ivory from the Orient. The walls were half paneled and half plastered, in the manner of the first floor, and several huge tapestries hung in the last bedroom.

"My mother did those," Constance said as she caught Aurora admiring them.

"They're wonderful."

"She was very good with the needle and taught me all she knew. However, my skill is not half as great as hers was."

The gallery led into a smaller, narrower gallery that twisted around another stairway, which Constance explained led down to the ground floor and then outside. Here there were still more bedrooms, although these were even more sparsely furnished than the previous ones, and other rooms whose original purposes were lost to time. The women passed several windows, narrower than a man's shoulders, and Constance explained these were part of the original fortresslike structure.

None of the rooms were the same size, and some of them were opened from another room instead of a gallery. One room opened onto another that had three doors, and beyond each door was still another room, each with two or more doors. Aurora was bewildered by the number of rooms in this maze. All looked much alike, and she saw how easily one could become lost.

The floor above, Constance said, was virtually identical to the one they were on, except that it had been closed for quite some time and was in need of repair; a precarious stairway led upward to a stone tower, which had been used a century or more ago in the defense of Grey Wood.

"Could I see the tower?" Aurora asked, excited at the prospect. "I've never seen a real tower. Oh, please, Constance?"

The widow was about to refuse, but then she smiled and shrugged. "Why not? Follow me."

Constance led her to a narrow staircase, and they ascended to the third floor. This floor was far darker than the one below, and dust billowed in great clouds as they walked through its halls. Aurora coughed, and Lucye squirmed in her arms. She didn't want to set her pet down, for fear she might lose her, so she put her in the pocket of her apron. After a few seconds, the kitten stopped moving, and Aurora looked in to see her napping.

Constance found a narrow door and pushed it open. Beyond was a spiral staircase of stone. It was narrow, dark, and damp, and Constance cautioned the girl to watch her step. Once, Aurora slipped, but she clutched a stone protruding from the wall and steadied herself. As they climbed higher, Aurora could feel the cold air seeping into her clothes, and she shivered. Finally, they reached a primitive-looking door. Constance put her shoulder against it and pushed. Slowly, it opened, and they climbed into the tower room.

If Aurora had thought the floor below had shown signs of disuse, this room appeared unvisited for well over a century. Dust lay piled in the corners, and heaps of rubbish testified to generations of rats nesting here undisturbed.

"I was only up here once with Geoffrey," Constance said.

"When I was a girl. He wanted to picnic here—the room wasn't in this state of disrepair. But we never did."

Aurora had moved to a slitted window and stared out at the rolling landscape below. Everything was white, except that here and there buildings, dark against the snow, sprung up like small mushrooms. She moved to another window and saw much the same scenery.

Constance put her arms to her chest and shivered. "It's cold up here. I think I'll go down now. Do you want me to wait for you below?"

Aurora shook her head. "I've seen enough. I was just curious."

As they descended the stairs, Constance glanced back over her shoulder.

"You can see how old the tower is—it looks more Norman than anything else. I don't know how old the original house—or castle—was, only that here and there we discover small reminders of its antiquity."

"Perhaps on a warm day we could go up there again," Aurora suggested.

"And picnic?" Constance asked wryly.

"Just to look."

"Very well, but in the meantime I have things to do downstairs. Will you come with me?"

Aurora nodded, realizing how in two days she was fitting into the routine of Grey Wood. On one hand, it was frightening; on the other, it was reassuring, and she needed that.

13

The following day dawned cold but sunny, and Constance deemed it an excellent time for the girl to see some of the grounds. This task was left to Dickon Tate, who willingly conducted Aurora on an extensive tour.

"The estate extends as far as you can see in all directions," Dickon said. They were bundled heavily against the cold crisp air, and his breath frosted as he spoke.

Aurora had left Lucye inside today, even though the kitten had wanted to follow her. It was simply too cold outside for the cat, she thought. She looked in the direction that Dickon pointed, and she slowly turned with him, staring across the snow-covered hills. This magnificent sweep was all part of Constance's estate. "It must be hundreds of acres," she said, amazed.

Dickon nodded. "Used to be more, but some's been sold over the years. Some's been sold to tenants. Still it's big, though most of it is still woods. The master didn't care that much for farming and preferred the land in its natural state."

Dickon led Aurora to the back of the house to show her the gardens.

"You can't see much now, what with all the snow, but it's a fine garden in the spring and summer. Come those seasons, you'll see." He nodded knowingly. "The mistress collects flowers from the garden and puts them all over the house, so the house almost becomes a garden itself."

From there they went to the various outbuildings, ending

with the stable where Dickon's young nephew, Edward, was in charge.

"We've only got a handful of horses now," Edward said apologetically, showing Aurora the horses munching on hay in their stalls. "We had more before, but the mistress has had to sell some off."

"Because of expense?" Aurora asked. She was surprised, believing that Constance, if not rich, was more than comfortable. But the widow had been forced to sell some of her land, as well as her horses. That didn't seem to make sense.

Dickon was staring fiercely at the boy, and the youngster shifted from one foot to another.

"Oh aye," Edward muttered vaguely, as if he'd already said too much.

Aurora had noticed a strange look pass between uncle and nephew and wondered what it signified. It was as if they were deliberately keeping something from her. And they had every right to, she reminded herself. After all, she was a newcomer to Grey Wood, and doubtless they were not sure she could be trusted. She wasn't quite a member of the household—anyway, not yet.

She reached out to stroke the nose of a small bay who was watching them with some interest. Aurora twined her fingers through the black mane; it wasn't as coarse as horses' manes usually were, and she thought that someone took very good care of the beast. Was it Edward, or did Constance find time to visit the stable?

"She's lovely."

"Aye, she's the mistress's own mount. Lord Blacklaw picked her himself."

"I see."

"Do you ride, mistress?"

"Yes, a little, although I've never been on anything as good as this mare. I learned upon the wide flat back of a farm cob."

"Those be good horses, too," Edward said, nodding to himself. "Stout of heart."

"Yes," she murmured.

"You'll be riding this one," Dickon said, stepping forward. He had been quiet for some time now, and Aurora had almost forgotten his presence—which, she thought, was precisely what he wanted.

He brought forward a leggy chestnut with a blond mane and tail. "He's big enough for your long legs," Edward said artlessly, "and gentle as well. You couldn't ask for a better mount, mistress."

"And was he also chosen by Lord Blacklaw?"

"Yes," the boy replied, although this time his tone was more cautious.

"Lord Blacklaw seems to be a fairly frequent guest at Grey Wood," she remarked casually.

"Upon occasion," said Dickon. "Now, we'd best be running along so that the boy can get back to his chores."

Aurora thanked Edward for showing her the stables, and she and Dickon walked back to the house and entered the sitting room. She handed her cloak to Dickon, and went to the fireplace, to warm her numb fingers by the flames.

"I'll send Betty in with something warm for you, miss."

"Thank you, Dickon."

She stood by the fireplace for a few minutes longer, feeling the warmth return to her body. She looked up from the flames as Constance entered the room.

"Did you enjoy the tour?"

"Yes, I did. I can hardly wait until spring to see the gardens."

"They are a lot of work, but lovely, I think. Some of the flowers are not from England but were brought to us by friends of my husband, and I think you will be quite surprised by them."

"You also have some fine horses."

"Thank you. We had more once—when my husband was alive—but I sold them. One woman could scarcely keep twenty head. After all, there was no one to exercise them any longer."

Betty came in with mugs of mulled wine and then left. "After we've eaten, I thought we would go to the still-room and you could help me with some of my herbal preparations," Constance said.

"I'd like that, Constance. I used to help my mother some, although she had only a few recipes, and I'm sure they were very simple compared to yours." It was the first time she had talked about her mother to Constance, and the woman had not pressed for many details. Aurora suspected that Constance would want her to talk about her past only when she felt ready.

They ate a simple midday meal of yellow cheese and a venison pie, flavored generously with nutmeg. A fruit tartlet followed, and the entire meal was washed down with several cups of ale. Afterward, they sat before the fire, with Constance doing some needlework, while Aurora dozed. The kitten had found her and was asleep on her lap. After a few minutes, the girl woke and apologized for sleeping, and then she followed Constance into the still-room, which was located on the other side of the kitchen.

This room was filled with jars of dried rose petals, dried sage and marjoram, nutmeg, yarrow, valerian, poppy seeds, and dozens of other ingredients used in the day-to-day existence of Grey Wood. Here, Constance made poultices for the sore stocks of the horses and herbal compresses for ill persons within the household. She also distilled several perfumes for her own use, and for sprinkling upon stored linens.

"We will begin with the basics today. In the future, I will also teach you how to perfume candles to guard against vermin and the plague," she said, as she replaced the top of the clove jar.

"I want to learn everything you can teach me," Aurora said eagerly.

"Good. I like a willing student. In the days to come I will also teach you how to make conserves, and jellies, and rose hip marmalade. All of this—and more—is very important for you to know if you are to be a noblewoman," Constance said.

Aurora realized with a start that her education had already begun. Constance shrewdly had said nothing about lessons; instead, she had simply suggested that Aurora help her; and all the while the girl was learning.

For the remainder of the afternoon she helped Constance prepare bags of sachet—powdered mixtures of dried lavender, rose petals, and cloves. When they finished, it was time for dinner. Afterward, Constance had Aurora read to her, and Aurora did so haltingly because she was nervous. But before long, they retired to bed. As Aurora waited for sleep, she was surprised to find herself wondering when she would see Giles Blacklaw again.

14

In the next few days, Constance encouraged Aurora to sleep as late as she wished. She said that the girl needed her rest, and there was nothing that demanded her immediate concentration. Aurora appreciated Constance's concern, for she continued to feel exhausted.

During the daylight hours, her time was spent helping Constance in the still-room or in one of the many other rooms that needed their attention.

Upon occasion the two women would retire to the sitting room in the late afternoon, where they sipped mulled cider and Aurora read aloud as Constance did her needlework. Her initial shyness having disappeared, the girl no longer stumbled over unfamiliar words, and many of the phrases became familiar to her. With the widow's encouragement, she looked through more of the old volumes. Constance recommended as lighter reading *Guy of Warwick*, *The Ship of Fools*, and *The Book of Riddles*.

The two women had planned a ride one day, but a snowfall postponed it for several days. Finally, the sun came out, and Edward brought their mounts around to the front of the house. He joined them on a third horse, and the trio rode away from Grey Wood, the boy's horse some paces behind theirs. Pausing at the crest of a hill, Aurora caught sight of a distant white ribbon cutting a long path through the woods.

"What river is that?"

"The Thames. We're east of London, in Kent. Where did you live?"

"North of London, I believe, in a village you wouldn't know because it's so small." For some reason her eyes were stinging.

"We're not far from Greenwich, although you can't see it from here. Grey Wood was the site of an old Roman encampment." Constance paused. "Aurora, do you know who the Romans were?" The girl shook her head. "Well, that shall be part of your education."

"Were they soldiers?"

"An assumption with merit. Yes, and they lived in the time of Our Lord, although when they came to England it was before the birth of Christ. They conquered several people here, pagans who worshipped great stones and sacrificed human lives, and in the end the Romans themselves were conquered, too."

"By the pagans?"

"By those who came from the land of the Vikings." She smiled at the other's blank expression. "I think I will enjoy teaching you history very much."

"Where did you learn this?"

"My father was a renowned scholar and desired that all in his family—women, included—be most knowledgeable, so that he could conduct intelligent conversations with them. Thus, he taught me everything he learned. My late husband, too, was something of a scholar."

"Who else lived in England?"

"After the Romans left, the Saxons settled here. They were a proud race, but they were peaceful farmers when the Normans arrived from what we today call France. A new reign began, a completely new way of living, with lords and underlings, and a strict system of fealty.

"My family—my mother and father, you see, were first cousins—was the le Greys, an aristocratic Norman family who came here as warriors some five hundred years ago. They fell in love with Kent upon first sight. King William granted to my ancestor, Robert le Grey, all the land that the baron could see from this hilltop. In time, though, the le Greys mingled with other families, some of them Saxons, and in the end the Westcotts became the ruling family." She paused. "They stood with York against Lancaster, and fought on Richard's side at Bosworth a hundred years ago; we have ever been the King's—and Queen's—faithful.''

''And your family now?''

''Alas, I am the last of the le Greys and the Westcotts. Much of the land you see now belongs to another Norman family, the de Juliers. Their ancestors, and mine, fought side by side.''

The three riders continued their way in companionable silence, while Aurora thought about what Constance had—and had not—said. She had sensed something odd underlying her words, but what it was, she couldn't say. She did notice that several times Constance gave Edward a significant look.

When the light began fading, they turned back to Grey Wood, arriving just in time for dinner. They dined upon roast chicken, pickled fish, and dried apples. Afterward, they drank cider, and Constance entertained her young guest by playing ballads upon the alpherion and singing in accompaniment. She soon had the girl learning the words, while she deftly plucked the instrument's strings. Other evenings passed in much the same way, and soon Aurora began work on a small piece of embroidery. Each night the scene beneath her hands blossomed with the application of the colorful threads.

As the days passed, Aurora felt a change in herself. One morning she sneaked into Geoffrey Westcott's closet to peer into the mirror she had seen there. In the silvered glass, she saw a different girl. The dark smudges under her eyes had disappeared, and her eyes no longer looked haunted. Her hair was restored, while her skin was soft and suffused with a healthy glow. She smiled at her image, an almost tremulous expression, and realized she had Constance Westcott—and Giles Blacklaw—to thank for this image.

Giles Blacklaw. Her thoughts had been filled with the man. Still she wondered what prompted him to save her from prison. And even while she was enjoying her new life, she wanted to know what would happen in the days to come. She suspected charity had played no role in her release. But, if not charity, then what? And she feared thinking too much about the future, lest her life change horribly and she return to Bridewell.

Too, she wanted to know more about Blacklaw himself, for

as much as she did not want to admit it, he intrigued her. But though she was curious about him, she asked no questions of Constance. She suspected that those questions would not be appreciated—she could not ascertain the precise relationship between Blacklaw and the widow. And while Edward might have slipped by saying that Blacklaw was a frequent visitor, since Aurora had arrived at Grey Wood, Blacklaw had only visited once, and Constance had mentioned his name twice.

Aurora had now been a fortnight at Grey Wood. This morning, she rose well before Constance and went downstairs. She worked for a while on her embroidery, the fanciful birds slowly beginning to take form, and then went to the library to read. Constance finally called her to breakfast, and as they were at the table, they heard a knock on the outside door. Almost at once Aurora recognized the special pattern of knocks Blacklaw had used the day he'd brought her here, and so she was not at all surprised to see him when he strode into the room. But when she saw his face set in a grim expression, Aurora knew her pleasant interlude at Grey Wood was about to change. But whether for better or worse, she couldn't tell.

15

"The human body," John Maxwell explained as he paced in front of the great fireplace, his hands locked behind his back, "is comprised of Four Humours: blood, phlegm, black bile and yellow bile. With these, the physician may then diagnose the patient's illness from the four qualities of the body—dryness, moisture, heat and cold—which correspond to the Four Humours. The physician may also prescribe treatment according to the imbalance of the humours, as in prescribing leaching when the body, too filled with blood, causes the face to turn red.

"It is the Ancients, of course, to whom we owe the present advanced state of our medicine, and who were the first to note the Humours. One of the most famous Ancients was Galen, who lived in Turkey more than a thousand years ago."

As Maxwell continued his discourse Aurora's mind drifted. A month ago her studies had begun in earnest, and of all the subjects Blacklaw insisted she know, this one interested her least of all. She didn't think it was practical. A much sounder policy would be to study herbs and their curative effects with Constance. She tried to listen, but couldn't concentrate, so she began studying her newest tutor.

He had a narrow face with a firm chin and wide mouth meant for smiling, although she'd rarely seen that expression on his face since his arrival. His brown eyes were wide-set and guileless. He wasn't tall, and in fact stood only a few inches taller than she. He was exceedingly slight of build, a thinness enhanced by the numerous days he had spent without anything more than a crust of bread for a meal. His was a kind and gentle scholar's face, she thought.

John wore a scholar's gown of plain brown cloth with long hanging sleeves. The open gown revealed a simple shirt of white and unadorned trunk hose, and she could see that the gown had been patched several times, none too expertly. On his feet he wore heavy leather shoes, once black but now turned grey from wear. Their silver buckles were polished, which surprised her. From the little he'd said about himself she suspected he was close to twenty. He told her he had been studying at Oxford until just a few years ago when his family fell upon hard times.

In these times, there was great suspicion toward even one's own countrymen, and the Catholics were feared above all other groups. John was the first son of a noble Roman Catholic family. The Maxwell lands, owned by his family since the time of the Conqueror, had been seized by the Crown, and thus the revenue from the tenants had ceased, leaving the family penniless.

With no choice left, John left the university, and since then he had made his living—a marginal one—by tutoring students who did not mind his choice of religion.

Aurora had been saddened by his story, and yet had not fully understood why this tragedy had befallen John. After all, why should the Crown take away the lands of nobles loyal to it? Innocently enough, she had asked him, and he had replied that it was something which he would leave to Blacklaw to explain.

So far, she hadn't asked Blacklaw; she was waiting until what she judged to be the right moment. Meanwhile, she listened to her other tutors.

In the past few weeks she'd had a succession of teachers, all of them noblemen or men of good birth. Hearing their life stories in varying detail she found that they, like John, had fallen upon hard times. Each tutor bore himself with pride and distinction, yet their once-fine clothes were shabby and patched. She realized that without Blacklaw, these men would have had little money; yet when she mentioned this to her benefactor, he brushed it away, as though he didn't want to acknowledge his kindness. Why did he want to seem harsher than he was? It didn't make sense to her.

"Aurora, you are not attending me," came a gentle remonstrance. Guiltily she looked up to see John Maxwell watching her. She blushed and ducked her head.

"I am sorry . . . I was thinking."

"And I suspect not about Galen, either."

"No." Her blush deepened.

"Have you read any of Lily for today?"

William Lily's Latin grammar was her basic text; although neither Maxwell nor Blacklaw expected Aurora to become proficient in Latin in the short time they had set aside for her education, they did want her to learn the basics.

"No," she murmured.

He sighed and closed his book. Then he sat down on a bench, and helped himself to cider from a mug.

"I think you've had enough of studying for today, Aurora. What do you say?"

"All right, John."

When he had first arrived, he had asked her to call him by his Christian name rather than Master Maxwell, for the latter made him "feel like an old fat burgher." She had giggled but acceded to his request. They were both aware that there was little difference in their ages.

"Is something amiss, Aurora? Usually you are quite attentive in your lessons."

She smiled and shook her head. "No, 'tis simply that my mind will not settle today."

" 'Tis the nature of the season, I believe," he said, "so close to midwinter and Christmas. There are many festivities that young girls such as yourself would wish to attend."

"Will Constance plan anything?"

"Surely, although it might be difficult now with . . ." His voice trailed off, and he glanced away.

"With what?" she prompted.

"Never mind, child." He shook his head, indicating that the matter was closed. He looked out the nearest window and saw the light smothered under the cover of dark clouds. "Well, 'tis late, anyway, and looks to be snowing soon. I suppose I should be leaving."

"Nonsense, you'll dine with us tonight."

Both Aurora and Maxwell jumped slightly and turned to face the newcomer. Neither had heard Blacklaw enter the room. He was dressed all in black, and he brought with him a whiff of the cold air outside.

"Have you given up studying so soon?" he asked. One eyebrow was arched, giving him a sardonic look.

She nodded. "I fear that my mind rests on other matters today."

"You've done well enough these past few weeks to end early today."

This was faint praise from him, she knew. But if she expected more, she wouldn't be getting it. She must be satisfied with these few crumbs.

"Now, what about dinner, John?"

"I shouldn't, Giles; I have other students to attend today, and they've been waiting for some time." He paused, and seeing that Blacklaw did not believe his flimsy excuse, he nodded. "All right, I'll stay."

"Good lad." He glanced her way. "Go inform Constance we shall have a guest for dinner tonight."

"Very well, my lord," she said in a meek tone. She could see the look of surprise on Blacklaw's face at her obedience, and inwardly she smiled. She rose reluctantly and left the room as quietly as her benefactor had entered it a moment before.

"What have you told her, my lord?"

"Nothing beyond that I wish to make her into a noble-woman."

"And she's asked nothing?"

"I did not say that."

Blacklaw carefully placed a log onto the fire and watched as the the orange and red flames swept upward. For several minutes the men were silent. Then Blacklaw sighed and sat in the chair by the fireplace, while John settled on a bench. The older man stretched his long legs and stared moodily into the fire.

"How does she fare?" Shadows from the firelight cast hollows in his eyes and along his cheeks, and John thought he had never seen a more forbidding man.

John rose and paced about the room, his hands behind his back. Blacklaw smiled gently at this scholarly pose, which

Maxwell assumed so easily and unconsciously. "Very well, I think, Giles. Even though I've worked with her for only a few days, she's proved a good student. Her mind is quick, and usually she's eager to learn. Today, though, she wasn't attending my lecture. I'm sure that's natural. After all, you've been working her rather hard in such a short time."

"Is that disapproval I hear?"

"What you do is none of my business, only that . . . I am concerned about her."

"You think I've recruited her for some evil purpose. Is that it?" Maxwell said nothing. "I have your answer. My purpose is not what you think."

"There are many possibilities, Giles."

"Yes, and you have fastened upon only a few. I think you have the mind of a Puritan sometimes, John, for all that you're a Catholic."

"As are you."

"That is something I will never forget," Blacklaw said softly. Before the two men could speak further, Constance swept into the room, followed by Aurora.

"You'll not mind a simple roast tonight, will you, John?"

"It sounds wonderful," he replied gravely. "I wish there was something I could contribute."

"Your presence is contribution enough," she said, dimpling faintly. "Aurora, come." They retired to the kitchen to oversee the meal.

Aurora would have preferred to stay with Blacklaw, but Constance needed her help. Betty had been basting the roast and now began assembling others parts of their meal.

"Is John so poor?" Aurora asked. She had found the napkins—precious luxuries—and held them carefully so that they would not get soiled.

"Yes. There isn't anything John could afford to bring, I fear. Once he brought a loaf of bread, but I think a student had given it to him as payment for lessons."

Aurora took down the plates. "I hadn't realized. . . . I know he came from a good family, who had once been wealthy."

"Don't they all." Constance sighed, and Betty stepped backward to permit her mistress to shift the cast iron cooking pot.

"Just as Lord Blacklaw comes from a good family?"

"You shouldn't be calling him a lord, child," the widow said mildly. She gestured to Betty to run to the still-room for cheese.

"But he is, isn't he?" Aurora persisted. "Even though he told me to use no title, I know he has one."

The woman sighed and brushed back a tendril of hair. "Yes, he does, if you must know."

Aurora felt a flash of triumph at this small success. One puzzle was solved, but its solution only indicated a larger mystery.

"Lord Blacklaw has fallen on hard times, like each one of my tutors." She looked to the other for confirmation and received it with a brief nod.

"I thought so," Aurora said.

"You think too much about the wrong things, Aurora. You'll doubtless discover that thinking and asking questions can lead to trouble. Now, bring those vegetables here. I'm ready to put them by the roast."

Aurora promptly did so, and within an hour the four sat down to a modest dinner of beef roast, a hare dressed in herbs, beets in vinegar, stewed turnips, and bread. It was followed by apple tartlets, which Aurora and Constance had baked that morning.

Blacklaw had brought ale with him, and as she drained her third glass, Aurora could feel herself becoming slightly lightheaded and less restrained than she normally was. Emboldened, she was prompted to ask a question.

"My lord, why did you take me from Bridewell?"

Conversation at the table ceased as Constance and John looked at him.

"It was a whim."

"I beg to disagree, sir. Teaching me to be a noblewoman is hardly the 'whim' of a serious man. I'm no simple-minded child who believes every story she's told."

"Indeed, you are not."

"Then why—"

"No, not tonight." He smiled at her, but the expression did not reach his eyes. Aurora was wise enough to drop the matter—for now, she resolved. But whatever his reasons, she would have them from him. Somehow.

16

Aurora's days fell into a pattern. Her lessons began shortly after she awoke, and she scarcely had time to breakfast before John Maxwell or another tutor appeared at the door, ready to start.

Aurora also began to be tutored in the art of being a lady. These lessons, given by Constance, were less formal than Aurora's other studies, and Constance proved a patient instructor. Thus, Aurora looked forward to these lessons more eagerly than she did to her regular schooling. Among the first instructions Constance offered were the table manners expected if Aurora were to dine with the Queen, or with anyone of a higher station. Constance said that often the manners of nobility were little better than an animal's, but the girl would distinguish herself by her refinement. Aurora learned to curtsey becomingly, to play an instrument—very important, Constance swore, for any man or woman to know because music was highly appreciated at Court—and to dally and flirt. She also learned, as it might be expected of her once she reached the worldly court, to play cards, chiefly gleek, primero, noddy, post-and-pair, and God-make-them-rich.

"This ability will not be over-appreciated by some, particularly among the men," Constance said, "but you must learn it to be accepted."

She, Constance, Blacklaw, and John sometimes played a group game in the afternoon. Her favorite was Purposes, a game of questions and answers, and she proved good at it, although not as good as Blacklaw. Blacklaw threw up his hands in feigned disgust and left the room when Constance suggested "draw-gloves." Aurora looked at Constance. These games were so new to her that they excited her.

"It is a game based on a race at drawing off gloves when certain words are spoken, and Giles does not think it a 'serious' game." Constance's eyes sparkled with amusement. "But then he is not a lady at Court and does not know that little of a serious nature is expected of one there."

Blacklaw taught Aurora to play chess, and in each game she was roundly beaten by him. She despaired, thinking she would never achieve any skill, but he shook his head and said that for an amateur she was not bad. It was small comfort to her.

But soon new delights took Aurora's mind from her inferior chess-playing: the next day, she began her dancing lessons.

"Dancing provides a young lady with exercise, as well as grace, a highly desirable quality in Court members," Constance said. "It is also considered a fine aid when you are seeking a husband."

"Am I to have a husband?" Aurora asked, somewhat startled.

Constance looked thoughtful. "I think so, although Giles hasn't selected anyone yet, my dear. Do you not wish to marry?"

Aurora hesitated. She didn't know what to answer. Yes, she thought she might like to marry, but only if she fell in love. Perhaps that was a silly notion for her even to think about. An arranged marriage was more practical, if far less desirable.

"I don't know," she replied truthfully. "I hadn't really given it much thought."

"Well, don't worry about it. You have other matters that concern you now." Aurora nodded but could not dismiss a small lingering worry.

As the days progressed, she learned all that would be expected of a young woman of her age and apparent breeding. Lucye aided her in her dancing by jumping on her feet and often tripping her, so that girl and cat would land in a heap on the floor. Constance would smile indulgently and suggest that Lucye should sit out the next dance.

Before half a year had elapsed, Aurora was proficient in both reading and writing and had begun conversing in simple French, a language she enjoyed for its nuances. Before her arrival in London, she had possessed only a rudimentary education, for she'd been taught with the other village children the basics of numbers, reading, and writing. But now, her horizons had broadened, and she began to see a world she had never known existed.

By the time she had been at Grey Wood for eight months, she began to wonder when her education would be completed—and what would come after that. Blacklaw took over the next phase of her education himself, moving her classroom outside with the good weather. He taught her how to hunt with a falcon and to ride a horse in a most elegant fashion.

The horse he led to her one bright August day was the tall chestnut with a golden mane and tail that Edward had said Blacklaw had chosen for her. The gelding fairly pranced, and Aurora eyed it nervously.

Blacklaw helped her up and then vaulted easily into the saddle of his own mount, and they rode away from the house. As she had frequently done in the past few months, she grew very aware of Blacklaw's closeness to her. As usual, this proximity made her nervous and she would fall silent, afraid that if she spoke she would stutter or otherwise make a fool of herself. They had gone some distance from Grey Wood when he turned his head and regarded her coolly. "You handle the gelding well."

"Thank you," she murmured. "I was taught by an excellent instructor."

A smile flickered briefly across his face. "That is true, but you also possess a special ability with horses and animals. I noticed it first with that kitten of yours—it won't come near anyone but you. And then there was that time when you held my falcon. I had never seen him so calm as when you began to stroke his feathers."

She blushed, pleased with his praise, which came rarely. "I like animals very much."

"So it would seem." Again he looked over at her, but this time he didn't speak. She wondered what passed through his mind at that moment, but she didn't dare ask him.

The road narrowed, so that they were forced into a single

file, with Blacklaw ahead of her. She studied his straight back and the proud way that he held his head, and was conscious of a deep ache inside. She wished that she could banish that feeling.

As if he sensed her thoughts, Blacklaw glanced backward. "Are you all right, Aurora?"

"Yes, fine, thank you."

In the distance she heard the muted cry of birds, and from a pond on the left there came the comical croaking of frogs. The sky was a deep blue, the air warm and fresh, and she was riding with Giles Blacklaw. What did that matter? she asked herself. She was alone with him; there was nothing more to the matter than that.

No, one part of her said, there was more, much more to the matter than that. Quickly Aurora thrust any such thought from her mind and concentrated on enjoying the ride. They rode for several more hours, and when the light began to fail, he suggested that they return. As they rode into the stable, she wondered how many more times they would be able to spend alone together, and she knew that somehow these times would be too few.

PART II

1583

1

Could an entire year really have elapsed? Aurora asked herself wonderingly as she sat by the window and stared outside at the great flakes of snow that fell in soft swirls. Lucye, now grown to a long, sleek adult creature, lay asleep by her side, and from time to time she stroked its soft sides.

The sky had remained overcast since she'd risen that morning, and she had suspected then that later in the day it would snow. She wasn't pleased about the snow, not today anyway. This day reminded her very much of the day one year before when she had been taken from Bridewell. Sometimes she felt as though she had been out of prison for well over a year; at other times her stay at Grey Wood had seemed brief.

To mark the occasion, she was going to prepare a special meal as a thank-you for Lord Blacklaw. It would be an elaborate meal for two only, designed to demonstrate the skills she had learned under Constance's tutelage this past year. She had thought of the idea a week ago when Constance said that Blacklaw would be returning to Grey Wood on this day but that she would be visiting friends in a neighboring house. The widow's absence meant Aurora and Blacklaw would be alone at Grey Wood, with the exception of the servants. There had been few occasions when she had been left alone with the man. Usually Constance stayed with them, or one of the many tutors, all of whom had been dismissed now that Aurora's education was finished. Only John came to visit from time to time; indeed, he saw Aurora far more often than Blacklaw did, for which she was not at all happy. And so, within a few hours Giles Blacklaw would be here again . . . after a month's absence on business, as Constance had explained.

What sort of business? Aurora wondered, drawing her finger idly across the frosty pane of glass. It left a smear, which she quickly breathed on and rubbed away with a corner of her apron. No one ever said what sort of business Blacklaw had or why he must go away for so long. And he never said a word about it when he returned. She had asked, certainly, after the first few absences, but Blacklaw had said he couldn't discuss it, and he had looked at her with that infuriatingly enigmatic smile.

He couldn't be more mysterious, she thought, and because she didn't know the answers to any of the questions that crowded her head, she was all the more intrigued with him.

She smoothed out a wrinkle in her skirt and smiled as she touched the soft rose material. It was one of the many new gowns she'd been given this past year. Gone were the old hand-me-downs from Constance; the press was filled with new clothing, much of which she had sewn herself. Beneath the gown, she could see her underskirt with the elaborate embroidery she had learned under Constance's instruction. Automatically her fingers went to the dangling earrings of matching rose stones set in her lobes. How she had changed in the past year—becoming so different, so much older. She rose from the seat, disturbing Lucye, who yawned, showing a very pink mouth, and lazily opened one eye.

"Yes, I'm going into the kitchen now. I have much to do, and you may come if you wish." Aurora smiled and scratched the cat behind an ear. She headed toward the kitchen, and within seconds she heard Lucye's soft padding as she trailed behind her. While it was only early afternoon, she had many preparations still to do, even though Blacklaw wasn't expected until evening. He nearly always came under the cover of night.

And wasn't that a little odd? one part of her asked. She shrugged, and began slicing the bread. She shouldn't be so nosy. His business wasn't her business. And yet she felt she had a right to know more about him. Had he not taken her from the prison and taught her to be a noblewoman? And because of this, weren't their lives somehow twined together? So she should know his business, even if it was illegal—for what other sort of business was so furtive, making a man as close-mouthed as Blacklaw? She didn't know what it was that drew him away from her, but tonight she was determined to find out. No matter what.

2

"I thought you wouldn't come this evening," she said shyly.

Blacklaw had just arrived, and stood now in the great hall, brushing off the flakes of snow that clung wetly to his shoulders and his hair. He handed his hat and gloves, as well as his cloak, to Dickon, who bowed and departed. Once more, this mysterious man was all in black; it was a color that suited him well, Aurora thought, reflecting the man's dark moods.

Aurora forced herself to keep her hands clasped in front of her. She didn't want to betray her emotions by letting him see her hands tremble. That they most certainly would have done now that he was here, and she was alone with him. Alone, except for the presence somewhere of Dickon, and Betty, Samuel and Peter, and Edward out in the stable.

He arched an eyebrow. "Oh? And why is that? Didn't Constance receive my letter? I wrote that I would be coming today."

"Oh yes, yes, she received it, but I thought . . . the snow," she explained, more than a little nervous now, "I thought it might keep you away, keep you with your—business."

His look now held amusement. "Indeed, is that what you thought?"

She answered quickly, almost breathlessly. "Yes, I thought that might be. Constance had said you were away this past month on business, and I thought it might be . . . business again . . . tonight which detained you because . . . business . . . often takes you away."

"My 'business,' as you call it, has been taken care of—quite satisfactorily, too."

"I am glad."

He followed her into the sitting room to stand before the fire. She handed him a large glass of claret, which he accepted gratefully.

"I'm numb tonight. It was a long cold ride from London."

She nodded, not knowing what else to say. So, he had been to London. On business. Still, this information told her nothing.

In the chair before the fire, Blacklaw lapsed into a thoughtful silence and stared moodily into the flames. Aurora sat opposite him, on the stool. The cat slept on the hearth beside her, and from time to time she leaned over to stroke the glossy fur.

What is he thinking? she wondered. About his business? About Constance? About herself? She doubted that. If she were ever to figure in his mind, one reflected, it was only as a pawn in some unknown game of chess.

And if that were so, one part of her asked, why did you go to the bother of making an elaborate meal for him? For that she had no answer.

Blacklaw raised his head. "Where's Constance? I haven't seen her yet tonight."

"She is away. Visiting," she added lamely, as if to clarify her answer.

"I see."

She took a deep breath and plunged forward. It was now or never. "My lord, do you know what today is?"

"A Wednesday, is it not?"

"Yes."

"Mid-November."

"Yes."

"I see. You want something more." He steepled his fingers as he gazed at her. "It is the fourteenth." He stopped, and comprehension suddenly lit his features. "I *see*. It was a year ago."

Aurora was surprised that he could recall the significance of the date; it was important to her, but surely not to him. It did not occur to her that Blacklaw might be teasing her.

"Yes," she replied almost primly, "it was a year ago today that you freed me from that terrible place, and to show you my gratitude, I wanted to prepare a special meal for you.''

"I see. And so Constance is not present with us tonight.''

"Ordinarily she would have been, Lord Blacklaw, but she wished to visit her friends now, before the winter's storms begin." She kept her eyes downcast. What she said was partly true, after all.

"It looks as though she might have encountered one already," he said with a faint twist of his lips. "Yet it should be clearing by morning, I think, and she'll have no problem returning home." He paused. "Ah, yes, I mustn't forget about your dinner, should I? And what are we having, and when shall we dine? I warn you that I am ravenous tonight.''

Dickon entered at that moment to inform them that dinner was ready. They retired to the small dining room, where Dickon served them a meal of roast duckling with apples and cinnamon, broiled fish, stewed rabbit, and rice pudding.

Aurora and Blacklaw ate without speaking. Aurora was almost too nervous to eat, fearing that Blacklaw would dislike the meal. But from time to time she sneaked a glance at him over her raised wineglass, and he seemed to be eating with relish.

When he was finished, Blacklaw carefully wiped his fingers with the napkin and smiled slightly at her. "A fine repast, Aurora. You will make some man a good wife.''

"And is that what I am destined for?" she asked lightly, although she felt a sudden constriction in her chest. Below the level of the table her hands clenched in her lap.

"That isn't your concern as yet.''

"When shall it be? I have lived here a year already, my lord.''

"Don't address me as that.''

"What else am I to call you? While you say you are no noble, you cannot deny the rank of your birth. You are a nobleman, no matter what you claim.''

Without speaking, Blacklaw pushed back the chair, the legs scraping loudly across the floor, then rose and left the table. Irritated, Aurora tossed her napkin down and followed him from the room.

She found him once more in the sitting room by the fire.

He had poured himself a mug of ale, and left one atop the mantel for her.

She ignored the ale and pushed her stool closer to the fire, then pulled the tapestry frame toward her. She picked up the needle, threaded it, and began applying herself to an elaborate design of flowers and vines interwoven among letters. The light from the fire flashed on her needle as her hand moved up and down with the stitches, and for many long minutes the only sounds in the room were the crackling of the resinous logs in the fireplace, and the slight rasp of her yarn as it was pulled through the material.

Once Aurora looked up to see the man staring at her, and when their eyes met, he looked away quickly. From that moment on she grew even more aware of his nearness to her. At times she fancied she could hear his breathing, and it seemed rough, as if he were slightly out of breath after running a great distance. She sneaked a glance at him from under her lashes, and saw that his face was flushed. 'Twas the fire, she thought, because he was sitting so close, or perhaps a result of the ale he'd downed so quickly.

Their uneasy silence continued. Once he seemed about to speak, but then he appeared to change his mind. Finally, after he had sighed several times, she could tolerate it no longer.

"Well, sir, what is it to be?" she asked, after she had finished one complicated section of scarlet flowers and berries. She allowed herself to glance up momentarily from her design.

"What?" He looked almost startled, as if his mind had been very far away.

No doubt on *business*, she told herself grimly. She continued plying her needle.

"I was merely inquiring as to which topic of conversation we would devote ourselves this evening? The subject of your high birth which you will not acknowledge, or the subject of my purpose in your 'business' which you will not discuss."

"My 'business,' as you term it, is none of yours," he replied shortly.

She lifted an eyebrow. "Indeed, my lord?" she murmured, aware of his irritated expression. "Can you say so honestly? Nothing to do with last year's strange scenario, in which you freed an orphan from prison and promised to make her a lady? I might add that you have generously fulfilled your promise. I have learned my letters and numbers and stitching, and can converse and flirt in French. However, now that you have 'made' me a noblewoman, am I to remain in this house, to use my new skills only occasionally? Or is there some other, darker purpose to which they might be turned?''

"You dwell too long on the matter.''

She stood up so abruptly that the tapestry frame tipped over onto the floor. She made no move toward the fallen frame, but stood with her hands on her hips and a scowl on her face. Lucye, startled, leaped to her feet, and arching her back, her ears flattened against her skull, she hissed at Blacklaw.

This change from Aurora's usual placid nature appeared to shock Blacklaw, and he stared at her as if he had never seen her before.

"I dwell on it *too long*, in your words, sir, because I do not know from day to day what is to become of me. I can think of little else because it haunts me. *What is to become of me?* Will you tire of this silly game to make me a lady? Was this the result of some wager, that you could take a country-born orphan and mold her into a lady? Do you intend—once you have finally wearied of me—to marry me off to the first man that comes along, no matter what my own desires might be? Tell me, sir, what you intend to do with me.''

"I cannot say.''

"Cannot? *Will* not.''

She dropped a brief curtsey.

"My lord. There is no use in continuing this one-sided conversation, so I will withdraw, for it is growing late and I have many things to do upon the morrow. I wish you good night.'' The expression on her face was as icy as her tone. Yet she felt a tightness growing in her throat, almost as if she wanted to cry.

He spoke again when she reached the door.

"Aurora.''

Against her will, she paused, one hand outstretched to the handle. Slowly her arm lowered, and she turned.

"Yes, my lord?''

"I am sorry.''

"Sorry?" Clearly she was bewildered. He seemed to be apologizing, and that wasn't in character.

"I enjoyed your meal this evening, and had no desire to anger you."

"Oh, indeed? I confess I am surprised. In the past year, my lord, you have given no thought to my feelings, so I do not understand why you should concern yourself with them now. Did you really not wish to anger me? I find that hard to believe. And now, I really must leave. Good evening."

Aurora stormed out of the room, passing Dickon who was coming out of the kitchen. He nodded to her, but she didn't see him. In a daze, she threaded her way up the stairs, unaware of Lucye patiently following her. How she found her way in the dimness she didn't know, but sooner than she expected she was safe in her own chamber.

Aurora stopped long enough to light only a single candle, then flung herself face down upon the bed, and sighed. The constriction had spread, becoming a burning within her face and hands and chest, and she shivered, as if she were suffering from a fever. Lucye jumped up on the bed and, curling up next to her, licked the girl's hand. Absently Aurora petted the cat. In a way, the girl supposed she was suffering from a fever. One of rage, of indignation, of . . .

All because of him. No, she mustn't think about him. He had bothered her enough tonight, more than enough, and in fact had ruined the evening. She had simply wanted to enjoy a meal alone with him, and perhaps to talk a bit with him later on. Perhaps, she thought, she had wanted to flirt with him . . . just a little. Certainly she hadn't intended questioning him about her future, nor had she intended to grow so angry.

She sighed and rose slowly from the bed. No matter how she might hate Blacklaw, she must not wallow in self-pity— and by all means, she mustn't wrinkle her gown. Her fingers moved mechanically as she undressed and hung up her clothes. Then she poured water out of the pitcher into the basin and splashed it onto her face and wrists. That seemed to revive her a little.

Somewhat refreshed, she crawled into bed and stared up at the dark ceiling. The cat curled up in the crook of her arm.

This night had been a failure, she told herself, and she hadn't helped it at all.

"Oh, Lucye, why must he be so impossible?"

But, if the cat had the answer to Aurora's question, she was keeping it to herself as she slept now, purring gently. Aurora smiled wryly. Tomorrow would bring a better day, she told herself. At least, she hoped so.

3

Downstairs in the sitting room Giles Blacklaw continued to sip his ale in a leisurely fashion. When he was finished with his mug, he drank Aurora's, which she had left, untouched, on the mantel. When that was gone, he poured himself another, and when that mugful was empty, he found a bottle of wine. He stared at the flames, and sipped the wine more slowly than he had the ale. He had no intention of getting drunk; as always, he would need a clear head for later.

He shifted, and his eye was caught by the toppled tapestry frame. For a few minutes, he stared at it, then finally bent over and righted it. He studied the careful and skillfully executed stitches along the border of curling vines. The rows looked even, and when he brushed his fingers across the thread, it felt smooth to his touch. Constance had taught the girl well; all of her tutors had. Perhaps his present problem was a matter of having taught Aurora—and her having learned—too well.

In a single year the girl had grown from a terrified, ragged prison urchin to a beautiful young woman, and in that time she had also gained the arrogance and pride of a wellborn lady. An outraged wellborn lady, he reflected. And the role suited her well.

Before tonight he had never seen her so outspoken, nor so vibrant. Tonight, Aurora's eyes had flashed angrily, her cheeks had been flushed; she had been so *alive*. Previously—except for one notable occasion—she had seemed passive, almost meek. Very soft-spoken, as if she were too timid to raise her eyes to meet his.

But tonight, after dinner, as they sat before the fire, she had looked at him, and he had felt . . . something . . . a charge like a bolt of lightning, and in that moment his opinion of her had drastically changed.

It would seem that she wasn't going to be as malleable as he'd expected. Also, he had reckoned on using her gratitude to him to influence her, but he now realized he might well be expecting too much. Aurora was no timid child with downcast eyes. She was a beautiful, vital creature, and tonight she had been—even at the peak of her anger—the most desirable woman he had ever seen. And that could be a problem.

Perhaps his attraction to her had been there all along, under the surface, never making itself known. Certainly it had influenced him when he'd selected her from among the prison children. But tonight, that attraction had made itself known, and now his job would not be as easy as it once had looked. The girl had her own mind, and it was more than apparent that she would express her opinions, no matter the consequences. Blacklaw admired that. He liked a strong woman. And yet, strength of character and independence weren't qualities he looked for in the noblewoman he created. Or were they?

For the answer to that bold question, he would simply have to wait. Only time would tell, and he suspected that the months to come would be anything but smooth and calm.

4

When Constance returned to Grey Wood the next day, Aurora confided little of what had passed the night before. Indeed, all she said was that Blacklaw had come for dinner and had been disappointed to find Constance away. If Constance suspected that anything unusual had happened, she did not say so. She simply asked if Blacklaw had told Aurora when he would return. Aurora was able to say truthfully that he hadn't informed her.

All that day and the next Aurora could not banish Blacklaw's visit from her mind. Over and over she replayed the scene, and each time she grew angry. She wasn't being unreasonable, was she? she demanded of herself. Didn't she have a right to know what Blacklaw intended?

That evening after dinner, when the two women were in the sitting room doing their needlework, Aurora looked at the other woman and said, "I need to ask you something, Constance."

The other woman didn't look up from her stitching. "Yes?"

"Why did you and Lord Blacklaw do what you did for me?"

Constance set her needle down and gazed at the girl. "Can you not accept that we have done it, and leave it at that?"

"No, because I think there is something more to it . . . a secret, that no one will tell me about. And I think I have the right to know. Sometimes at night I lay awake, worrying. Will you turn me out onto the streets when you both tire of me? Will you marry me off to some fat balding nobleman, who'll get me with child every year? What do you intend to do?'' She gave the woman a beseeching look.

"I wish I could tell you fully."

"Why can't you?"

"Because of Giles."

" 'Tis always because of him," Aurora said bitterly. "Are you his puppet? Can't you do something without asking his permission?"

"Aurora!"

Immediately Aurora was conscience-stricken, and she hastened to apologize. "I'm sorry, Constance. Truly I am. But you must understand how I feel."

"And you must understand my position. For the present I can say nothing, but when I am able, you will learn all. You must trust me for now, Aurora."

Aurora nodded, but did not feel relieved at the prospect of having to trust her future to this man and woman.

She must face facts, Aurora told herself one evening several days later. She liked Giles Blacklaw. Far more than she would have wished. But did she like him because of her gratitude? Or did she feel something deeper for him?

Was she intrigued by his strange light eyes, his good looks, his odd and engaging mixture of sardonic humor and perplexing sadness? Which was it? Or could it be both? That wasn't very reassuring.

Aurora knew that Blacklaw was some eighteen years her senior—almost old enough to be her father. Yet, Aurora did not think of him as a father; for the most part their age difference did not seem very great. But there were times when it seemed to span a century or more.

There were occasions when Blacklaw treated her like a servant. At other times, he seemed as fond of her as if she were his own daughter. And once or twice Aurora had seen a strange look in his eyes when he didn't think she saw him, and it was definitely not the look of a father for his daughter.

Aurora was confused, and she had no one to turn to except Constance. Yet she had already found she couldn't say much to the woman. No matter what, Constance would defend Blacklaw and his mysterious actions.

Were Constance and Blacklaw lovers? She couldn't tell. Blacklaw never seemed to stay at Grey Wood very long, and she rarely saw them together. Still, that didn't mean they weren't lovers.

She suspected that they had been lovers in the past, and that Constance might yet harbor fond feelings for him. If this were true, it would be difficult for Aurora to confide in Constance about her own feelings.

Once again, Aurora had no one to turn to; once again she was alone.

"Alone," she whispered in the comfort of her room, and tears stung her eyes. Lucye meowed and looked up at her.

Aurora smiled. "Alone, except for you, Lucye," she said, and hugged the cat to her.

Constance sat by herself in front of the fire. Aurora had gone to bed, and the older woman set aside her needlework, for she had other matters on her mind—important matters, which kept her thoughts in turmoil. Why did Giles want the girl? Constance asked herself, not for the first time.

When Aurora had come to her a few days ago and asked the same question, Constance had simply deferred to the absent man. She wasn't holding something back; she didn't know herself. In all the time they and the tutors had worked with the girl, Blacklaw had never volunteered any information. Certainly at other times Constance had hinted at his reasoning, but he had blandly ignored her. So Constance knew as little as the girl herself. But that would have to change, and soon, Constance thought. She had to know what Blacklaw planned to do with the girl.

With the young woman, she corrected herself. Aurora had grown in the past year; she was now a young woman, and an incredibly beautiful one at that.

At first Constance had suspected that Blacklaw was grooming the child to become his own mistress. But months elapsed between his visits to Grey Wood, so Constance knew she was wrong. Then she had thought he might wish to adopt the girl as a daughter, but that seemed to make no sense. Why would he want a child, when he had nothing left for the child to inherit? Giles might simply have taken the child out of the prison for charitable reasons; but that made little sense, either. After all, how would he have come to be in Bridewell? And why select Aurora? So, if his reason was not one of these, what was it?

Some months before, John Maxwell had told Constance that he was worried about the girl. Constance had smiled to herself, knowing that John's interest in Aurora was more than academic. John wanted to know what Blacklaw planned, and admitted that he had confronted him one evening. Giles had simply laughed at him, asking if the tutor expected some evil plan.

Of course, John had told Constance, he didn't think that; but she saw that he wasn't convinced of Giles' innocence. Nor was she. No one but Giles knew the course of his plan, and God only knew when Blacklaw would put it into action. Until that time, Constance could do nothing.

5

As Christmas approached, Aurora and Constance grew busy. They decorated Grey Wood with freshly cut evergreens, cleaned the house, and prepared a large banquet for the household and Aurora's tutors. It would be the first time that all of them had gathered together under the same roof, and Aurora was looking forward to the occasion.

As the weeks went by, Blacklaw came and went, mostly staying away on "business" more frequently than in the past. From time to time he stayed overnight, but during those weeks his visits tended to be rare. And although she had no desire to admit it, not even to herself, Aurora missed him greatly.

He's staying away because of what I said to him that night, Aurora reflected mournfully, as she untangled her tapestry yarn one evening. She had offended him, and because he didn't wish to further offend Constance, he was avoiding them and pleading that "business" called him away.

No, she hadn't offended him, the girl told herself. She had simply stood up for herself, because there was no one else to defend her, and despite its unhappy consequences, she would do the very same thing, had she the chance again.

She nodded triumphantly at the strands of yarn in her hand, and glanced up in time to see the puzzled look Constance flashed her way. She ducked her head and looked at her needlework pattern. The border of leaves and vines was finished, each stitch delicately made, but she had so much farther to go with it that she was beginning to doubt she would ever finish it. Why had she decided upon something so complicated for one of her first efforts?

She mustn't think about Blacklaw, either. It did no good at all. Suddenly Aurora yawned. She put a hand up to stifle a second yawn. She didn't think she could work any more on her needlework tonight. Her eyes were tired, the firelight seemed dimmer than usual, and her thoughts wandered away from her work. Already she had had to undo three mistakes, so perhaps she should just go to bed. She glanced over at Constance, who was reading, and waited for the woman to look up.

"I think I'll go to bed now. I can't seem to concentrate."

Constance smiled. "Go on, dear. After all, you've done a great deal today. I think your rest is well earned."

Aurora nodded, wound her yarn so that Lucye couldn't play with it, then set it down on the tapestry frame. She rose, the cat following, and walked toward the door. She paused to look back. She wasn't sure if she should say anything, but . . . but nothing.

"If Lord Blacklaw should arrive later, please tell him . . ." She hesitated.

"Yes?"

" 'Twas nothing, I fear, Constance. Good night." She smiled and slipped out the door.

For a long time afterward, Constance stared, frowning slightly at the door through which the girl had gone. *Now, I wonder what the girl intended to say,* she thought. *What did she want me to tell him?* She marked her place in her book with a finely stitched piece of cloth and closed the volume carefully.

There is altogether too much secrecy in this house, she told herself, as she shifted to look into the fire. *And Giles does nothing but encourage it, for he is a secretive man. No one speaks to anyone, and everyone acts on his own—the result is only more confusion.*

She smiled as she recalled the kitten—no, no more, the cat—leaving with the girl. It was almost uncanny, this attachment between the cat and girl. Some people with suspicious minds might read more into the matter. She would have to caution Aurora not to mention to anyone how the cat accompanied her everywhere, and how the creature seemed to understand what her mistress said.

She sighed and returned to her reading; nearly an hour had elapsed when she looked up and into the flames. A singular thought had just occurred to her. Could it be that young Aurora . . . and Giles . . . that the girl had somehow fallen in love with the man?

"No," Constance whispered aloud, and the room echoed with the small sound. No, it couldn't be possible—and yet if she told herself to open her eyes she saw that all of the signs were there, pointing to that most elusive and unexplainable of emotions. It had to be true; she could not doubt that Aurora had fallen—or thought she had fallen—in love with Giles.

Constance began to think about the past month, since her return from the brief visit with her friends. She had found Blacklaw gone from the house already, although he had written that he would spend a week or so with them; and in those times he'd visited since, he had seemed even more removed than usual. Constance had thought it the result of long work, but now she wasn't convinced of that.

And, the girl had seemed strange, too . . . even more quiet than before, and more than once Constance had seen Aurora grow misty-eyed for no apparent reason. Well, now it seemed there *was* a reason. A very good reason, too. The question was: Did Giles Blacklaw return the sentiment? Or did he remain ignorant?

Constance wanted—*had*—to know. But how she would find this out—particularly from a man like Giles—she couldn't begin to imagine.

6

Blacklaw did not appear at the house that evening. In fact, even though Constance expected him to arrive that day, he did not come to Grey Wood until some five days later.

Once more snow fell outside, the flakes large and wet, clinging to everything they touched. "You came much later than I expected," she said, as she helped him from his wet overclothes.

He glanced at her without speaking, then rubbed his cold hands together, and went into the other room to warm himself before the fire. He accepted gratefully the goblet of red wine she handed him, and took a long deep swallow of it.

"The weather delayed me. It was a miserable ride from London. My horse slipped several times, and I thought I would have to walk the last few miles."

"That was all?"

"Yes. Is there another inference there, Constance? I seem to detect one."

"There is." She hadn't seated herself since they'd come into the parlor and now she stood in front of him, her eyes gazing earnestly into his. "Giles . . . I have noticed that you have not been visiting us much lately, and that when you do, you cut your visit short. Pray tell me, why is that so?"

"Business," he replied crisply.

"Ah yes. Always business." She whirled away from him and the fireplace, poured herself a goblet of wine and sipped it as she stared at him over the brim. "I think there might be another reason."

"Oh?" He swallowed more wine. "And what would that be, pray tell?"

What nonsense was filling Constance's mind now? She had never questioned him so closely. Indeed, that was one part of their bargain . . . that she would never question his comings and goings, no matter the hour, no matter the circumstance. And now she played the role of the Grand Inquisitor. It didn't suit her, and he didn't like it.

"Aurora."

His throat tightened. "And why do you say that, my dear?"

He would have taken another sip of wine, but the goblet was empty. He rose and poured more wine from the bottle on the table, aware that his hands were trembling slightly. He kept his back to the woman so that she wouldn't see, and when he finished he returned to the chair by the fire.

He repeated his question.

"Because I have eyes in my head, Giles, that is why. I know that you are attracted to her, but you must leave the girl alone. She's far too young for you."

"Some far younger than she have been mothers for years."

"Giles."

"My only desire is to educate Aurora." Even to his ears his voice sounded overly formal. He sipped his wine, unable to meet her eyes. Constance's smile was skeptical as she looked at him.

"Perhaps that is so, Giles, and I do think you have done a commendable job in this past year. No one could know that she was not born a lady. And yet—yet, despite my complete desire to do so, I cannot believe you in my heart. I truly wish that I could. But for some reason I do not. I fear you may have some darker plan in mind." She waited, her eyes gazing at him intently. "Can you reassure me? Can you convince me of your good intentions?"

In answer, Blacklaw only smiled.

She whirled away. She poured herself another glass of wine, and in her anger the wine sloshed onto the table. "You are the most exasperating of men!"

"So I have been told."

Forcing herself to be calm, Constance turned around to face him. He did not seem at all repentent as he regarded her with a cynical twist of his lips.

"Watch what you do with Aurora, Giles. She is an innocent, far more naive than ever you or I were, far more than the women with whom you usually keep company. I do not wish to see her come to any harm, however unintentional it might be."

"With that I am quite in accordance with you," and as he lifted his wineglass in salute to her, he smiled sardonically. Constance was not at all reassured by his words.

7

John Maxwell and the other tutors returned to Grey Wood within a week, and Giles Blacklaw stayed at the house. The men met several times in private; neither Constance nor Aurora was allowed to attend these meetings. Twice Constance was summoned into the room with the men, and each time she stayed there for several hours.

On the fourth day, curious as to the nature of these secret meetings, Aurora lingered by the door of the study, hoping to overhear something. Suddenly she was aware of the sound of someone walking toward the door.

Quickly she dashed away, the cat at her heels, and sat down in the parlor and folded her hands as if she had been sitting there all along. Only a slight flush in her cheeks and a slightly quickened breath proved that supposition wrong.

The door opened, and Blacklaw emerged from the study. A few minutes later the tutors strolled out and came to the parlor, all of them wearing the most innocent of expressions, which frankly made Aurora all the more suspicious. There they poured themselves glass after glass of wine and ale.

The cat rose and stretched, then curled up once more at Aurora's feet.

John Maxwell came over to her and smiled. "That cat is a marvelous animal."

"How so, John?" she asked.

"She stays with you constantly—I've seen it myself. She

acts almost as if she were a dog. I've never seen such a faithful cat.''

"I think she believes she must be a dog, but so far no one has told her otherwise." She stroked the cat, who purred loudly. Aurora glanced up at John through her long eyelashes. It was a way of flirting, or so Constance had told her, and she meant to practice it now. She was also very aware that Blacklaw, even though he was talking to two of the men, was watching her intently. "Do you plan to stay long at Grey Wood?"

He grinned, then shook his head. "Alas, I cannot, although you know I would, if it were possible. But I have other work."

"Business," she murmured.

"I beg your pardon?"

" 'Twas nothing. I am disappointed to learn you won't be here with us long."

"I am, too."

"Time, gentlemen." It was Blacklaw, calling the others back to the study.

"I will see you later, won't I?" John asked the girl eagerly.

"I will be here," she said with a smile.

After they had returned to the study, Aurora waited for a while longer, then tiptoed to the closed door and pressed her ear against it. She heard the deep rumbling of men's voices, and she forced herself to distinguish them. One by one, she began sorting them out.

Peter was talking, and now the younger voice was John's. Now Blacklaw.

She frowned, trying to understand his words.

Someone else mentioned what sounded like persecutions. Religious persecutions? she wondered. Both Blacklaw and John Maxwell were Roman Catholics, as were most of the tutors, she suspected.

"That will soon end," said a voice—Blacklaw's.

There seemed to be general excitement at this pronouncement, then Blacklaw was speaking again. He was talking about something that would be done soon, something that the Queen herself would be unable to prevent.

What was the man talking about? she asked herself, but she scarcely had time to think more about it because at that moment she heard Constance calling her. Still, she vowed, she would return to listen later—if she had the time.

From the window of his room, John Maxwell watched Aurora. She was out in the snowy courtyard, completely unaware of him. She was bundled warmly against the cold in a cloak, stark against the whiteness, and she seemed to be singing to herself because he could see her breath frosting before her. She reached down and with a gloved hand swept a bench clean of its white coverlet, then sat.

He saw for the first time that she was carrying a bundle, and he smiled when she unwrapped it and the cat poked out her furry black head. The cat quickly withdrew back into the warmth of the cloth surrounding it, then Aurora released her, and the cat jumped easily to the snowy ground.

Immediately the cat lifted one paw, shook it, put it back, and then raised another to shake it. It repeated this process over and over, and all the while Aurora laughed. She called to the cat, who came to her at once, and jumped into her lap.

He smiled again, and tried to ignore the aching within his body for Aurora.

Across the courtyard, the sun glanced off the walls of the house, illuminating the windows and those who stood behind them. From across the courtyard, unseen in the shadows of another wing of the house, Blacklaw regarded John Maxwell as he watched the girl in the courtyard below.

The girl and cat were chasing one another, one moment the girl running after the cat, the next moment her direction changing with the cat loping after her. Finally, she laughed and picked up the cat and hugged it to her, then sat on the bench once more and carefully wiped the snow off the cat's paws.

All the while Maxwell stared at her, his heart in his eyes. To Blacklaw, it was obvious that the young tutor was in love with Aurora. That was something that would have to be discouraged. He would talk to Constance, see what she suggested. She might well accuse him of simply being jealous. And she might well be right.

PART III

1584

1

Spring came, and it was not only the daffodils and tulips and tiny blue crocuses that bloomed. Over the long winter months, Aurora had grown greatly in confidence, and she began to blossom into womanhood. She had lost the gauntness that had marked her in prison, and when she looked into the mirror she realized that she was beautiful—or almost so, because she couldn't believe she was as truly handsome as Constance was. Not even the appreciative looks of John Maxwell could fully convince her.

Still, Aurora was more than a little pleased by what she saw and by what she felt—even though at times she was confused by a strange mixture of newly awakened feelings. Particularly disturbing were the feelings that possessed her whenever she saw or thought of Giles Blacklaw.

She could never see him now without feeling a shiver go through her entire body, leaving it at once icy and hot; when his hand accidentally brushed hers, she would start violently, then blush furiously. She didn't know if he noticed her reaction, but she wasn't sure that he could miss it, or indeed that anyone else could.

What a fool she must look, she told herself, and yet she could do nothing to prevent these reactions, so she resigned herself to them. No other man she met affected her this way. She enjoyed John Maxwell's company when he was at Grey Wood, but she never longed to see him as she longed to see Giles Blacklaw.

In mid-April Aurora celebrated her eighteenth birthday. This was a special occasion for her—and not just because it was her birthday. With mingled alarm and wonder, Aurora finally realized that she had fallen in love with Blacklaw.

She found the man both exciting and mysterious, more intriguing than ever before. She yearned to hear his voice, to see him . . . to be touched by him. For weeks she kept her silence, suffering by herself. Her dreams at night were filled with him, with his deep voice, his infrequent laugh, his light eyes. By day, her thoughts turned to him more and more often, and she found herself becoming absent in anyone else's company.

Finally, she knew she could keep quiet no longer. She must talk.

One sunny spring afternoon, Constance and Aurora sat doing their needlework together in companionable silence. The windows had been thrown open to let the sweet fresh air in, and Lucye lay curled in sleep on a windowsill, although one eye opened from time to time to study the birds that flitted from one branch to another in the trees in the courtyard.

It was time, Aurora told herself, and opened her mouth to speak, but found she couldn't. Her slender hands were icy cold, as if she'd dipped them into a stream filled with melting snow, and she rubbed them to bring some warmth to their tips. She must say something while they were yet alone. She must not be a coward. She mustn't. She waited a few minutes more, then quietly cleared her throat and waited.

Constance glanced up from her stitching, and seeing the serious expression on the girl's face, set her needle down.

"Yes, Aurora. Do you have something you wish to speak to me about?"

Constance was too canny, Aurora thought, somewhat unsettled. Already she knew that the widow sensed her unease.

"It is an important matter, Constance." She kept her head down, afraid to look the older woman in the eye. "I have no one else to turn to, to talk to, and so thought to come to you."

"Go ahead."

"I have a secret."

"Yes?"

Aurora raised her eyes now, thinking she detected amusement in the other's voice, and yet Constance's expression was serious. Don't speak, don't speak! one part of her called wildly, but she knew she must. She took a deep breath, plunged in.

"I think . . . no, I know . . . I have fallen in love with Lord Blacklaw."

The expression on Constance's face did not change. She did not even blink. When the widow said nothing, Aurora asked if she had heard her.

"Yes, I did, and I am not surprised to hear your admission, Aurora. Indeed, I would have been fairly surprised had you not admitted as much to me at some opportunity."

"Oh."

"And that is your secret, as well as a problem to you. Correct?"

The girl nodded. "I don't know what to do now that I know this. He doesn't seem to notice me at all—beyond acting as my tutor, that is. I am no more than a piece of furniture to him."

Constance's lips curved into a faint smile. "I think you are more than that to him."

"What should I do?" Aurora asked, her voice plaintive.

"As for that"—here Constance's expression grew solemn— "I think there is only one course. You must disengage your heart."

"What?"

" 'Tis folly to love him, Aurora, because Giles loves no one but a woman from his past. Ah, you look surprised. You know so little of his past that you begin to think he has none, but that is far from the truth." She shook her head. "I have mentioned little to you of it, and deliberately so, but perhaps I should tell you now."

Constance stretched out one hand to the fire and watched the blue and yellow flames, then roused herself finally and looked at the girl.

"You are correct in your assumption that Giles is a nobleman. Or rather he was. Although I suppose one cannot truly be stripped of that. He is the son of a well-known Catholic family, powerful once in this land, and when he was a young man, scarcely even of age, he was betrothed to marry a woman of an equally great family whose land adjoined his family's. 'Twould have been a powerful match, an alliance unwanted by many in the nobility.

"Yet, being a youth with much intelligence and curiosity, he sought to somewhat quench his thirst for knowledge and went abroad to enrich his education. He promised his sweetheart that he would marry her upon his return. He was gone some time, although not long by what we reckon as years, and when he came home, expecting to be welcomed by his family, he found unexpected tragedy.

"His father had died a short time before, and his family was scattered across the land, some in hiding; the woman, although she was hardly more than a girl at the time, had married another. Giles' estates had been seized by the Crown, and he himself had been declared a traitor."

2

"A traitor! 'Tis a lie!" Aurora insisted hotly. She glared at the woman.

Constance nodded her head. "Yes, that it is, child, as we well know these years hence. Unfortunately, others do not believe that now, nor did they know then all of what truly happened. It has been nearly twenty years since this terrible thing happened; in those days, the political situation was as it is today.

"At times our Queen has maintained a tolerant attitude toward the various religions, but over the years, her ear has been filled with the advice of less tolerant men. She has grown ruthless to those she is convinced are her enemies. And real or imagined, those enemies grow daily in number.

"Somehow, the Queen became convinced that Giles was a traitor, and thus his lands were ceded to the Crown. From the moment he set foot in England again, he became a hunted man, his life forfeit. Instead of fleeing abroad as many others more prudent than he would have done, he stayed. To survive he has at times indulged in highway robbery and other less honest pastimes—all done, he claims, to beard the lion in the den. He exists on little, and is aided by those who are his friends."

"Such as you." Were these robberies the "business" that often called him away? Aurora would never have thought him a thief, and yet she knew he must survive however he might.

"Yes. I and other friends—who all remain prudently out of

sight. 'Twould prove fatal for us all if the government were to learn that Giles Blacklaw visits here from time to time.''

Aurora had never thought of his visits bringing danger to them, and now as she considered what the widow said, she realized that she still wanted him to visit Grey Wood, no matter what.

''But the tutors know of him,'' she said.

''Yes, and they are all men who can be trusted, for many of them are in similar positions.''

''And he helps them however he can, also.'' She remembered John Maxwell's words.

''Yes. Sometimes the help is slight, sometimes it is great. And so you see, since that time,'' Constance said, her voice lowering in tone, ''Giles has thought of no one else but the woman who betrayed him. The woman he once loved with all his heart, the woman he wishes to see once more and punish for the wrongs she did him.''

''But could he not go to the Queen and try to convince that he did not betray her or the Crown?'' Aurora's expression was as indignant as her tone. ''Surely, some sort of proof exists.''

'' 'Tis not as easy as that, child. Elizabeth has a temper as fierce as her hair is red, and 'tis not often that she softens and changes her mind once it is firmly made up. And I do believe, too, that once Giles tried such an approach, but that he was pursued before he could reach the palace and seek an audience with her. He has not since returned.''

''He must do something!''

''Child, do you not think he knows that? And yet, what is there to do? He is an outlaw.''

''Yet you help him.''

''Yes.''

''Why?''

''Because I don't like to see wrongs continue. Someday I wish him to be vindicated. That is why.''

''You are at risk, though, are you not? Even of your life.''

''Yes.''

''But you continue to help him, even hiding him within your home.''

''Yes, and I would gladly do it a hundred times over.'' Constance smiled. ''And he knows that, too.''

"Do . . . you . . . love him?" Aurora could scarcely breathe or talk for fear of what the other woman would answer. Her heart pounding wildly, she waited for the widow's reply.

"Love Giles? In a manner of speaking, I do, I suppose. I lost my heart to him once long ago, but he did not want it, nor my love, and so we have acted as friends since then. I think that is best with him. He has no love left to give a woman."

Aurora felt her heart sink within her chest; pain overtook her and she glanced away, not knowing what to say. Aurora had not expected to hear what Constance had revealed. And she wished that she hadn't. His life was tragic; he had been robbed of his youth, his inheritance, his love. 'Twas no wonder that he seemed so dark, so bitter.

Aurora cleared her throat. "I have one other question, Constance." The woman nodded for her to continue. "When he leaves for his 'business,' he goes to be a highway robber?"

"I think so, although there is more to it than that, and what that means, I really don't know. After all, Giles confides completely in no one. I know a little of this and that, but that is all. I confess, though, that I fear that his education of you is somehow connected to his mysterious business and to that distant, lost love."

"Oh." Aurora felt disappointed and angry.

"I don't understand how that could be, but 'tis something I sense."

Aurora looked down at her needlework. She was disheartened by Constance's words. He needed no one, she saw, not her, not Constance. No one. It was best that she learn that, though, before she had completely lost herself to him and perhaps made an even bigger fool of herself by declaring her love to him.

And yet, she asked herself, how did she know that Constance spoke the truth? It might be to the older woman's advantage to embellish the truth to suit herself and her own situation, and thus to discourage Aurora, a younger rival.

But what Constance had told her had the ring of truth. Acknowledging that made Aurora all the more defeated, and left her even more lost than before.

3

All the following day Aurora thought about what Constance had told her and its implications with regard to herself. By mid-afternoon she had convinced herself that—somehow—Constance was mistaken about Lord Blacklaw. And if Constance were mistaken, then it was only logical that Aurora had a certain chance, however slim, with him.

She knew she must act upon that chance soon—before she lost what courage she could muster, or before she allowed Constance to chip away at her already shaken confidence.

That day the tutors left Grey Wood again, giving no indication when they would return. Blacklaw entered the parlor to find Aurora and Constance hard at work on their stitchery.

He said nothing, but sat heavily in the chair, leaned his head back, and closed his eyes.

After a few minutes of silence, Constance rose and said, "I must oversee Betty for tonight's dinner." She nodded to the others and started to leave.

"Do you need my help?" Aurora asked.

"No, child, you stay here."

Aurora nodded, pleased to stay behind in the parlor. Silently she continued to ply her needle, snipping the threads when finished with a particular row. She had dressed with particular care that morning in a deep rose gown that made her eyes sparkle. She thought the color suited her well, and she was hoping to catch a few words of praise from Giles. From time to time, Aurora looked up to study him. Blacklaw was no longer dozing by the fire, but had picked up a book and was reading.

Suddenly, as if aware of her eyes on him, he stood up.

"I must leave now. It's a long ride back to London tonight, and I have much to do when I arrive."

Just as abruptly Aurora stood up. Emboldened by his slight smile, which she took for encouragement, she summoned her nerve and crossed to him. Knowing that her love shone in her eyes, she gazed up at him and slipped her arms around him.

The reaction on Blacklaw's face was unreadable. Then without warning he threw his head back and laughed. He removed her arms from his waist easily and patted her head paternally. Chuckling, he gazed down at her.

"Even though we fall naturally into the parts, I don't expect you to play the loving daughter, my dear." When she did not speak, he continued. "Conversely, you are much too young to flirt with me. You should practice your feminine wiles upon a young man, someone such as John Maxwell, who greatly admires you. He is far closer to your age, Aurora, and I think of a like mind."

Stricken, she stared at him as burning pain ripped through her body. Suddenly it burst within her, proving too much for her to control, and with a faint cry, she whirled and fled the room. The black cat arched its back, hissed at Blacklaw, then followed her mistress.

Once in the sanctuary of her room, Aurora dropped upon the bed, then put her head in her hands. The tears came now, quickly and warm, rolling down her cheeks into her mouth, dripping down her neck. She ignored her discomfort and concentrated on her misery.

What a fool she had made of herself. An absolute fool. And no doubt he was downstairs at this very moment, laughing at her. Doubtless, too, he would wait until Constance came back, and he would entertain her with stories of his ward's guile, and then they would both laugh, vastly amused at her naivete.

How could she have thought he was encouraging her, even so slightly? How could she have thought he considered her anything but at best a daughter, at worst, a simple ward. How? She was so blind, a blind and stupid fool, a simpleton.

It had taken so much for her to approach him . . . to touch

him. She shuddered, feeling the emptiness growing within her.

Lucye jumped up onto the bed and rolled over onto its back so that Aurora could scratch its stomach. She did so, idly, and the cat purred and rubbed its small head against the girl's hand.

Now, she didn't know what to think, how to act. How did he consider her? As a child? Simply a ward? All she knew was that he did not see her as she truly was. That much was apparent.

His touch as he removed her arms had been impersonal, and yet the remembrance of it made her ache. How she wished that his fingertips had touched her lips. She shivered and hugged herself, and more forlorn tears fell.

Never again, she told herself firmly, never again would she be placed·in that position. She resolved that she would never again approach him. No matter how much pain she felt inside when she looked at him. The pain of his rebuff hurt far worse. She wiped the tears away with her fingers, and touched her hands to her flushed cheeks. She felt as if she were burning up from a fever. The fever of love. She would have laughed, except that she hurt far too much. She drew in a ragged breath, then rose slowly.

She went across the room in the darkness and found the stand with the wash basin. She dipped her hands into the cool water and splashed it onto her face, then pressed her wet fingertips against her eyelids. After a few minutes, she felt a little better and her skin was no longer as flushed. Yet nothing had eased her inner pain; nothing would, she told herself.

She sighed deeply and turned away. As she crossed the room, she undressed mechanically, letting her clothes fall where she dropped them. When she was finished, she crawled into bed, her ultimate sanctuary, and lay there under the covers. She knew that Constance expected her to be downstairs for dinner, but she couldn't eat. Her stomach heaved and turned, and she would be unable to keep anything down. When the widow came up to remind her of the meal, she would simply plead illness. Surely Constance would understand that innocent excuse.

She wasn't in the least tired, but she knew that she had to

rest. She and Constance would be busy tomorrow; she needed to sleep, needed to forget what had happened. Lucye, still purring, curled up at Aurora's side and was soon asleep.

But try as she might, Aurora found that sleep eluded her. All her mind could do was replay the terrible scene before the fireplace over and over. Finally, exhausted, she fell asleep, but it was only to dream of Blacklaw and his cruel laughter.

4

Constance had watched the scene from just outside the parlor. Ordinarily, she never listened to the conversations of others, certainly never in this manner, but this time she had known it was important. When she had returned from the kitchen she paused momentarily outside the parlor and noticed that the door was ajar. Thus it provided her with a viewing space of an inch or so; certainly it was wide enough for her to hear what went on in the room.

Except that no one in the parlor was speaking. Giles read, while Aurora did her needlework. Constance was just about to push the door open and enter when Blacklaw leaped to his feet and murmured that he had to leave for London.

Constance watched their brief embrace. Certainly Giles had removed Aurora's arms at once, but not before Constance caught the tortured expression on his face as he did so. He wanted the girl, very badly, as badly as she desired him. Constance watched, incredulous, as Giles began to laugh. She stared, horrified, as the girl's face drained of color. Aurora looked almost as if she had been physically struck.

Then abruptly the girl was running from the room. Constance stepped back as the door was thrown open, but Aurora never saw her as she rushed past and up the stone steps. Moments later the cat followed, just as quickly as its mistress. Gile stood there, not moving, with no expression on his face, and yet Constance could see the pain in his eyes, the pain he would never admit to anyone. Taking a deep breath, she smoothed down her apron, counted a minute's time, and then pushed the door open.

"What is this?" she asked in what she hoped was a steady voice. "Leaving already, Giles?"

"Yes. As I was telling Aurora, I must return to London, and as you know, it is a long ride. I also have much business to attend to tonight."

His voice was only a shade less steady than hers, and now that she stood only a few feet distant, Constance could see the pain in his face.

"What a shame. I had hoped you would be able to stay for the night," she murmured. She glanced around the room and hated herself for what she asked now. "Where is Aurora?"

He did not look at her. "I believe she has gone up to bed."

"Bed? But 'tis early."

"I believe . . . she said something about being tired, and wanting to be able to help you tomorrow, so she wished to rest."

"I see."

He glanced at her oddly then. "Well, as I said, I must be going. I can delay no longer."

"Come back soon, Giles. We are always glad to see you," she said, and when she gave him her hand she made sure it lingered in his overlong.

Then he was gone. Feeling suddenly tired, Constance sat down in front of the fire and stared into the flames without seeing them. It was a terrible thing to admit, but she was jealous of Aurora. She was ashamed of it. Yet she could scarcely prevent it, could she? She had always thought of Giles Blacklaw as simply a friend, someone to turn to when she needed a sympathetic ear, as she had discovered more than once.

And now, to her complete horror, she had found out that the man meant far more to her. What was she to do?

She couldn't face Aurora, couldn't face Giles again. Or could she? She really had no choice. And like Giles, she believed that the girl was too young for him. And she, too, had seen the admiring looks John Maxwell had sent his student's direction.

Constance saw that her course of action was simple: she must distract the girl and Giles from each other. The only road to success, she knew, was to enlist the unwitting aid of John Maxwell.

As Blacklaw had anticipated, the return trip to London took many hours that night, thanks to the muddy roads left from the rain two days previously. When he reached the inn where he normally stayed on such trips, he was mud-splashed and chilled to the bone; he sat before the fire to dry his wet clothing. Much later, after several mugs of ale which helped to warm him, he finally went to bed. But once in bed, he did not sleep right away, in spite of his fatigue. All too clearly he remembered the feel of Aurora's arms as she slipped them around him. He had been shocked by the abruptness and boldness of her gesture, but certainly he hadn't been displeased. With a frown, he recalled his body's immediate reaction to her slim body pressed against his, to her closeness.

He shook his head. He must be strong, must remain so, and see his plans through to the end. Yet he was a man; nothing more.

Within a very short time, he had watched her grow from a gawky shy child into a beautiful woman. He had helped mold her mind as well. To his horror, he found that she was molding *his* mind. She was the subject of most of his dreams of late. Every time he drifted off to sleep, it was to dream of Aurora. He saw her beautiful face, tasted her red lips, and sometimes he stroked her white skin, reveling in its silky softness. . . . He must be strong, he told himself.

"Strong," he said aloud, and the word echoed in the tiny room, mocking him.

Strong . . . he didn't know if he could. She was a temptress, though unaware of her power. Like a hawk, he watched her every movement, listened to her lilting voice, saw her in his mind's eye even when she wasn't there.

It wasn't right, he told himself, as he rolled over onto his side in his lonely bed and closed his eyes. It wasn't right because all he could bring to her—all he could ever bring to any woman—was pain.

5

"Thank you, John, for carrying the basket, though it was hardly a burden."

Maxwell grinned at Aurora, set the wicker basket down where she indicated, and waited. Lucye leaped into the basket, nearly tipping it over, and the two laughed at the cat's antics.

Aurora was grateful for his company. Of late, she had been slightly ill at ease with Constance, and there were few visitors these days. There was no one to talk to.

But today was different. At mid-morning she had gone out into the garden to collect flowers; she was engrossed in gathering the numerous lovely blossoms for the vases inside the house when she heard someone hailing her. For a moment her heart beat wildly with the hope that it might be Blacklaw; but reason took over, and pointed out that the voice calling her was not his. Disappointment—and relief—had followed. After all, had he not laughed at her the last time they were together? And yet . . .

Clutching a handful of tulips, she stepped from behind a short wall bordered by trees and saw John Maxwell waving from the other side of the garden. She waved back at once and indicated that he should join her.

Once by her side, John remarked that he had come for her lessons, if she were so inclined; but if she wanted to stay outside, that, too, was fine with him. Aurora's tutors had gone on to other students, she took fewer lessons these days, and at times she missed them. Still, she had more than enough activities to fill her days now.

It was a beautiful day, she thought as she gazed around. Fleecy white clouds dabbed the azure canvas of the late April sky, and occasionally returning birds trilled overhead. The bright sun shone warmly on her face and on her forearms, for she had pushed up her sleeves, and the air was redolent of the myriad fragrances of the flowers abounding in the gardens of Grey Wood. Aurora told John she would prefer to stay outdoors.

She smiled at him. Yes, it was a good day, and John was a good companion—even if he weren't Blacklaw. Unlike Blacklaw, John had manners; he would never laugh cruelly at her. And neither did he inflame her.

John saw Aurora watching him. "Perhaps we could go riding."

"I would like that, John, but—"

"But what?"

He was so attentive, so willing and eager to help her in whatever task she asked of him, and it was obvious that he was attracted to her. Certainly she found his attention flattering; she liked the young tutor, but cared for him as a friend— nothing more. Yet she couldn't say that outright to him. Or could she?

"I don't know," she said at last. "I think I just want to walk and enjoy the sunshine."

He grinned. "Very well."

He was so agreeable—so unlike Blacklaw, who seemed to disagree with everything she said or suggested, and who used her for some devilish reason.

"I would enjoy being anyplace where I was allowed to spend my time in your company."

"John—" she began.

"No, please, Aurora, let me speak." He seemed to be struggling with some deep emotion. "I have to tell you that for a long time now I have admired you greatly."

Her heart sank as she realized what must be coming next. She must try to forestall it.

"I am highly flattered, John, believe me, I truly am, but before you speak further, I wish to say something also. I want you to look deep into your heart. I think you will find that you do not love me. Now, now," she said, raising a hand as he started to protest, "hear me through. I know you are quite fond of me, as a friend—*as am I of you*—but I do not think your heart is touched." She paused and gazed at him. "Am I correct?"

His expression was almost comical, a combination of sheepishness and contriteness and slight embarrassment. " 'Tis so, Aurora, although I do not wish you to believe that I think of you any less."

"I know you do not," she said softly, "and I welcome your true emotions. Good friends are hard to come by, John."

He nodded solemnly. "Then we will be fast friends. And you are not angry with me?"

"Not at all." She reached out and gave him a brief kiss on the cheek. "And now as friends, we must hurry inside, lest Constance think the gypsies have stolen us away." She turned back to the bench. "Come, Lucye, I won't carry you in the basket!"

The cat opened one eye, then closed it, ignoring its mistress's words. John laughed and carefully picked up the black cat and handed it to Aurora, then grabbed the flower-filled basket and followed Aurora. As they headed back toward the house, she turned to him and said, "John, you must speak to me truthfully now, as we are friends, and good friends are always truthful with one another."

He nodded, waiting.

"Was it Constance who suggested that you . . . approach me?"

A slight redness tinged his cheeks and he dropped his gaze. "Yes."

"I see." She smiled, even though she did not feel like doing so. Still, she wanted to ease his embarrassment. "I think she must have thought I was very lonely."

He looked relieved. "Yes, I think so."

She simply nodded, but she knew that the truth of the matter was quite different.

6

As summer approached, Blacklaw appeared at Grey Wood less and less frequently. Aurora told herself that she was glad to see so little of him, but she could not totally convince herself of that. She remembered with pain the evening when he had laughed at her—yet still she longed for him to touch her cheek, to kiss her lips.

She was being foolish, she told herself. Yes, she was foolish because she was in love. She felt, however, that if she had seen more of Giles she might convince him that she was no longer a child. But what good would that do? He would always think of her as he first saw her, she told herself miserably—as a poor, scrawny waif. She continued her lessons with John and Constance, but her idle hours were filled with daydreams of Blacklaw.

Blacklaw made one of his rare visits on a particularly fine June day, when the blue sky was free of clouds, and the golden sunlight danced across the pond in back of the house.

From an upstairs window Aurora had seen his approach, and had gone at once to her bedroom to change; she was waiting downstairs when he was shown into the parlor. She had put on a new gown, a crimson and gold dress that deepened the green-blue of her eyes. Her hair was pulled back and fastened with pearl pins, and she knew she was at her most alluring. She watched as his eyes swept over her appreciatively.

"Aurora, I have never seen you look so beautiful," Blacklaw

murmured, never taking his eyes from her face. "I am enchanted."

She was aware that she was blushing slightly, but whether from pleasure or something more she didn't know. She wanted to respond, but her tongue seemed somehow tangled. Finally, she shook her head, then looked him directly in the eyes.

"I am surprised to see you today, Lord Blacklaw," she murmured.

"Oh? And why is that?"

"You come here so infrequently that I thought you would stop visiting altogether."

"Do not worry about *that*," he said, his tone more than slightly ironic.

She lifted a delicate eyebrow, a gesture which he knew she meant to be entirely scornful, and which he found delightful.

"Indeed? Are you at Grey Wood because you have important business here? I think the time has come, Lord Blacklaw, that you explain your reasons. Why did you take me in, and why did you see to it that I received an extensive education? I thank you for that, for otherwise I would not have learned so much—if I had even managed to survive Bridewell." She did not shrink from the stony look in his eyes; she couldn't stop now. She had to know.

"Your previous explanation—that this is all 'a whim'— satisfied me when I was a child. But I am a child no longer. You do not see the change, but it exists. And I must know." She paused. "I also must know how to repay you." She was standing very close to him, aware of the rise and fall of his chest with each breath.

"The truth is not for you—now."

Irritated, she started to spin away from him, but not before he could reach out and catch her gently by the arm. She struggled to free herself, without much success, then swung around to face him. Her struggles stopped; they were standing so close that they almost touched, and they were both electrically aware of an almost tangible magnetic attraction.

Flustered, she took a step backward, but at the very same time Blacklaw took her into his arms in a breathtaking embrace. His lips touched hers warmly, passionately, and for a moment, just a moment, she was startled, but then the surprise melted away and she began to respond fervently. She had never felt this way before. Never had she been touched, or kissed, in this manner; within her, fire alternated with ice. At times she wanted to faint to escape the deep emotion roiling through her.

Instinctively her arms tightened around him, and she pressed herself closer. She wanted to be with him, touching him, even more than she already was, and she moaned slightly, and opened her mouth under the pressure of his lips. His tongue gently caressed hers, and she sighed at the exquisite desire she felt.

"Aurora. My love," he whispered, and touched the back of her neck with his fingertips. She shivered at the feathersoft caress.

"Giles." She reached up and began kissing him again, touching his lips, his cheek, his forehead. She ran her fingers across his high cheekbones and kissed him deeply.

So engrossed were they in the depths of their ardor that Aurora and Blacklaw barely heard the knock at the parlor door. But finally, flushed and slightly out of breath, they pulled apart; when Constance entered the rooms scarcely a moment later, she had only to take one look at their faces to understand what had gone on in the room.

Aurora saw Constance's unhappy expression and could think of nothing to say. She felt guilty, and although she didn't think she should, she could do nothing to prevent it. Aurora simply nodded to Constance and, with a glance at Blacklaw, she left the room.

Blacklaw did not speak, nor did Constance. The redness had faded from his cheeks, and he had regained his composure. When it seemed he was about to speak, Constance shrugged and departed. It had been inevitable, after all, Constance thought. What could she have said?

Blacklaw knew he should stay away, but he couldn't—not when she was there. He would continue to visit even though he knew it was wrong. Hadn't everyone told him? Had not Constance told him he was too old for the girl? Had not John Maxwell, with his disapproving puppy eyes, told him that he was making a fool of himself? Everyone had told him—except the girl herself.

Blacklaw waited to visit until the days when he knew

Constance would be gone, or too busy to linger to pay much attention to him, and then he would turn up suddenly at Grey Wood. During the pleasant summer days that followed, he sought out Aurora frequently. They took long rides through the woods and along some of the country lanes outside London. There were any number of fairs camped along the fringes of the small towns, and Aurora begged him to take her. Against his inclination, he did so—and found he enjoyed himself thoroughly.

Yet as they rode out together or walked around the estate, he found her watching him curiously. Whenever he asked her what was wrong, she would shake her head and say nothing was amiss. But he knew better; he knew that something was troubling her—and he had a good idea what it was. Before long, he would have to tell her.

7

One beautiful day in early autumn Blackwell asked Aurora to go for a long ride with him. She agreed, and as they left the house, the morning sky was still streaked with the lingering gold and salmon tones of dawn. For some time they rode in silence, which suited Aurora. When they were apart, she ached to be with him; but when they were together, she often found herself tongue-tied or confused.

The morning air was fresh and crisp and smelled of damp leaves. Sunlight glittered on dew-dropped spider webs spanning the air between bushes and trees, and off to one side, a small brown rabbit hopped away at the approach of the horses. It was still slightly chilly, for the sun was hardly above the hills, and Aurora was glad she'd brought her cloak along.

Because they planned a long ride, Aurora had packed a picnic—enough for breakfast and lunch—and she hoped to surprise Blacklaw. She sneaked a glance at him now, and saw that he was looking straight ahead. Would that he would look at her so intensely some time, she thought, permitting herself a slight sigh. Shivers ran down her arms as she recalled their one passionate embrace. She shook herself. Thoughts such as those couldn't help her.

At mid-morning, they paused by a quietly gurgling stream to water the horses and to let them rest for a few minutes. Aurora spread her cloak across the ground, then knelt carefully and took a cloth-wrapped package from the basket.

"Would you care for some cheese, my lord?"

He smiled. "Of course."

He crossed his legs eastern style and gracefully sat down a few inches from her, and her hand trembled slightly as she cut a wedge from the yellow cheese. As she passed it to him, their hands brushed—she jerked away as if she had been burned. Aurora dropped her eyes and cut a small slice of the cheddar for herself. She nibbled delicately at it, averting her gaze.

"You can look at me," he said, his voice ironic. "I won't bite."

She raised her head. "I am not afraid that you will, my lord."

"Then what are you afraid of?"

She stared into his eyes, and thought she read concern and understanding in those dark depths. Once again she looked away. She didn't know if she could trust him: He had said nothing of his purpose for her. Her body trusted him, but her mind did not. What was she to do?

Abruptly she rose to her feet. She had no intention of ruining their outing.

"Shall we go, my lord? I think the horses must be rested by now."

"Yes." He helped her up into the saddle, his touch faintly impersonal now, then mounted his own horse, and they rode away from the stream, the sound of it gradually dying in the distance.

The horses picked a lazy route, and neither Blacklaw nor Aurora was inclined to hurry them. In the trees overhead, the leaves were turning colors; brown and gold and scarlet, and red and green vines entwined shaggy grey bark. Here and there she could see occasional late-blooming flowers—the blue of asters, the dark pink and rusty brown of chrysanthemums thrusting through the carpet of dying grass.

Occasionally a bird sang far above them, and once Aurora heard the quiet pattering of some unseen animal in the bushes. The soft wind riffled through the leaves; Aurora smiled, fully happy. It was beautiful here, peaceful, and she was glad he had suggested the ride.

They rode on, and before long, Aurora realized that she was quite lost. She had absolutely no idea where they were.

She realized, too, that they had encountered no one since leaving the main road by Grey Wood. Blacklaw didn't seem apprehensive, though.

"Where are we, my lord? We aren't lost, are we? Will you be able to find your way back to the road?" she asked, somewhat nervously.

His look was filled with sudden amusement. "Of course I can find my way. I have ridden through these woods many times. Don't worry."

"The forest can play tricks upon one, and you may think you know the path when it is very well somewhere else." She gazed at him solemnly.

"Thank you, Aurora, but I know where I am going." His voice was flat.

And she knew from the way in which he answered her that she'd best not pursue the matter.

After another hour or so, they stopped for a lunch of cold chicken, duck, and fruit. Aurora asked Blacklaw many questions about the area surrounding Grey Wood, and he answered as best he could. It was a poor neighborhood, and those who lived there tended to stick by one another. That would be something, she believed, that helped Blacklaw in his late-night comings and goings.

As they sat back after eating, the warmth of the sun proved lulling. Aurora, suddenly sleepy, yawned behind a shapely hand and curled up on her cloak. Her eyes closed slowly, and for a few minutes, she listened to the comforting sounds of the horses as they cropped the grass nearby. Off to one side, she could hear Blacklaw faintly whistling. She tried to identify the tune, but it escaped her; she told herself that she would ask him later. She heard nothing more as she relaxed and slid quickly into sleep.

8

Aurora awoke at the touch of a velvety softness. When she opened her eyes, she was staring at the muzzle of her chestnut. She reached over and stroked the horse's head, then gradually sat up. She rubbed her eyes and yawned deeply. It was now later in the day, and the woods around her were growing dark. The sun must be close to setting, Aurora realized.

Why had Lord Blacklaw allowed her to sleep so long? He should have awakened her long before this. Slightly startled, she looked around the dim clearing and found her answer. Blacklaw sat, sound asleep, leaning against a wide tree trunk. Aurora crossed to him and knelt in front of him for a few minutes, watching him as he slept. His face had a repose that she had never seen while he was awake, and she was reluctant to disturb him, but she had no choice. Gently she touched his sleeve, and she felt the warmth of his skin through the cloth.

"Lord Blacklaw," she called in a low voice. "Giles. Wake up."

Instantly his eyes opened. "What is wrong?" He struggled to his feet and looked around the small clearing. "What is the matter, Aurora?"

"Nothing is amiss—except that I believe we have overslept."

He glanced at the lengthening shadows of the woods, and then looked toward the sky, from which the light was rapidly fading.

"I had thought just to sit awhile and watch you while you slept, but then my eyes simply closed of their own accord. I had not meant to sleep more than a few minutes," he said, a touch of irony in his voice. "I am afraid we will have to leave at once, if we're to find our way back."

Quickly the couple gathered the remains of their picnic, and within minutes they were mounted and leaving the clearing behind. As they pushed their way through the branches and brambles, Aurora hoped that they would not meet with a storm. The day had been clear earlier, but now the darkening sky had an ominous look. Autumn storms were not unknown here, Blacklaw told her.

"We must go on a little faster," Blacklaw called back over his shoulder, "to keep ahead of the storm."

As Aurora urged the chestnut to a faster trot, the animal suddenly stumbled. Unprepared, Aurora flew headfirst over the horse's head. When he realized what had happened, Blacklaw was off his horse and running back to Aurora, and cradled her in his arms.

"Are you hurt?" His free hand explored her arms and legs, checking for breaks.

In a daze, Aurora could still savor Blacklaw's touch, and she was reluctant to move.

"Nothing but my pride is really injured, I believe, although I may have some bruises." She shook her head, and pushed back her hair, which had come loose in the tumble, away from her face. "How is my horse? I hope he hasn't hurt himself."

Blacklaw went to check on the horse, and within a few minutes returned with news.

"I found the rabbit hole he stumbled in, and I fear he has come up lame."

"Oh no."

" 'Tis not a bad injury, and all he needs is rest, but we'll not be able to reach Grey Wood tonight. We're lucky he didn't break a leg."

"Yes." Aurora looked up at Blacklaw in the gloom. "Are you sure we could not reach Grey Wood tonight, my lord? I could ride behind you, and lead the horse, and we could travel ever so slowly so that he does not further hurt himself."

Blacklaw shook his head. "Nightfall brings too many dangers, particularly this far from a town. No, we cannot travel by darkness—particularly when one of the travelers is a woman, and one of the horses is lame. It would slow us too much.''

''But where will we stay?''

''I know of a cottage not far from here, where we shall be welcome. Let me help you up.''

Blacklaw gave her his hand and tugged her to her feet. He mounted his horse and pulled her up behind him, and then finally reached down for the lame gelding's reins. They made their way slowly through the forest, and as she rode, her arms wrapped him, her face pressed against his back, Aurora trembled slightly. She had never touched him like this, and she knew he was just as aware of her touch as she was of his.

As she listened to the strange night noises around them, Aurora was glad that he had suggested that they not ride straight through to Grey Wood. Too many sounds seemed foreboding and sinister to her, portents of evildoers waiting for innocent travelers. She would be glad to be indoors for the night, away from the forest that had seemed so friendly by day.

The couple rode for what seemed like hours, and Aurora began to grow weary. She realized that she was far more bruised from the fall than she had initially thought. Finally, when she thought she could ride no longer, Blacklaw brought his horse to a stop and pointed a long finger before him into the darkness.

''There's the cottage ahead.''

Aurora squinted, but she could barely make out the silhouette of a building. How Blacklaw could recognize it as a cottage, she didn't know.

''I have made use of it before,'' he answered, almost as if he had known her thoughts. ''I think it's safe, but I want to be certain. I will let you down here, then come back for you once I am sure it's all right. If I don't return, you must simply hide, and make yourself comfortable until morning. Then you will easily find your way back to the road.''

Aurora nodded and slid down off the horse. She winced as she reached the ground and her ankle turned slightly under her. She watched while he rode forward into the darkness, and the minutes she waited were the longest of her life. What if he didn't come back? No, she resolved, she mustn't think about it. Surely the cottage would be safe; surely there wouldn't be robbers . . . or worse . . . in wait. Surely.

She strained, listening for any sounds of struggle, but heard nothing but the soft call of a nighthawk and the gentle peeping of tree frogs. At last she heard the sound of someone moving through the underbrush; she stepped back behind a tree.

"Aurora."

She recognized the whisper at once. "Here, Giles."

How easily she had fallen into that practice, she thought with a slight blush.

" 'Tis safe. I'll get you into the cottage, and then look for some wood. We'll need a fire tonight because it's going to be very cool." Gently he took her by the hand and led her to the cottage.

They tied the horses in a lean-to behind the cottage and took off the saddles and bridles. After some minutes of bumping about in the darkness, Blacklaw found a candle. Aurora heard the scrape of the flint, then saw a flicker of light; within moments the room was suffused with a gentle glow.

"You wait here. I'll look for firewood."

"There's some already," she said, pointing to a small stack some feet from the stone fireplace. "Enough for several days."

"I need some kindling as well. I'll be back shortly." With a nod, he ducked out the door and left her alone once more. She occupied her time by investigating the cottage. There was only the single room, but a large one; above the fireplace she found a sleeping loft, with a ladder leading to it to one side of the door. Several shelves lined one wall; some of them held broken crockery. Piled haphazardly near the fireplace, Aurora found some bedding; on inspection, it proved to be free of insects and mice.

The room had two windows, through which the darkness from outside seemed to leer in at her. Aurora crossed the room at once and pulled the shutters closed. That would keep any unwelcome eyes from staring at them. She shivered, wishing Giles would return.

She had brought the picnic basket indoors with her; now she set it alongside a small table in the corner. She pushed aside the cloth and saw that some bread and cheese remained, as well as some wine. That would have to do for now. Within a few minutes Blacklaw returned with an armload of kindling, and once he was inside, Aurora pushed the bar across the door, locking them in.

"Are you afraid?" he asked, after he had dropped the kindling by the hearth. He knelt and began working with the twigs and weeds until he had a small blaze going. Aurora watched as he slowly added a few small logs that would not smother the fire. When she did not answer him, Blacklaw repeated his question.

She shivered again, unintentionally. "I think so. Just a little."

He crossed to her, and gently taking her by the hand, drew her close to the fire.

"It's warmer here."

She nodded, aware that he was still holding her hand. She could not raise her eyes, as much as she wanted to look at him.

"You mustn't be afraid," Blacklaw said, his voice soft and gentle. "Not tonight, Aurora."

And as Aurora raised her head and looked up into his face, she knew that she had nothing to fear that night. Nothing.

9

As the storm came up around them, Aurora and Blacklaw ate
the last morsel of cheese; now they sat before the fire, staring
into the dancing flames and listening to the rain dripping off
the thatched roof.

Aurora had been right to expect this storm. Not long after
their arrival at the cottage, they had heard thunder booming in
the distance; minutes later, the heavens had opened. She
shivered, thinking how close they had come to being caught
in the deluge. She inched a little closer to the fire.

"Are you tired?"

She looked up. Blacklaw had risen and was standing a few
feet from her, by the bedding. His tone sounded intense, but
his face lay in shadows.

"A little," she admitted truthfully. Her afternoon nap hadn't
refreshed her at all.

"Do you want this now?" He indicated the bedding with
an almost curt gesture.

"Perhaps I should lay it out now. Yes, I'll take the bedding. But what about you?"

He shrugged and handed the blankets to her, and she began
unfolding them by the warm hearth. She sat down, yawned
and smoothed a wrinkle on the woolen surface. She didn't
know what to do . . . what to feel. Perhaps she should try to
sleep. She was tired, but . . .

After a moment she lay down, but she did not close her
eyes. Rather, she studied Blacklaw, who had come closer to

142

the fire. The yellow light from the fire played across the planes of his face. A deep feeling welled up within her, and hardly aware of what she was doing, she sat up and in one fluid motion held out her arms to him. His head turned, and then he was holding her against him.

"Aurora."

The sound of his voice whispering her name sent a thrill through her.

"Oh, Giles." She looked up at him and smiled, her lips parted slightly; she waited.

He kissed her. It was a long kiss, filled with smoldering passion, and she shuddered with emotion as he brushed his fingertips across her cheek. His fingers traced the line of her jaw, then caressed the lobes of her ears, her soft eyebrows.

His lips were on hers again; then his tongue probed deeply, traced her lips, and caressed her own tongue. A warm tingling, far warmer than the fire only a few feet away, grew within her, and her fingers gripped his arms. She sighed, and her own small tongue darted out. He made a low sound of pleasure.

"You are beautiful," he said, his mouth against the back of her neck. She shivered as his breath brushed against her, tickling her slightly. "The most beautiful woman I have ever seen."

"No," she murmured, shaking her head a little. "I'm not beautiful."

He drew away slightly and, taking her by the shoulders, stared into her eyes.

"You *are*. I will never have anyone—not even you—disagree with me on that. Do you understand, Aurora?"

Her lips quivered. "I think so. But perhaps you should explain further."

"Gladly," he said with a mock growl, and began raining kisses on her cheeks, chin, nose, eyelids, mouth, forehead. Then his lips traveled slowly downward to her neck, lingering on her collarbone. Her eyes closed, and she gave herself up to the exquisite sensations that swept through her body until they reached the center of her passion. As she bent her head back, a small moan escaped her lips.

Gripping his hair, she pressed his face against her neck. One of his hands touched the swell of her breast, and tiny pinpricks of heat streaked through her bosom, almost as if his fingers were flames, igniting her to love. Inside, she ached; and she knew what she wanted—him.

Blacklaw turned toward her; she shivered slightly, and he rubbed her arms gently. Warmth—from the fire, from the friction of his hands, and from something more—coursed through her body, and she raised her lips to his. Again their bodies melted together as they kissed passionately. He was strong and warm, powerful and gentle.

"I must have you," he whispered, his mouth next to her ear, and she trembled at the feathery touch of his breath and at her desire. She drew back, and stared up at him; her throat was dry, and she struggled to speak.

"Oh, yes."

10

Aurora raised her hand to the fastenings of his shirt, but Blacklaw's fingers clasped hers.

"Please, allow me," he said, and gently kissed each fingertip. He took off her shoes and stockings and lightly touched the instep of her foot. A pleasant tickling sensation swept up her leg. He helped her to her feet, and with maddening slowness, began unfastening the hooks of her skirt. He pulled the garment away, laying it carefully across the table. For a moment she allowed herself to dwell on the well-practiced skill with which he managed women's clothing. Then all unpleasant thoughts were pushed from her mind as he undid the hooks of her bodice. Modestly Aurora crossed her arms. She still wore her chemise, but under his gaze she felt quite naked. Gently pulling her protecting arms away, he bent to kiss the soft skin above her breasts. His fingertips brushed each side of her neck, traced across her collarbone, and up to her chin.

"Raise your arms," he whispered; half-willingly she did so, and her lips parted slightly as she gazed at him; the chemise was pulled off lightly and tossed aside with her other clothing.

Backlit by the golden firelight that gave her skin a warm flush, she held her head high; her eyes met his as she stood naked before him. For a long moment Blacklaw did nothing but gaze, his eyes devouring every inch of Aurora's body.

"You are beautiful, Aurora," he said in a husky voice, and

he stepped forward to pull her trembling form close. His arms tightened about her, warming her, and as she listened to the beat of his heart it seemed to pound with the same rhythm as her own. His hands, gentle yet insistent, swept down her long straight back, trailed lightly to her thighs, and then returned to her back. The touch of his fingers excited her, increasing her trembling tenfold. Pulling away from him slightly, she looked for a moment in wonder at her own body, become alien. Her breasts seemed to have grown heavy, like lush, ripe fruit, and her nipples had risen to rosy peaks.

Man and woman sank softly, gently to the floor; his arm cushioned her against the hardness. The blanket beneath them seemed more comfortable than any bed in which she'd ever slept. His lips curved into one of his rare smiles, an expression that she would have sworn only a man in love could have, though his eyes were hidden from her gaze by the shadows of the firelight. He knelt to one side, and bending slightly from the waist, kissed her mouth, her neck, her breasts.

Moaning, she lay back as his tongue caressed the hard buds of her nipples. Pleasure—at once molten fire and icy flames—raced through her body, leaving her shuddering with anticipation, and she gripped his hair, pressing his face harder against her breast. His hands wandered. One stroked her breasts, teasing the bare nipples between his fingertips, sending barbs of pleasure through her stomach and legs, while the other hand rested for a moment between her breasts, then trailed downward until it reached the downy triangle between her legs.

He caressed those dusky lips, then sought and found the tiny bud of her desire. He stroked and brushed it with his fingers until her skin gleamed with a fine sheen of sweat, and she felt ready to burst with passion. Abruptly he pulled his hand away; Aurora cried out to him, wanting him to continue.

Smiling, he shook his head.

"What?" She couldn't believe that he would do this to her.

"One moment, my love," he said, giving her a quick kiss.

He stood and began to undress. Her chest rose and fell unevenly as she watched him methodically removing his shoes, coat, shirt, doublet. At last he was finished and pushed them aside in a heap. She swallowed quickly as she sat up and stared at him.

Never before had Aurora seen a man without his clothing, and she found Blacklaw's body at once foreign and moving— and utterly compelling. His shoulders were wide and strong, just as she had imagined, and the curve of his calves, the muscles of the arms, attested to his strength and agility. He was smiling at her yet, and her eyes slowly traveled downward, from his face to the tangled mat of dark hair on his chest, down past his flat stomach to his narrow hips and his penis.

She blushed slightly, and he laughed. She could not see enough of him. Emboldened by his encouraging smile, she reached out with one hand and stroked the muscles of his thigh. They were hard, like his lips when he kissed her, and she ran her hand down his leg. Then once more he was kneeling by her side.

"I've never seen a man undressed before," she said shyly as she smiled up at him.

"Do you approve?"

She nodded. "Oh, yes, I do. But only, I think, of you, Giles."

He chuckled, and bent to kiss her. Hungrily their lips met. Blacklaw pulled momentarily away. He kissed her hand, then bent and caressed her shoulder with his tongue. His studied touch sent thrills of pleasure tingling through her, and once more, languorously, she lay down on the blanket. He stretched out alongside her and wrapped one of his hands in her long hair; the other traced an idle line from her chin down across her chest to the honey-colored triangle.

His fingers urgently sought her, stirring a hot liquid response deep within her body, and she moaned as his highly skilled fingers deftly played her, flaming the prickles of desire that threatened to overwhelm her. With her eyes closed tight, Aurora arched her body closer to him, to his hand, and cried out as the world around her burst into a rainbow of startling colors. Shudders of delight rocked her body, shaking her free of earthbound concerns—she forgot everything but Blacklaw and her love for him.

When the shudders had subsided, she opened her heavy eyelids and looked with surprise at him as he smiled down at her. Her hair stuck damply to her cheek; carefully he brushed it aside.

"Are you all right?" he asked, his voice concerned. He stroked her cheek with gentle fingers. Oh yes, she was all right, she thought, just unable to speak; so she simply nodded against his hand, then shifted her head and kissed his palm.

She didn't know what to do next, didn't know if he expected her to speak or to remain silent. She wished she weren't so naive. As if sensing her confusion, Blacklaw said, "You must tell me what gives you pleasure, Aurora—just as I will, in time, tell you what gives me pleasure."

He shifted, and momentarily she thought he was pulling away from her, but she soon saw she was quite mistaken. He positioned himself carefully so that he could kiss the warm fragrant skin between her breasts, and knelt between her legs. He kissed her deeply, and hot, liquid desire overcame her once again.

His lips wandered across her, to the flatness of her stomach, her soft hips, her silky thighs. His kisses enflamed her, and she moaned. Her legs stretched, opened wider to welcome him, and she reached out, brushing his hair with her fingers. She stroked his dark hair, tracing the lines of silver, then gripped his shoulders; her fingers pinched as his lips intently sought and found her center of pleasure, and once again the fire of raining colors flared within her.

Silver and gold lightning arced behind her closed eyelids; and from the very core of her, that secret place of longing she had never known existed, a great cry came bubbling up. She arched her body upward, straining up and up, wanting it to last, and he buried his face within the warm depths of her. Spasms of pleasure burst through her body, rippled, twisted, and roiled, and when the trembling was finally past, she opened her eyes again to see him kneeling before her. A musky odor enveloped them; she thought it a truly wondrous scent.

Her heart itself seemed to ache as she stared at him, and she could almost have cried with joy. Never before in her life had she been so happy. She reached out with her arms and he came into them, and she held him against her damp body. For a long moment they did nothing but lie together, and it was the sweetest, purest moment she had ever known.

Then once again he was kneeling before her, and she was smiling at him. His skin glistened in the firelight, and shadows played across his muscular chest. She licked her dry lips and without a word held out her hand. He took it and guided her fingers to the hard length of him. She felt him, warm and pulsing, and she sobbed aloud. She had never seen . . . never touched a man . . . never imagined it to be like this.

Even as she caressed him, his manhood was hardening, throbbing and jutting against her hand; he moaned with pleasure as she stroked him. She rubbed her fingers up and down the shaft, touching the triangular head and the glistening dampness there, then gently raked a fingernail down the shaft. His body was swaying now, and her own paralleled its rhythm. Reaching up, she pulled him down to her, chest to chest. With great care he eased himself onto her, until she felt his hardness at the opening to the heart of her desire. But though the sensation startled her, she felt no fear.

"I do not wish to hurt you, my love," Blacklaw said as he stroked her breasts. He kneaded them, rubbing the pink nipples back and forth between his fingers. "But you must understand that there may be pain, because you are a virgin."

She nodded and smiled, and he kissed her passion-enflamed lips. His hands raced across her body, stroking and fondling, rubbing and tracing, and she caressed his shoulders, arms, back; she kneaded the muscles with her strong fingers. Then with one powerful thrust, he entered her, claimed her.

A sharp pain lanced through her and then, just as quickly, was gone, to be replaced by a flooding of sweet warmth as he began to move within her. With almost dizzying awareness Aurora realized that the earlier pleasure and the roaring fire he had given her were nothing in comparison to this. With growing wonder and desire, she raised her body to meet his. A sob was wrenched from his lips, and he caught her hair in both his hands and thrust swiftly, fiercely. They both called to each other.

Together the lovers rocked, their harsh, uneven breathing seeming to fill the room. Blindly they kissed each other, held on to one another as though they were about to be swept away. He murmured her name while she wept, tears of love falling down her burning cheeks. He kissed the tears away.

And they were about to be swept away, she thought, her

mind and body filled with the delightful feelings, the sensations that she had never imagined before. He murmured to her without words, called out her name, and then his breath began to come in short gasps. Her blood was liquid fire as her hips ground beneath his; surely she was melting, the flames eating away at her, but she felt only pleasure, no pain.

Together they pushed toward one, then withdrew momentarily, then came together again, their bodies locked in an ageless rhythm. They kissed, their tongues thrusting, pushing, caressing, and she moved her head and nipped him on the shoulder. He laughed, a low sound, and kissed her long on the neck, his tongue tracing the line of her throat. Then there was one last thrust, a thrust that seemed to delve to the very heart of her being, and around her the world burst into a thousand brilliant colors and joyous sounds and exotic scents, and she cried out as she gripped his shoulders.

For one incredible moment, a moment that seemed to last a lifetime, they were united—acting, thinking, breathing as one; Aurora could have wept at the sensation. Then gradually the feeling of suspension passed, and the delicious emotions were ebbing away, leaving the man and the woman shuddering with empyreal delight.

Slowly their breathing quieted until they breathed normally once more, until the world no longer shook, and his breath was warm against her cheek. They continued to lie without moving, clasped in each other's arms.

Weakly, Aurora nuzzled Blacklaw's chest, and in response his arms tightened around her. She felt drained, but pleasantly so, and she seemed almost to float. She didn't want to open her eyes, didn't want to see anything or do anything except lie there, satiated, in the darkness, with the warmth of the man covering her and the warmth of the fire to one side, with all the wonderful feelings that had been released for the first time within her body.

She decided that she would just lie there for a while, only a while, though, and rest, and enjoy and remember what they had done . . . but only for a very short while . . .

When she opened her eyes finally, Aurora saw that Blacklaw had shifted slightly and was propped up on one elbow, staring pensively into the fire. She wondered what he was thinking of; she did not think it was of their lovemaking, and that disturbed her a little. She felt reluctant to distract him, afraid that somehow she would, but she couldn't lie still forever. She stirred, murmured a little, and he glanced down at her.

"Did I sleep?" she asked a little guiltily.

He smiled and nodded. "It wasn't for long. Only a few minutes."

She smiled lazily and reached up to stroke his dark eyebrows, then ran her fingers across his high cheekbones and down to his lips. Slowly he kissed her fingertips, one by one.

"It was wonderful." She stroked his neatly trimmed beard, ran her fingers through it.

"Giles. I *have* heard you say my name before, you know."

"Giles," she repeated, and chuckled. She stretched, luxuriating. "I've never felt so . . . so wonderful." She laughed a little. "I'm repeating myself. Is that a silly thing?"

"It doesn't matter. I wanted it to be special for you, my dear. That's all that matters to me."

"It was," she whispered.

She reached out and brought him down to kiss her, and her arms tightened around him. They kissed for a long time, their mouths pressed hungrily together, and gradually the embers of her earlier passion began once again to glow. Pressing against him, she could feel the desire reawakening in his body, too, and yet he said nothing, made no gesture beyond the tenderest of caresses. She wasn't sure what to do now. Would it be too bold—too hoydenish of her—to indicate that she wanted him to make love to her again? What did other women do in such situations?

"Giles, I—" She stopped, suddenly not sure of what she'd been planning to say.

"Yes?"

"Would you . . ." Her voice trailed away. She didn't know how to say it.

"Yes?" He arched an eyebrow.

She suspected that he knew what she wanted, but wasn't about to help. Playfully she struck his arm; he grinned in response.

"Would you . . . that is . . . please, make love to me again?"

"Gladly, mistress."

With the effortless strength she had experienced before, he pulled her over on top of him, and once again took possession of her, body and mind.

This second time brought her more pléasure than she could have imagined, and none of the pain of the first time. The lovers made love slowly, each taking time to explore the other's body, to discover what the other enjoyed, drawing out the rising wave of exquisite tension till every nerve quivered. Deeper and deeper he thrust inside her, and she wrapped her legs around him, bringing him so close that they seemed to share one skin.

She had to have him! She cried out once, then she was shaken by uncontrolled shudderings, and their voices mingled.

Afterward, in the peaceful lull of afterlove, they talked in love voices, and finally, with Aurora's head cradled against Blacklaw's shoulder and their arms wrapped tightly around each other, they slept.

11

Aurora woke long before it was light outside, and in the half-darkness of the room looked at the man lying next to her on the bedding. Blacklaw was still sound asleep, one arm crooked under his head. She smiled tenderly and kissed his lips gently. Sometime during the night one of them had awakened a little, enough to pull up the coverlet, and Aurora snuggled beneath its warmth, reluctant to leave their cocoon. The night before had been wonderful—the best ever of her life—and although she hoped the gelding would soon be better, Aurora reflected, she was glad that her horse had come up lame.

She had never thought she would love, and had certainly never dreamed of loving a man like Giles Blacklaw. She shivered with the remembered pleasure of his body against hers. When she closed her eyes, she could feel his kisses, his caresses, and she knew that she was intoxicated with the very thought of him. She licked her lips and felt warmth in her cheeks.

Was it only the year before that she had been languishing in Bridewell? Who knew how long she would have stayed there if Giles Blacklaw had not rescued her? No, she wouldn't think about the prison. Not now, when she had all this pleasure to think about. She sat up slowly, then raised her arms above her head and stretched, feeling lazy as a cat. Suddenly a hand cupped one breast. She glanced down at Giles; his eyes were open.

"I wasn't sleeping," he said, "and the opportunity offered was too great for me to resist."

"Scoundrel," she said.

"Indeed." His fingers tweaked her nipple, and she stirred. "Come back to bed, and we'll make love."

"I shouldn't, Giles." She didn't know why; she wanted nothing more in the world than to be with him again . . . and again, time after time. His fingertips brushed slowly back and forth across the stiffening nipple; she groaned.

"Or should I? What do you say?" She cast a mischievous look at him.

"You should."

And so she did.

Some time later Blacklaw and Aurora finally rose from their makeshift bed. The morning was already well advanced by the time they had dressed and saddled Blacklaw's horse and were ready to leave.

As they left the cottage behind, Aurora felt a subdued regret settle over her. She rode behind Blacklaw, and thus could not see his expression, but she was sure his face was once more in its habitual stern lines. Whatever they had shared in the cottage seemed to have been left behind; they were now returning to Grey Wood. She could have cried, but Aurora was determined that she would not lose him . . . not his love; that she would find him . . . truly . . . again.

The man and woman did not speak on the ride back, and even though her stomach rumbled from hunger, Aurora said nothing. The closer they drew to Grey Wood, the bleaker her mood became. Since they had left on their ride the day before, she had thought nothing of Constance. Now—too soon—she would be facing the keen eyes of the widow.

The rain of the previous night had left the forest wet and Aurora was glad she had worn her cloak. She huddled beneath it, keeping her cheek against Blacklaw's back, reassured by his warmth. Once they were out of the woods, Blacklaw soon found the road, and it was mid-afternoon when they arrived at the house.

He jumped off the horse at once and helped her down, and before she could even speak, he had turned and was leading the lame gelding into the stable. Edward came out to meet him, and the two talked about the horse. Aurora waited for him, and when Blacklaw was finished, they both went into the house. There, as Aurora had feared, they found Constance waiting in the parlor.

A shaft of sunlight fell on her. She sat with her arms crossed tightly, and her face was stern. Aurora had never seen Constance wear such a harsh expression, and it frightened her a little. Nervously the girl glanced at her companion, who smiled affably at Constance.

"I hope you weren't too worried, and I suppose you want to know what happened to us," Blacklaw said, as he crossed over to the fireplace to warm his hands.

"No, I do not. I do not care to hear what excuses you have concocted for my benefit."

"Constance—" he began.

"No."

"My horse went lame last night," Aurora said eagerly. "She stumbled in a rabbit hole, and Giles—Lord Blacklaw— thought it best to stop for the night in an abandoned cottage. He feared robbers were abroad."

Constance glanced from Aurora to the man, but said nothing.

" 'Tis the truth, Constance."

"You were always glib, Giles. Always the silver-tongued one."

"Constance!" Aurora said. " 'Tis the truth, as God is my witness. I—"

Before the girl could say anything more, Constance threw a withering glance in her direction, whirled and left the room. Aurora sneaked a glance at Blacklaw. He wore a look of chagrin.

"She's hurt," the girl said.

"I know that," he replied shortly. "You don't fully understand, though."

"I understand that she's in love with you. Anyone with eyes can see that." Her words caused her stomach to knot up. What if he returned Constance's love? What if the things he had said last night were simply the words of passion? What if . . . no, she wouldn't think about that.

"Damn."

Blacklaw strode to the windows and stared out without speaking; Aurora went to him and stroked his cheek softly.

"I love you, Giles." There. She had said it; and now he

would either lie or tell the truth, and it didn't matter, as long as she heard the right words.

He smiled down at her. "I know, little one, I know." He bent and kissed her briefly, almost chastely, on the lips.

"You cannot keep your hands from each other for even five minutes in my absence."

They sprang apart at the sound of the harsh words, and turned to see Constance in the doorway.

"Yes, Constance?" Blacklaw lifted an eyebrow; there was no sense in arguing with the woman when she was in this mood. God knows, he'd never realized how puritanical she was. Certainly she hadn't exhibited such tendencies when they had been lovers. "What is it that you want to say to me?"

"I haven't thought about it a great deal, and I believe it is time that Aurora's lessons end. I am sure you have taught her nearly everything you now, Giles." Neither he nor Aurora missed the heavy irony in the woman's words. "I think it is time."

"I agree."

"Good. Then you must begin soon. Do you understand me?"

He nodded.

With a swish of her skirts, Constance turned and once more left. This time Aurora did not make a move toward the man. She waited for him to speak. She hadn't fully understood the exchange between Constance and Giles, but knew that her life was about to change once more. She could not suppress a shiver. For a long moment Blacklaw gazed at her. He made as if to speak, then kept silent. Finally, almost hesitantly, Aurora spoke.

"What did Constance mean—*it is time*?"

"Time for you to be introduced into London society," he said.

Fear stabbed at her insides. " 'Tis too soon!" she cried. "I don't know enough. I would make a fool of myself, Giles."

"No, my dear, you would not." He crossed to her and lifted her chin with two fingers. He brushed her lips with his, stroked her cheek. "In a few months time you and Constance will go to live in London, for you must demonstrate what you have learned."

Tears stung her eyes, and she shook her head. She was afraid, yes; afraid she wouldn't see him while she lived in the city. She knew that he could not move freely through the streets of London; how could he ever visit her?

"Ah, I understand. I will visit you often, child. Have no fear of that."

"But how will we find time to be together?" she asked plaintively.

"As for that," he said, bending his head to kiss her, "we shall always manage."

"But, why now?"

"Because this is an important time. Before many months the Court will be at Whitehall for Christmas."

Perversely she dug her heels in. "I don't have to go along with your plans, Giles."

His eyes glittered. "You do, if we are to continue seeing one another."

She nodded mutely, knowing he was right. And she realized, at that moment, that she would do anything for him, as long as they could be together.

12

Early in November, through the auspices of a discreet friend in London, Blacklaw found a house for Aurora and Constance to use during their stay in the city. Just over a month later the two women began to settle into the grand house along the Thames.

Aurora was fascinated by the long ride into the city through the snowy countryside. Streets of fashionable houses were back to back with streets of the meanest hovels. When their coach pulled up before the house they were to live in, Aurora gave a cry of surprise.

She had thought that Grey Wood was grand, but this house far surpassed it; to her eyes it looked just like a palace. Constance told her that the four-story residence was not nearly as old as Grey Wood. It was constructed half of wood and half of stone that fairly gleamed in the December sunshine. Aurora couldn't believe that they would be living in such a fine place.

Aurora stared in amazement as they entered the great hall, which was fully three times the size of the one at Grey Wood. The floor was inlaid with black and white marble, arranged in alternating squares. A massive fireplace stood off to one side; she thought it large enough, surely, to roast an ox in.

She didn't have much time to explore further; the servants soon brought their belongings in, and the rest of the afternoon was taken up with unpacking and settling in. Aurora's bedroom was much larger than the one she'd had at Grey

Wood, and this time it was at the far end of the corridor from Constance's. Aurora could not but feel that the arrangement was deliberate; she shrugged, knowing that it might be for the best.

The bed was larger, too, than the other, and there were many fine pillows piled upon it. She ran her hand across the delicate embroidery of the pillowcases, then smoothed the rich burgundy coverlet. The bed curtains were burgundy too, and of a heavy brocade with silver threads running throughout.

The bed lay near the fireplace, and Aurora was pleased to think of lying in bed, enjoying some of the warmth from the fire. Several pieces of light violet-colored Venetian glass stood on the mantel, and to one side was a tapestry of hunters and hounds pursuing a fabulous beast.

She wandered throughout the room for some time, looking at everything, examining the many fine articles within. Finally, when her clothes and personal items were put away, Aurora realized that she was tired; she decided to rest for a while. Lucye curled up next to her, happy to be with her mistress and out of the basket in which she had traveled to London.

Aurora lay, half-dozing, thinking about the story that Blacklaw had coached them in before they left Grey Wood. Their story was to be this: Aurora was a cousin of Constance's; Aurora's father, a minor nobleman, was traveling in Europe and the two women had come to London to await his return.

No one would question their tale, Blacklaw said, because communication beyond London was almost nonexistent, little better than the sometimes impassable roads. It would be virtually impossible for anyone to give the lie to it. He added too that there were any number of lesser noblemen scattered throughout England; no one could maintain a list of each noble and his wide-flung family. Aurora had nodded, her heart pounding from excitement and fear. For a few minutes Constance and Giles had conferred in tones too low for Aurora to catch. Then he came over to her and said farewell. Under the widow's watchful eye, he kissed Aurora on the forehead—rather like a father, she had thought, or a brother. She wished Constance away so that they could embrace.

He had escorted them out to the coach and helped them up; before the door was closed, Blacklaw had handed Lucye, in her basket, to Aurora. Momentarily their fingers had brushed, and she had blushed and dropped her eyes. She had waved until the house, and the man standing in front of it, could be seen no longer.

Constance spoke little during the trip, and for the most part dozed. Since the day that she'd found Blacklaw and Aurora embracing, Constance had remained polite, but not warm. Aurora was far too excited to sleep and could not keep from looking out the window; she was filled with questions, too, but she was reluctant to ask them. Finally, she decided she would venture one.

"Constance?"

"Yes." The woman opened her eyes and looked at the girl.

"Will Lord Blacklaw be able to visit us often in our new home?"

"No, I think not; he cannot come easily to London. It is too risky for him."

"Oh." She said nothing more, but she felt a painful stab of disappointment. She consoled herself with the thought that he would have to visit to see that his plans—whatever they were—advanced correctly. He would have to come to London, and more than rarely, too. That thought considerably cheered her for the remainder of the journey.

In her new, comfortable bed, Aurora drifted slowly off to a dreamless sleep; she woke a short time later, much refreshed. Rising, she went to the window to look out. It was close to evening, and she wanted to see all she could while some light still lingered. Her view was of the Thames below, and she smiled. Cries of "Eastward Ho!" and "Westward Ho!" carried to her ears as people walked down to the river gates to wait for boats to take them across the river. Swans, white as snow, sailed through the clear waters like miniature ships. Up and down the river Aurora saw dozens of boats: scarlet and gold barges that sailed to the Queen's court; little wherries that took passengers from the river gates to Westminster, to the Tower, to the other side of the river; boats full of hay, of corn, of casks of wine—and sometimes even filled with sheep, bleating nervously.

The waterfront was busy, even so late in the day, and for many minutes she watched as the boats docked, and the passengers left, or the wares were unloaded. She wondered if this activity would continue through the night or stop with the setting of the sun. Leaning out the window slightly, Aurora could see other fine houses up and down the river, and she wondered who lived there. Great nobles and their ladies, she told herself, lords and ladies she would meet . . . if she were presented at Court. Presently the Royal Court stayed at the Whitehall Palace in London for Christmas, and in mid-January would move—nobles, servants, and drudges—to either Richmond or Greenwich palace. With the coming of spring, the Court would be once more on the move; the nobility were fond of moving every few months or so.

Presented. To the Queen. Aurora shivered at the incredible thought and drew back inside the room, closing the window against the cold fog that was already rising from the river. She was frightened about appearing at Court, scared of being seen by the nobility. She feared they would point to her, laugh and denounce her at once as an impostor. What if the Queen discovered who she was? Might not Her Majesty punish such impudence? What if Aurora were sent back to Bridewell?

Never, she told herself; never again would she go there. She would kill herself first.

There might be an even harsher fate than Bridewell for an impostor. Aurora felt like one, too, and she wondered if all the education and training Giles and Constance had given her would ever wash that feeling away. Perhaps some day, but not now. Not when she feared the unknown.

Enough of this, she told herself with a slight shake. She had better things to think about—and certainly more cheerful ones. She glanced out the window and saw that the light had faded from the sky. Time to change her clothing and go down. Doubtless Constance would want dinner served soon.

She indulged, for a few minutes, in playing with Lucye. Then she changed and left the room, with the cat placidly following.

13

The following morning Aurora awoke refreshed and eager to
see the house. She rose at once, and after she had washed and
dressed, she was ready to explore. She left her room, and smiled
as Lucye once more followed her. The cat seemed to be adjust-
ing to the move quite well—perhaps even better than I am,
Aurora thought. As she went down the large winding stairway, she thought once more how different this house was
from Grey Wood. The ground floor was less gloomy, with
more windows in each room and along the galleries, although
the view was less appealing, unless one looked at the river.
There were fewer twists and turns in corridors and larger
rooms on the whole, all of them elegantly furnished with an
abundance of exquisite tapestries and much silver in evidence.

She counted fifteen rooms on this floor, divided almost
equally between the kitchen and its associated rooms, and the
dining rooms and chambers used for entertaining guests. Aurora made her way upstairs again. The second floor contained
eight spacious bedrooms, each with a small chamber adjacent
to it for servants; the third floor had twice as many. Certainly,
she thought, they would be able to entertain any number of
guests and never have to worry about running out of bedrooms.

Aurora finished her exploration and made herself comfortable on a window seat, with the cat by her side; she was
watching with great interest the traffic that passed below in
the street when Constance came out of her room.

Aurora smiled sweetly at her. "Good morning, Constance. How did you sleep?"

"Quite fine, thank you, considering that it was my first night in a strange bed. And you?"

"I don't remember a thing," Aurora replied truthfully. "I must have been asleep even before my head hit the pillow."

"Are you ready for breakfast?"

Aurora nodded, and followed the older woman down to the dining room. Its large, upright, rectangular windows faced the east, and long shafts of morning sunlight pierced the room. Dust motes danced in a shaft of light, and Aurora held a hand out to the sunbeams, which had almost a magical quality. Suddenly aware of Constance's faintly amused look, Aurora dropped her hand and quickly seated herself across the table from the widow. This was not like the warm intimate room in which they had dined at Grey Wood; this room could hold immense tables set for several dozen guests.

Blacklaw did not want to risk the danger of having a spy among the servants, so he had asked that as few outsiders as possible be brought into the household. Betty, Dickon, and Edward he knew and could trust; but strangers, he could not.

Spies. For what? Aurora had wondered, but she had asked no one. Yet the thought continued in her mind. What was Blacklaw's secret? That she was no noblewoman? That he was associated with the household? She wished she could ask Constance, but she feared that the widow would simply put her off, as she had so many other times.

Somehow Blacklaw and his discreet friends in London had found servants for Constance and Aurora, and suddenly, they had added six more people to the staff. Aurora giggled aloud at the thought that the new house was positively crowded. She had grown accustomed to having only a few people about at Grey Wood.

Aurora turned her attention to her meal—bread and cheese and milk, followed by dried fruit. Constance insisted that they follow a healthful diet even in London.

"We will finish settling in today, I think," Constance said, as she paused in the midst of buttering a chunk of bread, "although it will take weeks before everything is settled completely and to our satisfaction. Then we shall see what we

can do about going to Court. What do you say to that, Lady
Aurora?''

''I think it's all wonderfully exciting,'' Aurora said, her
eyes large. ''I cannot truly believe I'm living in London. It
seems like a dream.''

''Do believe it,'' Constance said, ''and pray that it becomes no nightmare.''

Aurora's smile faded, and she stared down at her plate.

The second night was harder for Aurora. Even though she
and Constance had worked hard all day in the house, she
couldn't fall asleep right away. She was disturbed and puzzled by the widow's grim remark at breakfast. And, as usual,
her nighttime thoughts revolved around Blacklaw and when
they would next meet. She regretted that they had only made
love the one time, and she wished deeply for an opportunity
to be with him again. These thoughts kept Aurora awake for
many hours; finally, when the night was nearly past, she fell
asleep, only to awaken just before dawn. Tired, and longing
for Blacklaw, Aurora was not sure that she was prepared to
work as hard as she had the day before.

To her complete surprise, the next few days offered Aurora
little time to brood about Blacklaw's absence. Constance,
busy arranging introductions, kept her well occupied.

Aurora had been surprised to learn that Constance had
friends in London; she had always thought the widow had
spent her entire life in the country. Constance penned several
notes and sent them around to her friends in the city, and
within a day they had their first visitor—an older woman who
had been a close friend of Constance's mother.

Lady Bartholomew was a woman of imposing stature, not
tall, but heavy-set; yet she moved with the easy grace of a
young girl. It was obvious that she dyed her hair red—to
match the good Queen's, she averred—and her eyebrows had
been plucked to a single line. Her cheeks were heavily rouged,
startling against the white of her skin; beneath lowered lids
that made her look deceptively drowsy, Lady Bartholomew's
deep-set brown eyes were very sharp. She was dressed in
black velvet, its severity offset by thousands of tiny white
pearls sewn along the sleeves and low neckline of her gown.
Rings set with diamonds and rubies glittered on each finger.

Aurora had dressed with care for this particular meeting in a gown of gold satin. She wore matching slippers on her feet and a simple necklace of gold links around her throat. Her hair was drawn back at the nape of her neck, secured by a few delicate pearl pins.

"What a pretty one," Lady Bartholomew wheezed as she gazed at Aurora.

"This is my young cousin, Lady Aurora, who only of late has come to live with me."

"Your father's or mother's side?" their guest asked as she sat squarely on the single chair in the room. It groaned slightly under her weight.

"My mother's," Constance replied smoothly. She had prepared an extensive background life for Aurora, and could answer most any question directed about the girl, as could Aurora herself.

Lady Bartholomew shook her head. "That le Grey family. As prolific as rabbits. I can't keep track of any of your cousins, Constance. Now, let me see, whom does she resemble? She has Catherine's hair, but Margaret's nose. Well, I can't make head nor tail of it." She laughed, almost a rusty sound, then turned her shrewd brown eyes on the girl.

"How do you find London, child?"

"Quite well, my lady," she replied, "although thus far I've seen little. The traffic outside is quite noisy, but I do like to sit by my window and gaze at the swans on the river."

"A pretty reply, and a pretty girl. You'll be having a pack of hounds sniffing out this little fox before the week is over."

"Anne!"

Lady Bartholomew grinned, revealing short discolored teeth. " 'Tis the truth, and you know it, Constance. The best thing for you to do is to get her to be a Maid of Honor. 'Tis the safest place in London for girls—although not completely infallible—for the Queen watches after them with an eagle eye."

"Excuse me, Lady Bartholomew, but what is a Maid of Honor?" the girl asked.

The visitor shifted. "Ah, you country folk. . . . The Maids of Honor are young girls of good birth whose business it is to make a decorative background for the Queen. The Maids walk with her in the gardens, play, sing, and read to her. The

Queen watches over their manners and morals as fiercely as if they were each and every one a daughter to her.''

"I think that would be an excellent position for Aurora, Anne, but how could I arrange it?''

"Don't worry. I'll take care of it. Just see that you bring her to Court within the week.''

"Very well.''

Their guest stayed only a few minutes more, but promised she would return in two days' time for a hearty meal.

"What did you think of Anne Bartholomew?'' Constance asked when the heavy-set lady had left.

Overall, Aurora had liked Lady Bartholomew, but thought she had best watch her behavior around her; the old woman saw far too much. "She seemed very nice, and very enthusiastic,'' the girl answered cautiously.

"Yes, she is that. She is a good friend to have at Court, too, particularly when one is in trouble. If she sponsors you, then you are in a fairly safe position—if such a thing exists at Court.''

"Does she know Lord Blacklaw?''

"She did once.'' And with that curt reply, the conversation was ended.

The following week, Constance had arranged for Aurora to meet some of the more important young men and women at Court. One day, these ladies and lords, all of them dressed most exquisitely in the latest fashions, took Aurora along on a falconing expedition. She enjoyed the outing into the crisp December air and snowy fields and the delicate sound of the small bells on the birds' hoods, which made her think of the church in her own village . . . a village that seemed more than a lifetime removed from her new existence. Aurora's remarkable empathy with animals was demonstrated once again, as the falcons grew calm in her hands. This remarkable feat was commented on by all in the party, and Aurora smiled to herself, pleased to be the center of attention.

She returned home, burbling with the news of the outing to find that Constance had more company—all visitors who had come to meet her cousin. Much to her own surprise, Aurora soon proved popular almong the Court members to whom she was introduced. She was elated with her success, and silently she thanked Blacklaw for insisting on her thorough education. She could never have made it without that, and each day she drew upon that store of knowledge.

"What do you think of London now?" Constance asked one night, as Aurora prepared to go to bed.

"I think it's wonderful, and I couldn't imagine not being in London now," the girl said.

"Be careful, though. Do not be too free," the older woman warned as she left to go to her own room. "Remember that there are always spies about." The door closed firmly behind her.

Spies. Aurora made a face. She knew nothing of spies, nor did she wish to know. She was enjoying herself too much. There was only one thing that would make her joy complete: having Giles with her.

She sighed. There was no sense in pining for things that could not be. When he was able to come to London, he would come, and not a moment before. However long it took, Aurora knew that the wait would seem too long to her.

PART IV

1585

1

"What did you give the Queen on New Year's Day, Maraline?" asked young Mary Prentice.

"A set of fourteen brass buttons edged with beige pearls," Maraline Chambelet replied. "They were *very* expensive."

"Of course," Mary replied. "*All* your presents are expensive!" She wore an unadorned gown of russet brocade with a gold silk girdle. Her plain face could have been pretty, except that usually her eyes were downcast, or she was blushing— she rarely smiled. Her only jewelry was a simple pearl ring on her right hand, a present from her mother just before her death. She was the quietest of the group of girls, the shyest too, and she openly worshiped Maraline. Mary's long, straight, light brown hair was a source of agony to her. At the English Court, red or blond hair was the style, and a woman born with another shade soon changed its color. But Mary was sure that if she dyed her hair it would fall out and she would be forced to wear a wig, an opinion that elicited much laughter from her friends—all of whom were blessed with red or blond tresses.

At seventeen Maraline was a blond beauty of frail appearance, with a thin, delicate face, a pouty red-lipped mouth, and a high white forehead that bespoke less of intelligence than it did of diligent shaving of the hairline. Maraline's large blue eyes, fringed with blond lashes, did not for a second convey innocence. She was far shorter than the other girls in her circle, but without a doubt she commanded them as leader.

She was the only daughter of an extremely wealthy family of minor nobility, and she was determined to marry exceedingly well.

She was wearing an expensive gown of scarlet velvet, its bodice and sleeves decorated with gold buttons and tiny seed pearls. The gown was open in the front to show a heavily embroidered brocade petticoat. In her pale hair, jeweled pins glittered.

"What did *you* give Her Majesty?" Maraline kept a serious expression on her face.

Mary's face went red, and she stuttered slightly as she answered. "A—an embroidered handkerchief."

"How . . . sweet." Maraline smiled, showing white even teeth.

"Th—thank you."

"You're quite welcome."

"And what about you, Roxanne?" Maraline asked, turning to a girl with dark red hair and porcelain-white skin. Roxanne smiled, a feral expression that did not suit her. Her eyes were pale blue, her nose thin and small, At thirteen she was the youngest of the group, but by no means the least developed, for her body was already provided with many generous curves.

"I gave Her Majesty a tapestry that I've been working on for well over a year—it was an expensive gift, too." Roxanne Norville's family were of higher station than Mary's; but because there were eleven Norville children, the family was no longer as wealthy as it had been. Roxanne was determined to marry better than her mother had.

"Well, Mary, you'll just have to think of a better present next year."

Mary nodded slowly.

It was customary at Court on New Year's Day for all members of the Court and the royal servants to give presents to the sovereign. Elizabeth received money, pieces of clothing, jewels, embroidered linens, sweetmeats, and novelties such as watches. Donors were rewarded with plate from the Jewel House appropriate to their standing in the royal household.

Maraline, as a favored Maid of Honor, was amassing a sizable collection of plate, something which she yearly calculated. She would have a large dowry soon, something she could use to attract a highly placed husband.

"There's a new girl at Court," Roxanne said, her tone crafty. She glanced at the others as if daring them to discourage her from talking.

"Oh?" Maraline lifted an eyebrow for effect. An exceedingly ardent suitor had once told her that she had the most exquisite eyebrows; to prove his love, he wrote a poem about them, and then set it to original music. Ever since Maraline had used that gesture.

"Yes, her name is Aurora le Grey. Supposedly she is a *lady*."

"Umm." Clearly Maraline was not impressed.

"Oh yes," Mary said eagerly, "I've seen her, too. She's very pretty. Not as pretty as you, Maraline, of course."

"Thank you. I haven't seen her, or heard of her. Why is that? Where does she come from?"

"From the country, I hear. She is a cousin to Constance Westcott," said Alice Vaughan, speaking for the first time.

Alice was the eldest of the girls, and at twenty she sometimes felt out of place with them, but she had no other friends. She was tall, with curly hair the color of ripe corn. Her brown eyes were wide-set, her nose snub, and she tended to wear browns and golds, having once been told these hues became her. She had a nervous habit of biting her fingernails, and often sat with her long thin hands clasped in her lap.

"Oh, that old woman. Well, the girl can be of little importance," and with that Maraline shrugged away any thought of a potential rival. But her pretended indifference did not mean that she wouldn't watch this "Aurora" person.

2

Aurora was too busy being introduced to members of the Court to notice that she was under surveillance. And for the past week, she had been pleasantly distracted by the awareness that she had a number of admirers. Some of these men were white-haired gentlemen whose granddaughters were often older than she; others were more her own age. Many were the sons of the lords at Court. Old or young, she found she enjoyed flirting with them.

She now used all the skills of the fine art of flirting that Constance had taught her to great effect, and she silently thanked the widow for being so persistent in her lessons.

To her great surprise she also discovered she wielded a great power over these men—they would do anything at her bidding. If she dropped a glove, they would retrieve it; if she wanted a certain volume of poetry, they would fetch it. If she were thirsty at a revel, they would procure cup after cup of wine for her. She had only to raise a shapely eyebrow, and a legion of ardent admirers would be ready to do battle for her.

She did not misuse this power, however, as some young women new to Court might have; she regarded this ability with some amusement because her heart lay with none of these gentlemen, no matter how gallant he proved himself. Her heart belonged to Giles Blacklaw.

After nearly a month had elapsed, and Aurora had begun to

think she would never see him again, Blacklaw did finally arrive.

Late one night, after an evening of dancing at Court, she went straight to her bedroom. As she undressed, Aurora looked out the window at the river, its silvery surface gleaming with moonlight; then she crawled into bed. She hadn't been dozing long when the soft sound of her door opening and closing roused her. She waited, her heart pounding, then whispered fearfully, "Who's there?"

Nearby a floorboard creaked, and then a warm voice close to her said, "Is that any sort of a welcome?"

"Giles!"

Sitting up, she flung herself into his arms. They kissed and held each other tightly, his fingers stroking her hair. Finally, after some minutes, they pulled away to catch their breath.

"I've missed you so, Giles," she said, her head nestled against his shoulder.

"And I you, my darling." He kissed her lips, then her neck, brushed her hair away from her face, and held her tightly. "And what have you been doing this past month? Keeping out of mischief?"

"Oh yes, Giles. But I've been having a wonderful time at Court, truly I have. I thought I glimpsed the Queen once, although someone told me it wasn't she. And so I have not yet seen her."

"Be careful, my little one, when you do finally meet her. She is a crafty old fox. She can see things that no one else does, although at other times she can be as blind as a mole."

She nodded, suspecting that he was referring to his own case. "I will be careful. And every night I have danced and seen plays and the most wondrous of things. I think London is truly marvelous."

"And you do not lack for admirers, do you?" he asked, his voice teasing.

"Well . . ."

"Confess now," he said, tickling her a little. "Confess, my little vixen."

"Very well. I have a few."

"A few?"

"Several."

"What?"

"A handful then."

He laughed. "Minx. You have no doubt enough admirers to keep you busy every night of the month."

"Not quite," she said ruefully.

"But almost, yes?"

"Almost." She paused. "And Lady Bartholomew, Constance's friend, comes to visit often. She says that she thinks I would make an excellent Maid of Honor, and she will be talking to the Queen about me!"

"Lady Bartholomew . . . the old lady?" She nodded. "Amazing, child. I am delighted that you are such a success."

"I would be more of a success, if you were by my side," she said.

He shook his head; she felt the motion against her cheek. "No, my darling, no. It cannot be."

She sighed. Perhaps if she grew acquainted with the Queen, she could talk to her about Blacklaw, make the monarch see reason where he was concerned. And then he could return to Court.

"And what of the news at Court, my love? What fine gossip can you tell me?"

"Not much, I'm afraid. I still don't know who everyone is, so it is hard for me to make heads or tails of what I hear—although I did learn from Lady Bartholomew—she does talk a great deal, doesn't she?—that one of the Maids of Honor had to return to her family home up north rather abruptly. Some say it was an illness in the family that prompted her departure, but others claim she is in the family way herself."

"Shocking," he murmured.

"You're laughing," she accused.

"Only a little." He paused. "Anything else, my dearest?"

"Only that the Court is to move in a week or so. We still don't know if it will be to Richmond or Greenwich. I don't care which—I haven't seen either."

"Both are rather remarkable," said Giles, "although I suppose the most interesting palace is Nonsuch."

"Why do the Queen and Court move so frequently? The Court will be at Windsor in April, and by Royal Maundy it returns to Whitehall, and during the summer the Court is removed from London."

"There are numerous practical reasons—those of sanitation. And no palace can support all those people for an entire year. During the summer, remember, London is hot and disease-ridden. Then, the Court leaves for health reasons."

"I see."

"Will you be leaving with them?"

"I don't know. I don't know that I am a member of the Court yet. And I'm not really sure that I wish to be one," she added. Suddenly, her eyes widened. "But if I must go with the Court, then you and I will not be able to see one another."

"Don't worry, child. Something can be arranged. Believe me." He stroked her hair, then kissed her gently on the lips.

"Very well."

"Do you remember hearing anything else?"

"What do you mean? Oh, there are the usual grumblings about Mary." Elizabeth's cousin, who ruled the Scots, was disliked by many of the Court members—not only for having married a French prince, but also because she was a Roman Catholic.

"The usual? But nothing out of the ordinary?"

"No."

He smiled at her puzzled look. "I may no longer be at Court, but I do care to hear what is said there. Thank you, my sweet, you have done a good job. An excellent job. You must continue to listen—and watch. That is very important."

She wanted to ask him why she must continue to listen and to watch and be so careful, but tonight she didn't want to know, she didn't care—she sensed that the reason was not that he no longer stayed at Court; but tonight she didn't want to know. She just wanted to be with him, with her own love.

"Giles."

"Yes, my dear?"

"Love me, please."

"Gladly."

He began kissing her. His lips traveled across her eyelids and cheeks, down her neck to the soft swell of her breasts, and she threw back her head so that he could kiss the hollow of her neck.

Greedily her hands sought to unbutton his shirt. She ran her hands through the thick hair on his chest, shivering with excitement. Breathing hoarsely, Blacklaw shifted, slowly pushing her back down on the bed. He stood and quickly undressed.

As he knelt once more on the bed, his warm lips sought her bare breasts, and his tongue caressed and teased her nipples. She felt the tiny buds tightening with his exquisite attention, and she moaned with pleasure as his hand slipped between her thighs. He kissed her lips, then nibbled at an earlobe. Her legs opened at once to his gentle touch, and he caressed her till she felt she would explode with desire.

Wanting to please him as he had pleased her, she reached out, and taking his hardening manhood in both hands, she stroked its solid length, feeling its warmth enflame her. Velvety soft, yet hard, it throbbed against her, and he shivered.

Aurora moaned softly as his hands traveled across her legs, her stomach, her breasts. She arched her back and he slipped a hand behind her, gently massaging the small of her back. She felt so wonderful when he touched her—no matter how little, no matter where. She didn't want him to go away, even though she knew he must. She wanted him to stay, wanted to love him again and again, through the night and day.

Hot liquid feelings, wickedly delicious, welled within her and burst brilliantly, scattering barbs of pleasure throughout her body; then built up again, always cresting larger and larger each time. Finally, when she thought she could stand the tingling and aching no longer, she called his name, and Giles rolled on top of her and slipped effortlessly within her.

Rhythmically he thrust within her, seeming to delve deeper and deeper. She twisted below him, and their hips met, parted, met again. She felt as though she were being split in two, and all the while the pleasure intensified, growing hotter and hotter. His hands roamed across her stomach, her breasts, her face, and softly he called her name. A white heat built within her, grew, and threatened to explode; he pulled back slightly.

"No, no," she cried out, gripping the hard muscles of his back with all her strength; then he plunged deep within her. The heat glowed, and suddenly around her everything was light. Her nails dug deeper into his skin as she arched up to meet him, but he only held her tighter. She bit her lips, tasted the saltiness of blood, just as there was a roaring in her ears and her world burst apart in the illumination of a million suns.

Her soft cry of release mingled with his, and they rocked together. Slowly their movements stilled until they held each other limply in damp arms. The heat cooled ever so gradually, and she breathed deeply, trying to catch her breath. For a long time the lovers did not speak or move; then at length he stirred, making a low sound of satisfaction. He reached down and kissed her still enflamed lips. His were cool against hers, and she breathed deeply of his musky odor. They rested in their embrace, not moving, not speaking. She thought she had dozed for a few moments, and then she stirred.

"Giles?"

"Again?" She nodded, and he chuckled.

Their lovemaking progressed much more slowly than before, with each trying to bring the other to greater heights of passion; Aurora thought it more wonderful than ever, if that were at all possible. When they lay still, spent and worn, their senses sated at last, they drifted in and out of languid sleep. His hand stroked her thigh, and she snuggled closer to him.

Across the room the windows were pale rectangles now, and the faint songs of birds could be heard in the distance. Already hoarse calls from the river drifted up to her window.

"I must leave," he said.

"No, don't. Not yet, Giles." She grabbed his arm gently. "I'll make you stay—I'll make you a prisoner of love."

"You have already done that, Aurora." He kissed her lips and sat up. "Indeed, you have. But I fear that I must leave before the light of dawn, else someone might well see me."

She knew he was right, but she didn't want to see him go. "I wish you could stay."

"So do I, but I cannot." He rose in one graceful motion and began dressing. When he was finished, he bent over the bed and pressed his lips against her forehead. "I will be back. I promise you that, my dearest."

She nodded and hugged him, then watched as he slipped from her room. She pulled the covers up to her neck, and forced back the tears welling up. It wasn't the end of the world, after all. Not really. But why did it feel like it?

3

January snows forced the Court upriver to Richmond. On
their way to their new home, Constance had explained that
the great palace had once been the site of Sheen Palace,
favorite home of Edward III and Richard II. A century ago, a
fire had gutted most of the old building; Henry VII built a
new palace, and for once he spared no expense. When the
royal residence was finished, he renamed it Richmond—after
the title he had held before he became King.

Soon after her arrival, Aurora went exploring. She discovered that the royal quarters, or Privy Lodging, were decorated
with fourteen turrets, pinnacles and ornamental weather vanes,
and that the chapel—unlike any parish church she had ever
seen—had pews. The most wondrous feature of the palace
was the tower, and after she had climbed the one hundred
and twenty steps, she looked out to see a wonderful view of
the winding Thames and of Hampton upriver, and a haze to
the east—London. The fields lay like a patchwork of brown
and white, and everywhere she looked she saw trees, rolling
hills, and the glimmer of sunlight on the Thames. The wind
up here made Aurora cold, and she wrapped her arms across
her chest and hurried down the steps.

She joined Constance in her rooms, to warm herself before
the fire and to relate what she had seen from the Tower.
Aurora sat down on a stool by the hearth, and Lucye jumped
up onto her lap and settled down for a nap. The two women

talked for some time; when Constance grew tired, she bade
the young girl good night, and Aurora left for her own rooms,
adjacent to Constance's.

Alone, Aurora lay in the darkness for some time, then
slipped out of bed and padded across to the window. It was a
beautiful night, and the Thames gleamed silver in the moonlight. She wondered where Giles was.

Two nights later, a revel was held to celebrate the arrival of
the Court at Richmond. Aurora was especially excited that a
masque was to be presented. She took her time dressing,
finally selecting a new, quilted yellow gown with red sleeves
and white lawn yoke and ruff, a black felt hat with its crown
in folds, adorned with a blue ostrich plume. She wore blue
velvet shoes. Around her neck she had a rather plain necklace
of gold links, and only one ring upon her hand.

When she was ready, she picked up her feather fan, bade
Lucye good evening, and knocked upon Constance's door. It
swung open at once.

"You look magnificent!" Aurora exclaimed. And truly the
widow did. She was attired in a red gown, its skirt opened to
show off an exquisite petticoat in pink and silver, trimmed
with fringe. From her waist hung a small handmirror, her fan,
and a small ball of scent enclosed in silver. Her shoes were
red, and jewels glittered in her hair and upon her hands.

"Thank you. I thought I should make a good impression
for us tonight. The Queen will be there—and she will be
thinking of what Lady Bartholomew said."

"Do I look all right?" Aurora asked anxiously. "Perhaps I
should change?"

"Child, you look fine, simply fine. Please, don't worry, or
you'll spoil your evening."

"Very well, Constance. Are you ready?"

The widow nodded, and they walked to the staircase.
Aurora was nervous tonight, but more serene than she would
have been a few weeks ago. During that time Constance
seemed to have forgiven her. They spent many hours together, talking about this and that. At no time did they
mention Giles Blacklaw.

Downstairs, the palace's great hall was an incredible sight.
The immense room, already crowded with chattering lords and

ladies, knights and ambassadors, entertainers and servitors, was lit by thousands of candles, and the light, diffused by the room's size, was golden. Musicians played softly at one end of the hall, while the other stage had been set up near the Queen's throne.

Aurora watched everything, bewildered by so much activity. Constance introduced her to more people, and during the masque they sat together in one of the front rows. Aurora enjoyed staring at the costumed lords and ladies of the Court speaking their lines. The masque was a comedy, and the Queen was one of the most appreciative members of the audience.

From time to time Aurora sneaked glances at the sovereign. Dressed entirely in red, white, and gold, she was magnificent, too. Her ruff was amazingly detailed, sewn with pearls and diamonds, and her red hair gleamed in the candlelight. The Queen's hair was a wig, or so Constance had said, but that did nothing to take away from Aurora's impression of Elizabeth. The monarch was no longer young, yet her white face was unlined, and when she laughed, which was often, she looked far younger than her years. Her deep blue eyes were shrewd, and they reminded Aurora somewhat uncomfortably of a hawk's.

Eventually the rather lengthy and altogether silly masque was finished and the impromptu actors and actresses received great adulation and strong applause from their peers. Constance and Aurora rose to their feet, and in the crush, Aurora became separated from her companion.

As she wandered slowly through the huge hall, Aurora began to realize just how large the royal household truly was. She'd seen dozens of people thus far—and not a single one did she know, even though since December she had had countless introductions. There must be hundreds and hundreds of people in the household, and she marveled that anything was ever done properly.

A handful of girls close to her age continued to stare at her until she began to wonder if she might have met them once and forgotten it; one of them, a pale blonde dressed in green and silver, glared at her, and Aurora looked away. She was beginning to feel a little uncomfortable and wished she could find Constance, when she heard her name being called.

"There you are, child!" Constance laid a firm hand upon Aurora's shoulder. "I have been searching all over for you. Come, there is someone I wish you to meet."

Aurora nodded, and obediently followed the other woman.

Beyond a cluster of older men stood a young man. He was dark-haired with a handsome, narrow face, and he appeared to be close to Aurora's age. As the two women approached, the young man turned toward them and smiled sunnily.

His eyes were a pleasant shade of grey; his beard, light brown with some red in it, was neatly trimmed, as was his moustache. He wore somewhat more somber clothes than did the other young men around him, and yet he was striking.

"Richard, this is my cousin, Aurora le Grey; Aurora, this is Richard de Sayreville."

"How do you do," Aurora said, smiling faintly and extending her hand.

"Charmed," he said, "utterly charmed," and he bowed elaborately over her hand "I did not know your cousins were so beautiful."

Constance smiled at him. "Ah, but my young cousin comes from the country, and that makes all the difference, Richard."

"Indeed, it does," the young man said.

Aurora arched an eyebrow. "What utter rubbish," she said, and to her delight the young man laughed good-naturedly.

"There's no rubbing Richard the wrong way," Constance said, "for he is the most even-tempered person I've ever known."

"Thank you, although my father says otherwise." He made a slight bow. "I hope that I have always proved accommodating."

"I will leave you two children now, for I see an old acquaintance across the room." Constance flashed a smile at him and began threading her way through the crowd.

Aurora knew that Constance had introduced her to Richard in the hope that he would take her mind off Blacklaw. Aurora wasn't sure that it was going to work, although she had to confess that Richard de Sayreville seemed a most pleasant young man. At that moment she was far less lonely than she had been all evening.

"I take it that this is your first time at Court," he said.

"One of the first times, yes, although I've never been to anything this formal before. I have lived all my life in the country and just before Christmas came to live with my cousin Constance."

" 'Tis a shame that London has thus far missed your fair face; the city would have been all the brighter for it."

"You are most outrageous, sir."

"I am speaking the truth." He grinned. "And what of your parents, Mistress le Grey?"

"My mother died when I was young. My father is currently traveling abroad, but plans to join us in London sometime later this year, if time permits." She had practiced her story many times before, but had only had to say it a few times, and she felt a little awkward. She hoped that he hadn't noticed. "And you, sir? What of your family?"

"I am, alas, the only child who has survived beyond infancy, and because of that my mother has tried to shelter me all my life. She has not always been successful at that, for my father feels I must experience everything in life—pain and suffering in particular."

He was smiling as he spoke, but she saw that his eyes were quite serious, and she wondered what sort of man his father was.

For some minutes the young couple watched the others around them dance. When one air had ended and another was about to start, Richard asked her to dance. She found the young man an exceptional partner, and was glad she had learned her dancing lessons well.

As the pair moved about the hall, Richard introduced her to his friends, and Aurora was once more aware of the baleful stare of the short blonde. Once she whirled abruptly, convinced that the young woman was only a few steps behind her, but when Aurora turned, the girl was busy talking with her friends. Aurora frowned.

"What is amiss?"

"Who is that girl?" she asked, indicating the other with a nod of her head.

"Oh, her," he said, his tone flat. "She's no one of importance. Come, Aurora, let us dance again—the musicians are playing my favorite melody."

Richard and Aurora remained together until Constance finally found her again and said it was late and that they must leave. Aurora was surprised at her own disappointment. Still, she was tired; she wasn't used to all this dancing and drinking of fine wines, much less talking with hundreds of ladies and gentlemen. Stifling a yawn, she bade Richard a good night and left with the widow.

As they went upstairs, Constance glanced over at her young charge. "He seemed very taken with you, my dear."

"Oh?" She had particularly enjoyed Richard's company tonight, but she could not—and would not—look upon him as a beau, no matter what Constance wanted. Still, she liked him more than any of her other admirers.

"Yes, and the de Sayrevilles are a particularly good family. The mother is an intelligent, gracious woman. Lord de Sayreville can sometimes prove overbearing, but he is still quite handsome and just as charming as his son."

Aurora said nothing.

"Are you paying attention?"

"Yes, Constance, I am."

"Well?"

"I liked Richard quite a lot. Only . . ." Her voice trailed off.

"Only what?" Constance's voice was sharp.

"Only . . . I don't know." Aurora shrugged. "I am not attracted to him in that way."

"Sometimes matches are made not upon the attraction between persons, but whether it would be advantageous to both. May I remind you that you have no dowry, and cannot afford to be too choosy."

"I did not know that one of the aims of my coming to London and Court was to look for a husband."

"All young unmarried girls must have this done," Constance said rather primly.

"I see."

"I rather thought you would."

"Constance." They had reached their rooms now, and Aurora stared at the widow.

"Yes?"

Aurora pitched her voice low, so that they could not be

overheard. "Do you think that Lord Blacklaw will ever be allowed to return to Court?"

"No."

The answer was flat, emphatic.

"But surely—"

"No. Giles cannot come to Court. If he were to do so, it would mean his death. It is as simple as that, Aurora."

Aurora paled. To that blunt statement there was no response.

4

Not all at Court were as enchanted by the new beauty as
Richard de Sayreville. Slowly, over the weeks to come,
Aurora grew steadily more aware of this dissenting opinion.
Each chance meeting with the young blonde woman—and
such meetings were frequent and inevitable in the closeness of
Court society—made Aurora increasingly uncomfortable. She
didn't know what she had done to incur the young woman's
anger; they hadn't even been introduced until the week before. When they did meet, Maraline Chambelet was barely
civil.

"There is our new country cousin," said Maraline Chambelet, indicating Aurora as she entered the room. "One can
almost smell the barnyard scent clinging about her yet."

The girls surrounding Maraline giggled—all except Mary,
who glanced nervously at her friends.

"What is wrong, Mary? Do you fear she might overhear?"

"N—Not at all. I just thought th—that . . ." Mary looked
down at her shoes.

"Th—thought what?" Maraline mocked.

"That she looks rather pretty. I—I had thought she would
look like a cow or something . . . You know, because she's
from the country."

"Like a cow?" Roxanne said. She laughed, the sound high
and unpleasant.

"She is rather tall, though," Alice said. "Almost as tall as some of the men."

"Yes, how unpleasant to see eye to eye with them." Maraline commented. "After all, how can she flirt with them?"

"I hear that Richard de Sayreville is in love with her."

"Oh, Alice, Richard de Sayreville is in love with anything that wears skirts."

Prudently Alice remained silent; she knew Maraline had particularly harsh words for the young son of that noble family. Why this was so, she didn't know, unless of course he had spurned her.

Roxanne shrugged. "Everyone hears that sort of thing when a new girl comes to Court, but I haven't heard anything really . . . good . . . about her, have you? I mean, those who've met her think she's very charming." She made a face.

"I've heard something, though." Mary's quiet statement made them look at her.

"Yes, what is it?"

"I hear that she has a cat, Maraline. A black cat—and she talks to it."

Slowly a smile spread across Maraline's fair face as she looked at her friends; understanding Maraline's mind so well, Alice and Roxanne began to smile, too. Only Mary did not know what was going on.

"Don't look her way," Constance said to her charge. "Ignore her."

"It's very hard." Aurora did manage to keep her eyes from flicking in the direction of the blonde girl. "What have I ever done to her? Why does she treat me like her enemy?"

"What you have done to her is simply this: you are at Court. For her kind, that is enough. And because you are here—and have attracted considerable attention among the men—you have established yourself as a rival of Maraline Chambelet."

"That's silly!"

"Perhaps, but that is the way of women such as Maraline. I warn you—do not turn your back when she is present. Without compunction she will stab you—figuratively, and perhaps even literally. It has been known to happen, even among the nobly bred. But whatever you do, you must not attack her in public, nor can you give her any further cause to malign you. You cannot afford anyone noticing you that much. Do you understand?''

Aurora nodded.

''Good.''

They wandered away to the refreshment table to partake of the fine wine and delicacies there, and as they did so Maraline turned to watch the two women carefully.

Over the course of the next few days, Aurora grew increasingly aware of Maraline's malevolent interest and forced herself not to stare at the girl, although it wasn't always easy, particularly when Maraline made catty remarks to her friends—remarks which the blonde made sure that Aurora could overhear.

At one point Aurora's eyes filled with tears, and she knew she had to leave. She returned to her rooms upstairs and lay down on the bed. Lucye ambled over to her, turned over onto her back and purred loudly. She rubbed the cat's stomach as she thought about Maraline. What was she to do? If she ignored Maraline, the girl still talked about her; if she approached her, doubtless Maraline would then have more ammunition against her.

''Oh, Lucye, what am I to do?''

The cat purred more loudly and idly opened one eye to gaze at her mistress.

Aurora laughed and pulled the cat to her and held the purring bundle very close.

What she must do, foremost, is to continue to be seen at Court and be polite—in other words, to outsmart Maraline at her own game.

5

Richard saw how much Maraline upset Aurora and he counseled her to ignore the other girl. "She's not important. After all, no one listens to someone like that."

Aurora smiled ruefully. "I think you are a little naive, Richard. It is women—and men—like her who manipulate everyone."

He raised his eyebrows, a gesture that reminded her of Blacklaw. "Naive! Me? I have been at Court far longer than you, my country miss—may I remind you! I was practically born here and have lived within the Court confines all my years."

She laughed. "*All your years*, Greybeard? You may have lived here for many, many years, but that fact will not change my opinion. You are an innocent."

"In one respect, perhaps."

"Very well," she agreed. She did not enjoy arguments, not even a mock-battle one; these things could quickly become all too serious, and right now she was concentrating on the other woman. She watched Maraline for several minutes. "She's aware that I'm looking at her, isn't she?"

"Of course."

"Then I shan't." With a shrug, she turned her full attention to Richard and smiled at him.

"Thank you," he said with a half-bow. "Now, we can continue our conversation in a civilized way—with your face turned in my direction."

"Richard."

She thumped him on the arm with her fan, then took the arm he offered, and they strolled away.

Tonight they had played backgammon, and Richard had proved an excellent instructor; afterward they had played riddles with the others of the Court for several hours.

Richard was particularly adept at fathoming the riddles, a skill, he said in an undertone to Aurora, that he had learned from his mother.

Then had come a late dinner of venison and hare, quail and poached fish, and now, full from their delicious dinner, the young couple strolled about the great hall for exercise.

Aurora nodded to several people she knew, and smiled at one old gentleman, who winked.

"Oh, I see I have a rival," Richard was quick to say with a grin.

"Oh, well, Lord Danby is quite a flirt, but not a serious contender. I do not think he has marriage on his mind."

"And as well, for he's seen four wives buried in child-birth."

"Not something I wish to happen to me, thank you very much."

They stopped at a refreshment table, where Richard procured wine for them. As they strolled and sipped their wine, Aurora glanced sideways at her companion. He really was quite handsome, and amusing, and very, very attentive.

"Richard, may I ask a question of you?"

"Of course."

"What religion are you?"

He gave her an astonished look. "Why, I am a member of the Church of England, of course."

"I see."

"And are you?"

"Yes, I suppose so, I mean yes." She sipped her wine, hoping to cover her slip.

"You suppose so?"

"We are not overly religious in my family. My father and I had our own chaplain, but when my father went away, he dismissed the chaplain."

"Ah."

Relieved by her own quick thinking, Aurora took another sip of wine to cool her flushed face.

"Why do you ask?"

"There is something that puzzles me. Doubtless, you do not know this, being *city-bred,* as you are so quick to tell me"—and here she smiled—"but it is our custom to be very tolerant of others, particularly those of other faiths. Yet, to my great surprise I find in London—and most especially at Court—a terrible hatred of the Roman Catholics. However, where I came from, many people that I knew and loved and greatly admired were of that faith, and were decent citizens, faithful to the Queen, and not the devils that those here paint them. Why are the Catholics so despised? What have they done—or not done—to incur this enmity?" She had only to think of Maraline Chambelet to know that someone didn't always have to do something wrong to inspire hatred.

"You choose a difficult topic, Aurora." He tapped his fingers against his glass. He sighed. "A most difficult topic."

"I'm sorry."

He smiled slightly. "Let me try. If this grows too muddled, please let me know." He sipped his wine, then began. "Less than a century ago, all of England was of the Roman Catholic faith. But the Queen's father, Great Harry, wished to divorce his first wife to marry another. The Catholic Church refused to recognize the divorce, and so the King broke with it to establish our own Church of England. There was a great backlash against the Roman Church and the Pope; monasteries and nunneries were dissolved, churches torn down, and much of what was formerly owned by the Roman Church went into the coffers of the Crown.

"Of course, the Protestant Church did not stay whole forever, and sects began splintering away from the mother church—among these were the Puritans, who adhere to a strict form of Protestantism and abhor any hint of 'Popish' things. Others have been influenced by this thinking, as well, and have come to regard Catholics as the source of all troubles.

"It does not help," he went on to say, "that the Queen's half-sister, Mary, is a Catholic. Many Protestants were punished to great excess in her time.

"When our Queen came to the throne, there was much rejoicing because she is a Prince of our Church, and she was urged to be harsh with the Catholics. She has always been moderate of faith, and tolerant, but Parliament is riddled with Puritans, and her advisors urged her to take a firm stand—to build the confidence of her own subjects, and so she was forced to take action. Roman Catholics were forbidden to hold their own services; religious images in churches were destroyed, altars were removed, and entire Catholic families— noble and common—were persecuted and their lands seized.''

Aurora remembered what John Maxwell had told her about his own family, and she recalled, too, that Blacklaw's lands had been seized by the Crown.

Richard went on to explain that there was fear of invasion by a foreign power—in this instance, the Pope, the Catholic Spanish (Philip II having been married to Mary Tudor), and the Catholic French, England's traditional enemy; and in particular by the Queen's Roman Catholic cousin, Mary, Queen of Scots, who was next in line to the throne and whose first husband was a French prince.

''It *is* very complicated,'' Aurora admitted.

Richard nodded. ''This fear has been greatly heated by several assassination attempts upon the Queen in the recent past.''

Aurora gasped. ''But, who would want to kill the Queen?''

'' 'Twould seem any number of people. Fanatical Puritans, who think she's been too lenient with the Catholics; fanatical Anglicans, who think she gives in too much to the Puritans and the Catholics; or fanatical Catholics, who bear a grudge against her. We live daily with this great fear, and when she travels she has with her many guardsmen.''

Fanatical Catholics . . . did Giles Blacklaw fall into that category? she wondered. Certainly, he did bear a grudge against Elizabeth. But he would never do such a terrible deed. Would he?

''And thus reason has been turned into unreason,'' Richard said with a sigh.

''If the Queen is tolerant, surely she must realize she has hurt many people.''

''I'm sure she knows that, but 'tis a matter of hurting a few as opposed to many.''

''But what if someone . . . a Catholic, perhaps . . . were a loyal citizen and something terrible had happened to him because of one of these laws. Couldn't someone talk to the Queen to make her see reason on this matter, in this one case?''

Richard laughed. ''Now who is being the innocent, Aurora? He shook his head. ''I am sorry, but it doesn't work that way. Certainly I know many Catholics are loyal subjects—as are many Puritans and Anglicans. But.''

''Ah well, I suppose it was a good idea.''

''Yes, and tried, I might add, without any success, by countless others through the years. I fear,'' he said, looking around to make sure that no one stood by them and could overhear, ''that the Queen only sees and listens to what she wants to.''

Aurora took a sip of her wine, then caught a flick of movement from her eye. She glanced to her right, and saw Maraline. Aurora, with a stab of fear, wondered how much of this conversation the blonde girl had overheard—and how much she might twist to her own use.

6

"How is she doing at Court?" Blacklaw asked. He stretched his legs out in front of him, and rubbed a hand across his weary face. He had ridden most of the night in order to reach Richmond before daybreak. He would stay there for a few hours, ride east to London, and then be gone, all of his work accomplished before the first rays of the dawn sun struck the spires of London's churches.

He had only just arrived, disguised, and he had come directly to Constance's rooms. After she had asked a few routine questions about his own business, he'd turned the topic of conversation to his young charge and her recent court debut. Constance handed him a glass of wine and slowly sipped her own as she considered his question.

"She does very well, Giles."

"Thank you very much." His tone was dry.

"She is a credit to your teaching, for no one could tell that she was not nobly bred. Sometimes I think she must have been an orphan taken in by that woman; or perhaps her father was a gentleman. I have never heard her mention her father."

"It is not uncommon for a noble to beget a country bastard."

"I know . . . and she does show fine breeding in her face. That is one of the reasons you chose her, was it not?"

He nodded.

"There is only one cloud upon this otherwise perfect horizon."

"Oh?"

"Yes. Unfortunately, that vinegar-tongued Maraline Chambelet has seized upon Aurora as her chief enemy and vents her poison unmercifully. So far, Aurora has borne it well."

"Damn. Of all the things to happen now."

"I know. I have told Aurora to ignore the girl, although 'tis hard for her when Maraline is so obvious in her dislike. She doesn't understand why the bitch does what she does, and I fear we will have to watch that girl closely. I mistrust her greatly."

"So do I." He sighed and took a swallow of the dark wine. "I hear that she is a slut—that she will take any man—as long as he has wealth."

"Of that I have no doubt. She is a cunning one. But, enough of that. Aurora has proved exceedingly popular among the men at Court."

He frowned slightly, as if disapproving, then shrugged. "That's good to hear. I want her to be able to move confidently around these people, and for them to trust her implicitly."

Constance smiled. "One young man in particular is taken with her."

"Oh?" Casually he studied his wineglass. "Who is it?"

"I disremember his name at present," she said, lying effortlessly, "but he is only a year or two older than she. They make quite a handsome couple—he dark, she fair—and after the masque they danced most of the night. He promised to come see her, and so far he has kept his word."

Blacklaw said nothing, but there was a thunderous look on his face.

"He is a well-spoken lad, of a very respected family, and—"

Blacklaw set his glass down so forcefully that it shattered. "That's enough, Constance." He stood up and ignored the shards. "I must go. I have much to do before dawn arrives."

"Very well. Shall I tell Aurora that you were here tonight?"

"No . . . not this time. Another time, I'll come and visit her."

"It is dangerous for you, Giles."

She stood and moved across the room, and as Blacklaw was about to leave, she took his hands in hers, and looked up at him.

He paused, then bent and kissed her briefly on the lips.

Then he swung his cloak around his shoulders, secured the mask upon his face, pulled low his hat, and was gone, closing the door softly behind him.

Why hadn't she told him the identity of the boy? she wondered as she crossed back to the fire. Why? When he had wanted Aurora to meet Richard de Sayreville.

Constance shrugged, and began readying herself for bed.

"Father," said Roxanne Norville one evening as they sat together for a few minutes before going to bed.

"Yes?" Rupert Norville looked up from the contemplation of his ale. It was apparent that his daughter had received her dark red hair from him; and his heavy build foreshadowed Roxanne's probable increase in bulk as she grew older. His eyes were a pale brown, touched almost with yellow, and although he was just thirty-three, his hair was streaked with silver.

"I have a question to ask of you."

"What is it, pet?" Norville was surprised; Roxanne questioned little in life, taking after her mother in that respect, but perhaps she was expanding her knowledge at Court.

"How does one tell a witch?"

Stunned, he set his ale glass down.

"What?"

"I mean, Father, if one suspects that someone is a witch, how does one tell?"

"That is a serious charge, my child."

Her pale blue eyes widened innocently. "I know, Father, and I do not ask this question lightly."

"There are many different aspects of a witch. Usually, it is an old woman."

"Could it be a young woman . . . even a girl a little older than myself?"

"Yes. Generally she lives alone out in the woods, and has been known to cure—or curse—her neighbors. She knows little of Christianity."

"Cannot witches live in towns as well?"

He nodded. "And generally, witches have a familiar."

"What is that?"

"An animal that acts as a companion in their dark deeds."

"Oh," she gasped. "I know such a girl, who has a cat as a pet. A black cat."

"That isn't all that unusual."

"But she talks to it, Father, and it understands her as if it were a human—and follows her about as if it were a dog."

Intent, he leaned forward, hands resting on his knees. "Tell me more."

Roxanne smiled.

7

"And how do you find our fair city, Country Cousin?" asked Maraline in the sweetest tones Aurora had ever heard, and which surely could not be her normal voice. No one talked that way. Or did they?

Aurora looked up from her needlework. "I like it very well, Mistress Chambelet. I think London is a most wondrous place, and I think Richmond is the most beautiful place on earth."

They were all spending a quiet evening at the palace, and for that Aurora was pleased. She was very tired.

"Yes, so it is. I understand that in a week or so we leave for Nonsuch. That is quite a remarkable place, too." Without asking Aurora's leave, the blonde girl sat down on a second stool next to her and glanced at her tapestry. "You do needlework very well. Your stitches are uniform; it's all very pretty."

"Thank you." Aurora wasn't sure that the other had meant her remark as a compliment, but she was determined to be polite to this girl, no matter what.

"I do not seem to have the patience for such trifles. It seems so . . . domestic."

"It isn't as easy as it looks," Aurora said. "The thread can twist and it breaks easily. You must take care and work with it slowly."

"Yes, I can see that."

A few minutes passed in silence, then Maraline sighed

deeply, dramatically, stirred and looked at Aurora, who continued her stitching.

"I could not help overhearing your conversation with Richard de Sayreville a fortnight ago," Maraline offered casually. Aurora remained silent, only her fingers and the needle moving, but inside her her heart sank. She had hoped that Maraline hadn't listened.

"I was surprised that you did not know more about religion."

"My father is a tolerant man," Aurora said with a silent smile, "and those around me as I grew up were both Protestant and Catholic. They were always my friends, and loyal to the Crown. My father saw no reason to speak against our Catholic friends."

"Then your father is a fool," the other girl offered slyly.

"I think not."

"Only a fool believes that the Catholics can be treated like the Protestants. Only a fool would trust them."

"Only a fool speaks in such general terms about something not understood."

Maraline's cheeks flushed a bright red.

"I have known both Catholics and Protestants in my life, and neither have proved to be superior to the other," Aurora said evenly. "May I remind you that the Protestant religion came from the Catholic?"

"I know that. And I know something else as well, Country Cousin."

The other's tone was altogether too sly for Aurora. "What?" she asked, somewhat uneasily. Oh, why hadn't she listened to both Constance and Richard? Why had she engaged in an argument with this girl?

"What do you know?" She tried to keep her voice calm, but it was difficult. Did the blonde somehow know that she wasn't who she said she was, or that she knew Giles Blacklaw?

"Why should I tell you?"

"Maraline, don't be foolish." The girl's cheeks flushed again. Now, thought Aurora, I'm being the foolish one, and inwardly she sighed, knowing it was too late to end this conversation decently.

"It's very, very important what I know, and I might tell someone."

"Unless?"

Maraline smiled, a deceptively innocent expression. "No, there is no unless, Country Cousin. I just might whisper into a few ears that I suspect you are a Catholic sympathizer."

Aurora stared at her, and began to respond, then stopped, unsure of what she precisely was. Yes, she knew Catholics who had been wronged, and she thought they had a true complaint against the government.

"I am an advocate for neither one religion nor preaching against the other, and I cannot understand why the members of both religions cannot live peacefully side by side. And that is all I intend to say upon the matter tonight." She turned back to her needlework.

"We shall see about that."

"Ah, Maraline, I see you have introduced our new friend to the manners of the city."

Maraline whirled around.

A young woman, perhaps a few years older than Aurora, stood nearby, a faint smile on her pleasant face. She was by no means a beauty, but she had the kindest face Aurora had ever seen. Her brown eyes were large and wide-set and intelligent, her nose was straight, her lips firm, her chin resolute.

Her dark brown hair was dressed in a plain style, and her gown was a deep burgundy with an unadorned white collar at the neck. She wore few jewels, only a simple pearl necklace around her throat, and a single pearl in each ear. Her black leather shoes were low-heeled. Aurora thought she was very elegant. Her hands were small, with long, deft-looking fingers.

"Oh, it's you, Mistress Priss."

The newcomer continued smiling. "As you wish, Maraline. You were saying?"

"Nothing at all." She turned to Aurora. "I will talk to you again . . . alone." Without a further word, she rose and left, offended.

"Thank you," Aurora said warmly to the stranger, "for your timely rescue."

"You were looking a little dismayed. Maraline, for all her manners, is a most impolite creature."

"Well, thank you again. I have not the name of my rescuer."

"Faith Hopewell at your service," the young woman said.

"And you are Aurora le Grey. I have heard much good about you."

"You are most kind."

"No," the woman said, her eyes twinkling, "simply stating a fact." She glanced toward the retreating back of the blonde. "You must watch her."

"So I have been told."

"Good advice, but even more so now, you must watch her closely. She dislikes me, and any I defend, and now she doubly dislikes you."

"But she doesn't even know me!"

"From the beginning Maraline saw a rival to other men's attentions in you. It doesn't matter," she added when she saw Aurora's looks, "that you are no flirt. She doesn't understand anything but flirting and manipulation—both of which she excels in."

Before Aurora could speak, the girl looked across the room.

"I see my father and mother, so I must leave, but I will see you again, will I not, Mistress le Grey?"

"Yes, and thank you, Mistress Hopewell."

"Please, call me Faith."

"And I am Aurora."

They exchanged smiles, and the young woman moved across the crowded room to her parents. Aurora watched the trio for some minutes; all three were dressed in dark, simple clothes; Aurora wondered if they were Puritans. Finally, she turned back to her needlework. But she was no longer in the mood for it, so she simply stared into the flames, and hoped that nothing would come of this encounter with Maraline.

8

"Faith, what am I to do?" Aurora asked. Lucye was curled up in her lap. Faith, who had come into Aurora's rooms a few minutes ago, raised an eyebrow.

"Do about what?"

"I hear rumors now, concerning myself."

"Maraline."

"I have no proof."

" 'Tisn't needed, alas. Her hand is surely in this matter. What do the rumors say?"

"They accuse me of being a Catholic sympathizer, among other things."

"Are you?"

"I believe they have the right to practice their own religion, just as the Anglicans and the Puritans do. I don't understand why another's religion is so bothersome to some people."

"Some people have nothing better to do with their lives than meddle in others' lives."

"Oh, here's Richard now. Good afternoon." Aurora smiled sweetly at him as he bowed over her hand. "And do you know Faith Hopewell?"

He bowed in her direction. "Yes, we met some time ago."

"Please, sit down, Richard."

He did so, taking the stool only a few feet from her. "You are looking very serious today."

"I have heard rumors concerning myself . . . traced, I have no doubt, to Maraline Chambelet."

"Her."

"Yes. Faith and I were discussing what I could do. Do you have any suggestions?"

"Deny nothing yet, for it will make many suspicious. I should think that if these stories grow too much worse we must seek out the Queen."

"Oh, we couldn't," Aurora breathed. "She is far too busy."

"Yes, she's busy, but Maraline is a member of her retinue, and Her Majesty should know if one of her Maids of Honor is not comporting herself with dignity. That would bear directly upon Her Majesty."

"What do you think, Faith?"

Faith leveled her no-nonsense look at the young man and woman. "It's an excellent suggestion. Remember, too, please, Aurora, that Richard and I are your friends, and we will stand behind you no matter what arises."

Aurora smiled gratefully at them. Secretly she wondered what the two would think if they knew she was at Court under false pretenses. Who would be her friend then?

The rumors continued circulating at a Court renowned for its hunger for gossip. Some of the tales returned more than once to Aurora's ears, greatly altered and embellished along the way by more sophisticated gossipmongers than Maraline Chambelet. All were designed to humiliate her. She knew that she couldn't speak privately with Maraline—not after their last conversation—and so the only thing she could do was to hold up her head in public and to act as she had always done before. She prayed that her actions would speak more strongly than vicious words.

Aurora wished she knew what to do. She longed for advice—where was Blacklaw? She missed him greatly. It had been some months since he had visited her, and she missed his voice, his touch, his kisses. She did not know that since his last visit to Aurora, he had visited Constance several times.

9

In spring the Court moved to Nonsuch. If Aurora had thought Richmond unique, she quickly changed her mind when she saw this palace. It was not far from Richmond and Hampton Court, and Henry VIII had had the Surrey village of Cuddington wiped out and the palace built on the site.

Here was an incredible mansion with an overwhelming profusion of turrets and pinnacles, unusual clocks and ornate chimney-pots, cupolas, mock battlements, elaborately carved slate, Parisian plaster casts, and florid icing-sugar rococo. In Henry's time, the religious house of Merton Priory had been demolished during the dissolution of the monastery, and hundreds of tons of stone had been carted from the Priory to Nonsuch to provide building materials. The palace was built around two courts. The inner court was entered through a gatehouse and up a flight of steps. The upper section of this inner court was half-timbered and decorated with excellent plaster work. The far side of the inner court, facing the renowned gardens, was formed by a long range of buildings between two octagonal towers; and the upper stories of these towers were pavilions with countless windows. The pointed, leaden roofs were topped by pinnacles and vanes. Common lands in several neighboring parishes—some 1,700 acres—had been enclosed to make the two parks; these were subsequently stocked with over one thousand head of deer.

Aurora fell in love with Nonsuch Palace when she saw it for the first time. It was like a magical palace from long ago, from some exotic land. No matter how others at Court might laugh at what they called Henry's Folly, she thought it superb. Once again, as she had done at Richmond, she took herself upon an informal tour of the palace, and was amazed at the nooks and crannies she found within the building. There were all sorts of intriguing rooms, leading to round-about corridors and galleries, all of them sumptuously furnished. She saw tapestries of breathtaking detail, silver and gold plate of master workmanship.

Once again her quarters were adjacent to Constance's, and within a week Aurora's day-to-day life at Nonsuch settled into a regular pattern, much as it had at Richmond. She saw the same people—and heard the same vicious tales concerning herself. The number of rumors seemed to have increased, and finally Aurora went to Constance with the matter.

"If it grows too awkward at Court, we can always return home for a while."

"Won't the others here think that's cowardice, or at best, believe the rumors are true because I've run away from them?" Aurora asked.

"Yes, 'tis possible, although not all may believe that. Maraline Chambelet doesn't have the ear of everyone at Court."

"Then what do you counsel me to do?"

"Wait. She'll tire of the game, since you're not responding, and after a while, she'll turn to someone else, some other victim. All you can do is be patient; just wait."

Just wait, Aurora thought. It sounded so easy, yet she feared that it would be a long time before Maraline tired of her petty game.

10

"How do you find Nonsuch?"

Startled from her reading, Aurora looked up to see Maraline standing near her. The blond girl was smiling, which worried Aurora. She didn't like it when the girl sought her out on these quiet evenings.

"I like it very well. And you?"

"I think it's far too Oriental. It's not a good English palace."

Aurora said nothing.

"Cat have your tongue?"

"Not at all. But there's nothing more to say." She would be polite, she told herself. She *would*, no matter how difficult it was.

"Speaking of cats . . . ." The other girl's voice trailed away as her smile widened.

"Yes?"

"I understand that you have a cat as a pet."

"Yes," Aurora replied cautiously. How did Maraline know? Aurora supposed she had mentioned it to two or three of her acquaintances at Court, and somehow it must have found its way to Maraline. "There is nothing wrong with that, is there? After all, there are others at Court who have dogs with them."

"Oh, there's no problem at all. What color is she? I do so adore cats!"

"She's black."

"Ooo, I imagine she's very pretty."

"Yes."

"And so very clever, too." Maraline leaned closer to her. "Does she do any tricks?"

"No."

"None at all?"

Aurora shook her head. Even if she had taught Lucye any tricks, she would never admit it to Maraline. She didn't know why she didn't want to talk about the cat with the girl, who did seem genuinely interested. It was just that she didn't trust the blonde.

"I'm so disappointed. I was hoping you could show me some of her tricks."

"No, I'm sorry."

"Oh, well. Do be careful with your cat, though—cats have been known to disappear at Court." And with that somber statement Maraline gave her a quick smile and left.

What did she mean by that? Aurora wondered. Puzzled, she returned to her reading.

Late in April the Court moved to Windsor Castle, the home of English royalty for longer than any other building in England. In 1080 William the Conqueror had built the mound as the central citadel of the fortress. In the early days, the Castle was no more than a wooden Norman keep within a ditch, protected by stone stockades, and the King spent much of his time there, hunting in the forests to the south.

Henry II had commissioned the first stone buildings, including a stone keep on the mound, while the first king to adapt the castle to a comfortable residence was Edward III. Over the centuries more buildings and towers had been added to Windsor. A chapel begun in 1472 contained delicate window tracery, flying buttresses, and elaborately carved stone vaults. Henry VIII had done little to change the royal apartments, and many of the courtiers thought that Windsor was a bleak place compared to Richmond or Nonsuch. Elizabeth, however, liked the castle, finding it safer than her other palaces.

Once more Court life settled into a routine. Aurora marveled that anything was ever accomplished by anyone at Court. It seemed that every few weeks or months the Court was moving, and the disruption of moving and getting settled usually took several weeks.

After the move Aurora saw little of Maraline—which made her all the more suspicious. She didn't like it when the blonde girl made overtures of friendship, but neither did she like it when the girl was nowhere in evidence. What could Maraline be up to?

"Don't worry," Faith said when Aurora mentioned her suspicions. "If she's not around, then we truly have occasion to rejoice. There is no hint of trouble, so it must be as we all thought. Maraline has tired of this game."

Richard seconded Faith's opinion, and even while she listened to the reasonable voices of her friends, Aurora couldn't dismiss her uneasy feeling.

In late April another masque was held, and Aurora was invited to act one of the parts. She was thrilled but nervous at the prospect. The night of the performance came, and she acted her part well, earning much praise from her many admirers, and from Constance as well.

Afterward, Aurora took Constance aside so that they could talk privately.

"Have you heard from our traveling friend of late?"

"No, I have not. Not for some time, that is." Constance did not mention the several times Giles Blacklaw had come to see her. She did not want to hurt Aurora. Her initial anger had faded, and now she wanted to protect her young charge.

"I wonder where he is."

"Business," said Constance with a smile.

"Yes, business, no doubt." Aurora responded with a smile, but it was forced. She was uneasy about his long absence.

"Also," Constance said, leaning close to Aurora so that she could whisper, " 'tis more difficult to get into Windsor than the other palaces. Do not look to see him very often here."

Aurora nodded, knowing that Constance was right, but finding she missed Blacklaw all the more.

On the eve of her nineteenth birthday, Aurora overheard a conversation that upset her.

"I've heard the most exciting news!" Roxanne Norville said to Alice Vaughan.

"What is it? Do tell me everything!" the second girl demanded.

"My father has just returned from London and reports that a highwayman was shot and killed on the road to Tyburn."

"Oooo," breathed Alice.

"I haven't all the details, but I'm sure we'll hear more later tonight."

"I wish I'd been there," Alice said. "I would have liked to have seen him shot."

"Father says there was blood everywhere!" Roxanne's eyes were gleaming, and she licked her lips. Aurora looked away in disgust. The two girls walked away, and as the conversation faded, Aurora heard only that the highwayman rode alone. Her thoughts turned to Blacklaw.

All evening Aurora waited anxiously to hear more about this incident, and pressed each traveler who arrived at Court for more information. Finally, one traveler who had witnessed the robber's death and who had come to Court just an hour before, was able to give her more details. The description of the robber filled her with dread and despair.

She thanked the man in faint tones, then left and went upstairs to Constance's quarters. There she found the widow, and, pleading a headache, asked if she could return to Grey Wood. Her companion, seeing that the girl was pale, asked what was wrong, but Aurora could only shake her head and say it was a touch of the megrim. Constance said they would leave in a few days if she wanted. Aurora nodded numbly, then fled to her rooms.

She collapsed on her bed and the tears flowed like a stream. Undammed, they came, until she shook with emotion. Not even Lucye's consolations could bring a smile to her mistress's lips. Terrible thoughts tumbled through her mind. Her love was gone . . . killed . . . gone . . . never to lie once more within her arms, or to kiss her.

Aurora cried as she had never cried before, and finally, hours later, she fell into an exhausted sleep.

11

Something soft and insistent brushed against her arm, and Aurora woke instantly and slapped at the thing, thinking it must be a spider. However, it proved to be warm and quite human—a hand, lightly resting on her arm, had been shaking her.

She sat bolt upright in bed. Fear surged through her as she tried to keep calm. "Who is—"

"Giles."

"Giles!"

With an unbridled cry of joy, Aurora flung herself with wild abandonment into his arms and smothered his lips and cheeks with kisses. She clutched him tightly, almost fiercely, then said in a low voice, "I thought that you were dead. I heard of the highwayman being shot and killed just the week before, and his description matched yours, and because I hadn't seen you in so long, I was sure it was you."

"For a while I thought I would be," he said, his tone dry.

"What happened? Who was killed? Why were you delayed so long?" She settled back against him, his arms around her.

"I rode out that night as well. A trap had been laid ahead of time, for this highwayman and I worked the same stretch of road, although he was new to it. As fortune would have it, he arrived before I did, and the Queen's waiting troops shot him dead. I was riding along the road when I heard the sounds of musket fire from far up ahead.

"I deduced what had occurred, then turned around and

returned to London without delay. It was only later the next day that I was able to hear a description of the dead highwayman, and discovered that he looked like me.''

''Thank God it wasn't you,'' she murmured.

''My exact feelings,'' he said dryly. He ruffled her hair, then dropped a kiss upon her shoulder. His arms tightened around her. The cat rubbed against them, then dropped to the floor and padded across to the warmth of the hearth. She turned to face him. ''I'm so glad you're here. However did you get into the castle?''

''I have my ways,'' he said with an odd smile.

Her lips met his, clung possessively, tasted the wonderful flavor of him. ''I want you. Now, Giles. Please.'' Her fingertips brushed his lips, his cheeks, pushed through his hair.

The lovers kissed again; his tongue gently probed her lips, and as she opened her mouth to him, their warm breath mingled. With his tongue he gently explored the soft depths of her mouth, tickling and tantalizing her. She moaned softly and clung limply to him. She had missed him greatly, and had ached for him so intensely. She could feel desire building in her, raging through her body.

Her fingers tightened until they became almost a part of his arms. Her breathing quickened, beating a tempo with his, and the only sound in the room was the crackling of the fire and their combined breathing. Blacklaw drew back a bit. She touched his high cheekbone, outlined by the yellow firelight, and he slipped under the covers with her, and she giggled, finding that he had already shed his clothing.

''I was prepared this time, '' he said with a smile, and she laughed.

He laughed, too, and pushed back the covers. He knelt in the bed and stared down at her, limned by the faint light. He ran his hands down her smooth sides, across her stomach to her thighs, then back up to her bosom where his fingertips brushed the smooth globes of her breasts. He pushed the breasts together and tweaked her nipples. The tickling sensation within her increased until her stomach knotted with tension. A moan slipped from between her lips. He leaned down then and lightly kissed the tip of one breast, his tongue just playing across it; the delicate touch made her sigh again and again with pleasure.

Her hands, still behind him, tightened convulsively, and her fingernails dug into his buttocks. He cupped her breasts, brushing against their tips with his slender, whipcord-strong fingers. The tender red peaks rose and firmed at his incitement. Again he drew back to gaze down at her body . . . her slender neck, full breasts, narrow waist, the creamy lengths of her legs. He bent and kissed the inside of her left thigh, then his mouth inched downward as he continued kissing her leg. And when he had reached one delicate foot, he switched to the other leg, moving upward ever so slowly.

She watched him from under half-lowered eyelashes and giggled softly when one of his kisses tickled her. He paused to gaze up at her, then his mouth moved to the right, and he was kissing the very center of her being and passion. She closed her eyes as the liquid feelings swirled within her, and were released as his tongue lapped at her. She cried out once, then his tongue caressed her navel, then her breasts. His fingers idly caressed her stomach as his mouth fastened on her breast, and he licked at the nipple.

She continued to stroke his hair, his face, his shoulders, at times dragging her nails lightly across his skin. She heard a sharp hiss as he inhaled, exhaled, and she smiled, knowing the hot passions rose in him as well. Even as he continued to kiss her breasts, his fingers fled south, seeking warmth, and she groaned with pleasure as he stroked her womanhood. His tongue flicked out, caressed one tiny rosebudlike nipple; he nibbled at the bud, and she seized his arm.

"Giles. I want you. I love you." Another moan of pleasure escaped from her.

One long finger traced the line of her lips, then trailed down her chin to her neck. He kissed the hollow there, his lips cool.

She ran her tongue across her lips, so hot from her passion, and trembled at his incredible touch. Then he let himself down, his body half over her, and slipped one of his legs between hers, moving it back and forth, using it like a hand to fan the glowing ember of her desire into a flame.

He covered her—face and neck, breasts and stomach and legs—with kisses that burned. She moaned and gripped his hair in her hands, exclaiming softly with each caress, then murmuring his name. Her hands explored his shoulder, chest, back, as he continued kissing her.

Aurora reached down between his thighs, taking his rigid shaft in her fingers. She stroked its throbbing length, and he sighed deeply. Her fingers rubbed along the smoothness, and she felt his manhood pulsing in her hand. She ran her fingers across the tip, touched the droplet there, cupped him in her hands. His breathing came faster now, and his manhood thrust through her fingers, back and forth. She trembled at his power, and her legs widened in response. She moaned as he slid into her, and she wrapped her legs around his, drawing his body closer to her. With a fierce cry from deep within he thrust.

She cried out, grabbing his shoulder and kissing him. She arched her back as he thrust again, deeper still, and he moaned, a wild animal sound. Their bodies were slick with sweat, and they rocked together, their movements becoming more frenzied.

When he briefly pulled away, their skin seemed to have melted. His kissed her face, her ears, her throat, and stroked her breasts, all the while murmuring endearments. Then he pushed deeply inside her, and she called out to him, then cried out as her center of delight opened. They rocked, thrust, slipped away, came closer together, became one living entity.

Even as desire flamed within her, an arching pleasure burst through her body, rippling wave after wave through her very being until she was shuddering with delight. He called out loudly in his passion, his body rigid and still thrusting, and time slowed for them, keeping the lovers encapsulated in a perfect moment where they alone existed, they alone mattered.

She wanted this perfect moment, this closeness, to last. But even now the moment was past, their eyes were closed against the tempest of their ardor, and she was clutching at his shoulder, clinging to him, and sobbing, deep-throated, with passion. Within seconds the passion had ebbed, the violent tremors stilled, and their lips met in one more kiss.

12

Afterward they dozed for a few minutes, but were soon talking. It had been so long, and she had so much to tell him.

"I don't know where to begin," she admitted. "I have so much to say. You were gone so long." The accusation could be heard in her voice.

He did not respond to it, but rather said, "Then begin at the beginning, my love. Are you enjoying your life at Court?" he asked, raising himself up on one elbow so that he could see her in the faint firelight. He had already slipped out of bed to toss another log on the fire; the cat on the hearth merely opened one eye, then promptly went back to sleep.

Her lips curved into a smile. "I would enjoy myself more if you were here with me."

"I think not." He kissed her lightly. "That hasn't answered my question at all. Now tell me what—and who—you have been seeing. I wish to know if my prodigy is a success."

"I think I must have met everyone at Court—or so it seems, except for the Queen, of course. Constance says I am not yet ready for that experience, although I have caught glimpses of her several times. I met an agreeable young woman my age, or somewhat older, I suppose, and we have become fast friends. Her name is Faith Hopewell. Do you know of her?"

"I know of her father and mother, both of good family. Stephen Hopewell is a man to be trusted, if you ever need help. He stands by his word, unlike many others at Court."

She wondered at the cause of the irony underlying his words and wanted to ask him, but sensed that this was not the time. So many other times he had simply brushed away her questions. Why should tonight be any different?

"She and I have been seeing one another fairly frequently, and for that I'm glad. I think that Court, for all that there are many people here, could be very lonely without a friend. There is another woman here, though, who is not my friend. Maraline Chambelet. Apparently I have done something to offend her, although what it is I do not know."

"I think with that one you needn't do anything to earn hatred."

"You know her then?"

"I have heard of her."

"I think she is the one who is spreading rumors about me now, although I really can't prove it. But who else could it be?"

"What rumors are these?"

She laughed, although not as lightly as she'd intended. " 'Tis no need to worry, my love. She and I had a . . . disagreement . . . concerning religious matters. That is all, I assure you. It was shortly after this that I began to hear the rumors."

"Be careful, Aurora. Such disagreements have led to far worse than rumors."

"Constance has already warned me about Maraline, and so has Faith. And Richard, too, who dislikes her most intensely."

"Richard?"

She heard the interest in his voice, and considered the thought that he might be a little jealous. She smiled to herself. She wasn't opposed to his suffering a few pangs of jealousy.

"Yes. Richard de Sayreville, another new friend of mine. He has also been most helpful at Court these past weeks. He and I and Faith are often together and spend many long hours reading to one another, or riding, or even walking through the palace."

"De Sayreville."

She didn't like the way he said the name, giving it a sardonic twist.

"You know him?"

"Not the boy, my dear. Only the family. Once I knew the father . . . and the mother." His face was expressionless as he asked, "Have you made the acquaintance of Lady de Sayreville?"

"Not yet, although Richard wishes me to dine with his family soon. His parents have been away from Court for some time at their country estate and have only just returned."

"By all means, you must keep that appointment." His voice was neutral now, and he had rolled away from her and lay with his arms behind his head. "I am sure you will be provided with much amusement. The de Sayrevilles were always known for their diverting ways. I should have known that you would meet that family almost immediately." He spoke in a musing tone, more to himself than to her.

Aurora sensed that Blacklaw was struggling with himself, almost as if he wanted to say something to her, but he wouldn't. Or couldn't. And she wanted him to know that he could speak honestly to her. She touched his arm.

"Giles."

"Umm?" He sounded half-asleep now.

She was sorry to wake him now with her question. "Is there something about the de Sayrevilles that you should tell me?"

"No."

"I thought—"

"There is nothing to think. The de Sayrevilles are just another family from my past. Now come lie in my arms and go to sleep, my love, or I shall be forced to cover you with kisses."

"I think I would like that very much," and she rolled closer to him.

13

As he had done previously, Blacklaw left Aurora's bed well before dawn. She fell into a light slumber, but rose early, shortly after dawn, and felt as though she had not slept at all. She washed and dressed mechanically, and took her breakfast with Constance a short time later. She wished she could confide her happiness at Giles' visit to her friend, but that was impossible. And Aurora knew how Constance felt about Blacklaw.

But even that might be changing, Aurora told herself. Hadn't she seen a rather handsome older man paying court to Constance for the past few weeks? Perhaps it was nothing more than a mild flirtation. But it might be something much more serious; for Constance's sake, she hoped so.

All morning Aurora was kept busy. In early afternoon she excused herself, and returned to her rooms to change. She longed for a nap, but she was to meet her friends at two for a ride. As she walked toward Richard and Faith, Aurora yawned.

"Are we such poor company?" Richard asked teasingly as they walked toward the stables.

"Not at all," said Aurora, yawning again.

"I think the lady doth protest too much," Faith said cheerfully.

"No!"

"You see!" said Faith with a triumphant look to the young man. They broke into laughter, then Faith studied her friend more closely.

"Are you well?" she asked, concern in her voice. "You look pale."

"I am tired," Aurora replied truthfully. "I didn't sleep much last night."

"Excited about our ride?"

"Something like that, Richard."

The three laughed again. Soon the others of their party arrived, and they mounted their horses and rode away from the palace. In the mild spring weather they rode several times a week through the beautiful woods around Windsor.

Soon after Easter, the Court removed to Greenwich. As they sailed down the Thames, Aurora felt a tingle of excitement. Who would have thought, two years before, that the ragged, frightened child of Bridewell would live in four different palaces in the space of a single year?

Greenwich Palace, which lay in a great loop of the Thames, had begun its days as Bella Court, built by Henry V's youngest brother. In time the house passed to Queen Margaret of Anjou, who added glass to the windows and had the floors covered with terra-cotta tiles. The exterior was ornamented with pillars sculpted with her heraldic flower, and a pier was built to allow access to the river at all stages of the tide. Once Bella Court was acquired by the Crown, the name was changed to Placentia, or Pleasance. In 1485 Henry Tudor changed the name again, to Greenwich Palace. He had the entire building refaced with red brick; his son, Henry VIII, added a jousting yard and an armory.

Queen Elizabeth, who had been born at Greenwich, remained very attached to the house and saw further improvements made. She was a proponent of a great navy, and as the palace lay close to the royal dockyards, she frequently stayed at Greenwich.

Aurora knew that the stay at Greenwich was only for a few months. In the summer the Queen and her court would make the famous—or infamous, depending on how one regarded them—yearly processions. The purpose of these royal processions was to take the monarch out of the sweltering city during its hottest months, when many nobles returned to their estates.

Rather than stay in her own palaces and pay for what her courtiers ate and drank, Elizabeth liked to visit various nobility scattered throughout England—all of whom would foot the bill for her and her immense royal household. There would be no reimbursement for the host out of the Queen's coffers. What the host did, he did because he was a good and loyal citizen, even if he were bankrupted by the royal visit.

Once the procession began, the de Sayrevilles would return to their northern estate, and they would not return to Court until the autumn. Aurora knew that if she were to meet Richard's parents, it would have to be soon; and she longed to meet them, to penetrate the mystery of Blacklaw's attitude.

14

It was only a few weeks later that Richard arranged for Aurora to meet his parents. She was particularly nervous about this meeting, but she didn't know why. Richard was just a friend, wasn't he? Or was he something more? No, she told herself, he couldn't be. Not when her heart was given to Blacklaw. Yet at times Richard seemed to intend more than a friendship; and certainly Constance appeared to consider him a proper suitor for Aurora.

Richard's ardent liking only served to confuse Aurora further. She really liked Richard, but she didn't love him, not as a would-be husband.

The day she was to dine with the de Sayrevilles she took a long, hot bath, washed her hair and then combed it until it gleamed. She chose a gown with a full skirt of wine-colored velvet. The bodice was wine and grey velvet, its sleeves trimmed in silver lace, and with tiny silver buttons in the form of seashells. Around her waist she wore a silver girdle, from which she hung a small silver mirror and a fan, the latter a present from Constance. On her feet she wore black slippers.

She met Richard in a private dining room and glanced around anxiously.

"They're not here yet, but soon will be." He smiled easily. "You look beautiful tonight, Aurora—as always." The candlelight touched the silver pins in her fair hair and made them glitter as she moved her head. He bent over her hand and kissed it.

221

She smiled. "I do hope they like me," she said, then instantly regretted her words when she saw Richard's smile widen.

"I have no doubt that they will."

Now, she thought, she could almost wish that they would take an instant dislike to her. But it was not to be. In a matter of minutes, the older de Sayrevilles arrived.

Aurora took an instant liking to Philippa de Sayreville. She was of medium height, and still slender after many years of marriage. She had long, dark hair pulled back away from a delicate, ivory-colored face with large blue eyes. Richard's mother appeared hardly older than her son; she was quite beautiful, Aurora thought, but she looked sad.

Philippa was attired in a dark red gown, its bodice and graceful long sleeves laced with gold braid, and wore several gold rings on her fingers.

Aurora found Richard's father, Thomas, a strikingly handsome, slightly stocky man with a white-blond beard and moustache neatly trimmed and as yet untouched by grey. Like his wife, he had blue eyes, but there any similarity ended. While hers were warm and open, tinged a little with sadness, the light blue of his were touched with ice, and when his gaze lingered a little too long on her, Aurora felt a shiver, as though a cold hand had swept across her spine.

The elder de Sayreville was dressed flamboyantly in green and gold, his outfit emphasizing his broad shoulders and narrow hips; gold jewelry glittered on his chest and on his well-kept hands.

Aurora was surprised to see how little Richard took after his father, but supposed that might be all to the good—particularly as the evening wore on.

"Good evening," Thomas de Sayreville said, executing a low bow over her hand. "I am most charmed to meet you, Mistress le Grey, having heard so much about you from my son."

Aurora smiled politely, hiding her discomfort; the way this man stared at her made her feel as though he were undressing her.

Within a few minutes Thomas De Sayreville began talking about his favorite subject: himself. Inside of an hour Aurora had learned all she wanted to about his abilities in swordplay, hawking, and horsemanship, as well as his exceptional musical and poetical talents. The man was also extremely conceited about his own looks, pausing at times before a mirror in the hall to smooth his beard and admire himself.

Thomas de Sayreville soon displayed another unpleasant trait. To Aurora's great distaste, he revealed himself as a domineering man, ordering his wife and son about as if they were nothing more than servants. Philippa had hardly begun to eat her meal when Thomas demanded that she leave the table to fetch something for him.

Distinctly uncomfortable, Aurora looked down at her plate and said nothing. Richard said little in his mother's absence, and Aurora thought he was displeased by his father, too. When Philippa returned, she talked with her son and Aurora, directing few of her comments to her husband.

Theirs was not a happy marriage, Aurora concluded, and she wondered why they had ever married. Perhaps long ago, before Richard was ever born, Thomas had been a different sort of man, and perhaps Philippa had loved him then. Obviously she did not now, nor did Thomas love his wife. Aurora could see the contempt in his eyes whenever he glanced Philippa's way, and she found herself feeling sorry for Richard.

To add to her consternation, Aurora was horrified to realize that Thomas was flirting with her during the meal. Embarrassed and more than a little unsettled, she kept her eyes on her plate and responded to his questions as briefly as possible.

Afterward, when he bowed over her hand again, and kept it in his own for far too long, she had a most uncomfortable feeling that something important—and terrible—had just been planted in this meeting.

"What is it you wanted to see me about?" Thomas de Sayreville demanded.

Rupert Norville stretched out his hand; de Sayreville ignored it.

"I'm glad you've come. I know you are a busy man," Norville said. "And I know you've been away for a while, so I thought you should know."

De Sayreville arched a blond eyebrow as he sat in the chair before the fireplace. "My dear fellow, you keep saying I should know—know what?"

"About that girl—Richard's friend," Norville responded.

"Aurora le Grey?" De Sayreville's tone was sharp; he pulled his eyebrows together in a frown as he thoughtfully stroked his moustache. He had just met her the night before and thought she was a pretty sort, although altogether too quiet for him, and he wasn't sure why Richard was attracted to her. But then, the boy had always had odd tastes.

"Yes, that's the one." Norville took a deep breath. "There are hints about the Court that the girl may be involved in something . . . dark."

"Dark?"

"Witchcraft."

"Proof?" The fool. Norville was a superstitious man, with scarcely any breeding, much less a brain to call his own. Witchcraft, indeed. What mischief was he up to now?

"She has a black cat—her companion—that she talks to. She scarcely goes anywhere without it, and it appears to understand her."

"I see."

"There's more."

"I don't doubt."

"I heard this from Roxanne."

"Who heard it from whom?"

"The other girls—Maraline among them."

Ah, Maraline. De Sayreville indulged in a private smile. He should have recognized her fine hand in this matter.

"Well, I shall look into the matter, Norville, but until then I would say nothing to anyone else. Is that understood?"

"Oh yes. Good to see you again, Thomas." Norville nodded and left, glancing quickly left and right, as if fearing someone would see him.

So Maraline was letting it about that Aurora le Grey was a witch, eh? No doubt he could use that information to his own benefit. He grinned.

15

Constance knew that it would be only a matter of time before Queen Elizabeth would begin the first of her annual processions, and if she were to see that Aurora was to be presented, she must do it soon.

Aurora told her friend that she thought she wasn't ready, but Constance shook her head. She knew better than that.

" 'Tis simply a case of nerves," she stated matter-of-factly. "I had them, too, when I was your age and about to meet the Queen."

Aurora nodded and swallowed quickly, hoping that her stomach would soon settle.

For the next week, the seamstresses worked night and day on her gown, and she found herself sleeping less and less each night. Even at mealtime she was distraught, and ate only a little. When the special night finally arrived, Aurora was so nervous she could barely dress, and Constance had to help her.

"How do I look?" Aurora asked, when she was finished. She whirled around, then stopped and looked at the other woman, waiting.

"You look . . . beautiful. Truly beautiful." Indeed, Constance had never seen her look so enchanting, and it was hard to reconcile this pretty face with the haggard one of the girl released from Bridewell. Aurora's gown was made of white velvet, its bodice a silver material sewn with tiny pearls. Thousands of seed pearls decorated the gathered sleeves, and on her feet she wore white slippers. A necklace of perfectly matching pearls graced her neck, and tiny pearl and diamond studs gleamed at her ears.

Constance had kindly dressed in a dark brown gown she had already worn once before at Court. Tonight she wanted nothing to detract from the presentation of her young companion, and she wondered what Maraline's expression would be when she saw Aurora. The other girl would not be pleased.

"Well, my dear?" Constance asked, smiling gently. "Are you ready?"

"Yes. I think." Aurora took a deep breath and smiled. Not for the first time that day, she wished that Giles were there.

"Good. We'll go now."

Aurora nodded and tried to still the fear in the pit of her stomach.

"There aren't many ahead of us, which is good," Constance whispered as she peered around a stout woman standing in front of them. "She won't have time to grow bored."

Aurora nodded, unable to speak. She and Constance had been downstairs in the great hall for some three hours now, waiting with the other young girls. Her Royal Highness, they had been informed when they arrived in the great hall, would begin the presentations at nine, and not a second earlier. And so they had waited, Aurora trying hard, and none too successfully, to conceal her nervousness, which was doubling by the moment, tripling by the hour.

What if the Queen took one look at her and laughed? Or decided that she didn't want Aurora in Court? How would she be able to bear it? Yet, a voice within countered, Maraline remained at Court. Surely if Maraline could, Aurora would.

As the line diminished, Aurora stepped forward, and to her great distaste, saw that Maraline was standing with some other girls close to the Queen. The Maids of Honor, then.

She looked away, but not before she saw the blonde glance coolly toward her and say something to one of her friends. But she didn't have long to think about the other girl, because all at once, or so it seemed to her, Constance's hand was on her arm and she was being propelled before Elizabeth of England.

The monarch sat upon a large throne. Her fiery red hair

was elaborately dressed. Her eyes were a bright blue, slightly hooded, and were not the type of eyes that missed much. Aurora was reminded, as she had been on first seeing the Queen, of a hawk; it wasn't an unpleasant association, either.

While the Queen was not the beauty she had been in her youth, she was still very handsome, and there was a great presence about her. Her wide forehead bespoke great intelligence; her skin was white as snow, no doubt the result of the thick makeup she wore. Her cheeks were bright red, almost as if she were blushing continually, and her lips were painted a deep red.

The Queen wore gold—her gown was of a heavy brocade, with red and gold threads interwoven throughout, and sewn to it were hundreds of pearls, topazes, and rubies. Any slight movement by the monarch caused the gown to shine like a small sun. Her immense ruff was starched and white, and its edges were trimmed with gold braid. Jewels were everywhere adorning the Queen's hair, her ears, her fingers, and her thin neck.

"So," Elizabeth said, after a moment of studying Aurora, "this is the young girl—your cousin, is she not?—that you were telling me about, Lady Westcott." The blue eyes raked over her, missing no detail.

"It is, Your Majesty," Constance replied.

Aurora swept a low curtsey. "Your Majesty," she murmured.

"A polite child, I see. Hasn't been too long at Court then." The blue eyes flashed with warm humor, as Aurora's lips lifted involuntarily in a half-smile. "What is your name, child?"

"Aurora le Grey, Your Majesty."

"Le Grey?" The Queen's sandy eyebrows drew together in thought. "God's teeth, I know that name somehow. A noble from the north, perhaps? Or does my memory serve me?"

"My father is William le Grey, and he is currently away, traveling in foreign countries. His interest is in exploring."

"Ah, one of *those*. I have many of them at Court." The Queen's eyes went to a tall dark-haired man to one side of the throne, who bowed when she glanced at him. "God knows who sent them to me, the Devil or the Lord—I don't know."

There was polite laughter at this from those standing around Aurora, the most laughter coming from the man. Aurora wondered who he was, and thought she must ask Constance afterward. He did not seem at all intimidated by the Queen, and in that singular way he reminded Aurora of Blacklaw.

"Well, I am glad to see you, child. Do not be shy around us. Do visit us again."

"Thank you, Your Majesty." She swept another curtsey, and then Constance was taking her by the arm and drawing her away.

Once they were some distance from the throne, Aurora took a deep breath and leaned against a wall. She was shaking, and she clasped her trembling hands together.

Constance smiled and patted her hand. "You see, 'twas not half as bad as your mind had painted."

"I suppose not," she said slowly, "although I'm glad it's over. She is quite impressive, Constance. Thank you for presenting me."

"You're quite welcome, my dear. Yes, she is impressive and can be very compassionate if she takes a liking to someone. But she has a very long memory. Do not ever cross her and make her your enemy. She never forgets—or forgives."

Aurora nodded, although she thought it unlikely she would have much to do with the Queen after this. With Maraline's influence, she did not think she would become a Maid of Honor.

"Who was that man I saw by the Queen?"

"One of her favorites. Sir Walter Raleigh, an explorer of some note."

"He reminded me of Giles a little." There. She had said it.

Constance smiled. "Yes, he does, doesn't he? Now, let us find something to drink."

Aurora nodded, and followed the woman to the refreshment table. Now that the presentation was past, she thought, what worse could there be?

16

The warm summer months soon gave way to the cool of
autumn days, and a masked ball was planned at Court, now at
Windsor again, for late September. Everyone at Court spoke
of the event and nothing else. Faith and Aurora began planning their costumes weeks in advance.

"There is no other choice for you, Aurora!" Faith exclaimed
at once when they sat down to decide their costumes. "You
are so beautiful that you must go as Iris. You will have all the
men at court falling in love with you."

"You are too kind by half, Faith! Iris, the goddess of the
rainbow? I think she would need a very elaborate costume,
and I'm not sure that I could do it. Perhaps I could go as
Aurora, goddess of the dawn."

"No, no, that's your name! You must choose something
altogether different."

Aurora smiled, wondering what Faith and Richard and her
other friends at Court would say if they learned Aurora wasn't
her real name. She didn't often think about it, because in the
years since she had been taken out of Bridewell, she *had*
become a new person. Aurora le Grey. And whatever, and
whoever, she had once been, she no longer was.

"Very well, I will be Iris. But what of you, Faith? Who
will you be?"

"Echo," the other girl said matter-of-factly.

"No, no," Aurora said at once. "You can't be the nymph
who loved another in silence—unless of course, that is true."

She peered at her friend's reddening face and lifted an eyebrow. "Oh, do I sense a secret here?"

"Not at all, Aurora! But, perhaps you're right. Echo isn't appropriate. But what *should* I go as?" Faith's eyes would not meet hers. "Mayhap . . . I know! *I* shall go as Aurora!"

Aurora laughed. "Yes! That's perfect!"

From that day on Faith, Constance, and Aurora worked diligently on their gowns. On the night of the ball, they dressed carefully, taking nearly three hours in doing so. Constance was attired as Lamia, the Libyan Queen beloved of Jupiter, and the girls declared she was as beautiful as the real goddess. Faith was dressed from head to toe in a soft lemon yellow, while Aurora's gown was of soft rainbow hues of blue, lavender, dusky pink, and yellow. The three women slipped on their masks and went down to the Great Hall. The large room was awash in the golden light of thousands of candles.

They were neither early nor late, and yet they had been preceded by hundreds of courtiers and their ladies, all dressed in the finest furs, silks, and jewels, all adorned in truly exotic costumes.

Constance, claimed for a dance by an old acquaintance, left them almost at once; Faith and Aurora slipped carefully through the crush, staring at the men and women, trying to identify each one. They were successful with some but they failed with many others. The elaborate costumes—and equally elaborate masks—concealed too much.

Finally, after some time, they grew tired of this game and moved across to the refreshment tables to sample some of the delicacies arrayed there. They gazed in wonder at platters piled high with cuts of beef, pheasant, venison and chicken; they stared amazed at cakes in the fanciful shapes of fishes and stars, and bowls of ripe, exotic fruit.

As Aurora nibbled at a sugared almond, she glanced sidelong at her friend.

"So, you pine for someone."

"Aurora!"

"Shh! Tonight, I am Iris."

"Very well, Iris, but this is hardly the time to talk of such matters."

"Ah, but 'tis an excellent time, I think. Which one of these excellent gentlemen is it?'' She peered around at the masked courtiers.

'' 'Tis none of th—'' Faith stopped. ''You tricked me,'' she accused.

''Only a little.''

The two friends laughed, and Aurora handed her friend a piece of marzipan shaped like a pear.

''Here. Tell me of your lost love later—when we are alone.''

Faith nodded, and before she could speak, a gentleman dressed in gold, and whose ruff was edged with pointed gold lace, and who wore a golden mask in the shape of the sun approached them and bowed low.

''May I have this dance?''

Aurora smiled, recognizing Richard's voice. ''Of course, Sir Sun.''

He took her hand, and led her out toward the other couples. As they danced, he gazed at her. The directness of his look made her somewhat uncomfortable, and as she sipped she was relieved when the music ended. He claimed her for the second dance, and the third, but for the fourth another gentleman cut him out, and for that Aurora was thankful.

She danced all evening, only pausing a few times. Once she sat down with a glass of wine, and she looked around for Faith. She found her dancing with a young gentleman. He reminded Aurora of someone; but she didn't have time to reflect on it, because another dancing partner was bowing low over her hand.

Toward midnight, in need of a rest, Aurora found solitude behind a pillar. From this secluded spot she could watch and relax just a little. She sipped her wine and smiled at the beautiful sight. Who would have ever thought she would be attending a masked ball?

A hand fell lightly upon her shoulder, and with a gasp, she whirled.

A tall man wearing a plain black mask edged in crimson stood behind her. He was dressed all in black, except for the one touch of red, and at once she knew who it was, and her heart leaped.

''May I have this dance, Goddess?''

"Of course . . . er, I don't know who you are supposed to be," she said.

"Hades, come to collect his bride."

"Persephone was his bride, not Iris. You have confused the two stories."

"So I have," he murmured, and she knew that he was smiling.

He took her hand and led her to the other couples, and they danced together. Not once did she take her eyes from Blacklaw. This was the first time they had met in some time, and whenever their fingers brushed lightly, fire shot through her. She burned at the mere sight of him, she wanted him so very much, but she could do nothing but wait . . . wait until after the masked ball. And perhaps then they could make love, at least be together for a few more hours.

While they danced, the lovers talked of many things, mostly light subjects, and finally he took her by the arm and guided her out onto the balcony. The autumn night air was crisp, and the full moon rode through a sky of black velvet, sewn with tiny diamonds. Moonlight gleamed on the ribbon of the Thames as it wound past the castle. The sweet breeze swept away the stuffiness of the hall.

Yet Aurora paid scant attention to the sight below her. At once she whirled around to face her dancing partner.

"You are exceedingly foolhardy for coming here, my lord."

"I couldn't stay away, my love."

He stepped forward, lifting his arms to embrace her, and just as she was about to move into them, they both heard a sound nearby. Aurora sprung back, while Blacklaw dropped his arms.

Maraline, her mask in one hand, stepped out onto the balcony and blinked at them.

"Oh, my, I hope I have not interrupted a serious discussion." She laughed a little, and her voice was high, and she sounded as if she had been drinking.

"Not at all."

"Oh, it is you, Aurora." Maraline giggled. "I didn't know you were here."

"Nor I you, Maraline." Aurora's gaze slid to Blacklaw, as if to warn him to keep quiet.

"I don't believe I know your dancing partner here. He is quite tall and handsome."

"Handsome? Why, you cannot see his face. He might be as ugly as a troll, Maraline."

"I think not," the girl said sweetly. She giggled again.

"As for his name, why, tonight he is Lord Hades," Aurora said, taking his arm.

Maraline said nothing, but shivered as if the breeze were cold.

"Now, if you will excuse us," Aurora said coolly, and left the balcony with Blacklaw. She did not see, but rather felt, the other woman's eyes on them. She was furious that Maraline had interrupted them.

Once again within the crowded hall, Aurora glanced at Blacklaw, but he shook his head slightly to indicate that this was no time to discuss what had happened. As he led her into the opening steps of another dance, he bent close and whispered, "I will come to you tomorrow night."

After the dance, he relinquished her reluctantly to Richard, and after that, Aurora lost track of her clandestine lover. She was disappointed that he did not ask her to dance again, but supposed he must have thought it best to leave.

It was after four in the morning when Aurora and Constance returned to their rooms, and Aurora, her fingers numb with exhaustion, was barely able to pull off her gown. When she finally managed to undress, she dropped her gown onto a chest, pulled the pins from her hair, then tumbled into bed; but despite her exhaustion, she couldn't sleep.

Aurora smiled to herself. Tomorrow night she would see Giles again. At least they would be together, no matter how short their time for love.

She was uneasy about the chance encounter earlier with Maraline. Surely she could not know who Aurora's partner had been from what she'd heard; there was no way for her to identify him. Doubtless Maraline would think that the tall man was simply a secret paramour. She hugged herself then, thinking of his visit to come, and soon fell asleep, dreaming only of Lord Blacklaw.

17

"Tell me again what you saw and heard," Thomas de Sayreville demanded.

Maraline, nude, with only a sheet covering her to the waist, lay in bed, while de Sayreville, half-clothed, reclined beside her.

He raised himself up on one elbow now as she repeated the scene she had witnessed on the balcony. Unfortunately, she had made a slight noise that had alerted the couple to her presence. Only by her quick thinking had she been able to convince them that she had been drinking heavily.

"That was clumsy of you," de Sayreville said, as he fondled her full breasts.

"I know, Thomas," she pouted. "But at least I did hear something for you."

"Yes, but of what significance is it, I wonder?" Idly, not really aware of what he was doing, he pinched her aroused nipple until she squeaked in pain and batted his hand away.

"Tom, be careful. I bruise easily."

"Umm," he said, lost in thought. "You are sure it wasn't my son?"

"Oh no, it wasn't Richard. I saw him inside talking with friends, just before I saw her slip out onto the balcony with the other man. That's what caught my attention. What a deceitful little c—"

"That's enough, love," he said, pressing his hand hard

against her lips. "You know that I don't like it when you are crude."

Her eyes filled charmingly with tears, so he removed his hand and kissed her waiting lips. His hand strayed down past her breasts, under the sheet, and made a rough thrusting motion. Frowning becomingly, she jerked her head away.

"You know that I wish you wouldn't do that immediately."

"Why not?" His smile was lazy; his eyes cruel. "I'll stick you soon enough, my love. Why not prepare you?" She pouted again, but her soulful expression did not move him, and he laughed. Under the sheet his hand moved back and forth rhythmically, and Maraline began to squirm as his fingers passed over the moist musky triangle, and slipped in and out of the center of her womanhood. Her legs opened wider, and he smiled again. He kissed her hard on the lips, drawing blood.

"Come into me," she whispered. "I want you now, Tom. Now. You know I'm hot."

His hand continued to move, then abruptly he pulled it out from under the sheet and rubbed a wet finger against her lips. She licked his finger, then sucked on it, all the while giving him a pleading look.

"Tom, please."

"Go to sleep, wench. I want to think." He stood and moved across to the fireplace.

Glaring at his back, Maraline pulled the sheet up to her neck, and slipped her hand under the covers. De Sayreville ignored her and her subsequent moans of delight.

So, Lady Aurora had been seen at the masked ball earlier in the night with a man whom Maraline could not identify. And Maraline possessed an excellent eye for faces. Damn that he'd worn a mask. A man identified only as Lord Hades. An appropriate nickname, if what Maraline said about Aurora le Grey were true.

And the man had not spoken, either, she had said. The other girl had been quick to ensure that he did not. Thus, his voice might have betrayed his identity. But how? Would it have been a voice that Maraline would have known? Perhaps, perhaps not. Certainly this was a most interesting development. Indeed, most interesting.

For some reason he didn't understand, de Sayreville didn't

trust the le Grey bitch. He sensed something very wrong, and now this liaison with an unidentified man only seemed to prove his hunch correct.

He smiled. He knew other ways of gleaning information. He glanced over at his mistress, whose self-passion had dissipated. She seemed to be sleeping, but he knew otherwise.

As he crossed the room, he threw off the remainder of his clothing; reaching the bed, he ripped back the covers. In feigned horror Maraline screamed, and tried to cover her naked body with her hands. He laughed, a cruel sound that echoed in the room, and struck her across the breasts with a ringing slap. His hand left a red imprint, and she giggled, and as she twitched her hips, she reached out and pinched the reddened head of his already hardening penis.

Without delay, he threw himself down upon her and buried his face in her. He raised his head when she cried out for him to stop; then grinning ferally, he raised himself up, and rammed into her.

Her scream of pleasure mingled with his moans of release.

18

The following night the man waited in the shadows and watched the rooms. He had been told to wait all night, if he must, and he would do so to earn his fee. His alert eyes did not miss the stranger who looked carefully about and then slipped down the darkened corridor. The watcher pressed himself into the corner, then waited. The other man knocked at a door which opened quickly, and went in.

The watcher waited for some time, then crept toward the rooms. He grinned at the closed door, knowing it would be locked, then walked down the corridor, turned the corner, and looked around to make sure no one was there before pushing a stone block. An immense door slid open with a minimum of noise. Inside was a dusty hallway, littered with dried leaves and the old bones of rats long dead, and as he made his way through the maze there, he continued to grin.

He found the right place within seconds, having memorized the layout of the corridor. Crouching, he put his eye to the small hole in the wall. He could hear a woman's quiet voice, followed by a man's voice, speaking her name softly.

Aurora.

But as much as he listened, he could not make out the words. He waited, hoping they would say something that he could take back to the man who had hired him, but they did not, and when he heard finally the sounds of love, he grinned, wishing he could see them rolling about as they rutted.

Sometime later, he left the secret corridor and returned to

his original spot to watch. As he waited, he brushed the grey dust from his clothes. Before long, the door opened quietly and the stranger slipped out of the room. The watcher followed discreetly. It was apparent that this man knew the palace well, too, because he used none of the main hallways, but followed disused corridors. Once outside, the stranger mounted a horse, and so the watcher lost him.

Still, he thought, de Sayreville would not be displeased to learn that young Lady Aurora had had a male visitor.

The watcher waited outside the rooms every night for a week, but he did not see the man again. At his master's instructions, he continued waiting, and was finally rewarded on the ninth night. The pattern was the same as before.

The stranger, who took such pains not to be seen, did not return for three days, and then after that it was two weeks before he appeared. And after that, a month. All this the watcher reported in great detail to his master, Thomas de Sayreville, and each time de Sayreville rewarded him handsomely for his efforts and bade him continue his watch.

"So," said Maraline, as she sat upon her lover's lap, "the girl is visited each night."

De Sayreville sighed. "Not each night. I have told you that twice. The man's visits are sporadic. They have no pattern, as far as I can see." He frowned, and tapped his fingers on the tabletop.

Maraline wiggled, trying to get his attention, but he ignored her. Suddenly she laughed. *Poor pious Richard is already cuckold,* she told herself, *and how he will blush and then turn pale with anger when she tells him what his beloved Aurora is.*

Once more she chuckled. Maraline had her own plans for the only son of the illustrious family. She intended to marry Richard, yet remain the mistress of the elder de Sayreville, thus doubly ensuring that she would benefit handsomely through the kindness of both men. It would take at least two of them, anyway, to satisfy her appetites.

"What will you do, love?"

"I must find out who that man is. I think it might well be used against Lady Aurora. That, and the information concerning her black practices. Do you not agree, my dear?"

"Oh yes," she breathed warmly into his ear, then her tongue flicked out and caressed his earlobe. "And I would enjoy seeing that bitch tumble from favor. The Queen has seen her several times, and talks highly of the pious little bitch."

He grinned. "Maraline, my dear, there is nothing quite like jealousy to make a woman like you show her true colors."

She laughed. "Yes, I admit it. I am jealous, but not for long."

"That is true." He poured himself a glass of wine, which he shared with her. "In the meantime, my dear, I have another job for you."

"Which is?"

"Foster more rumors about the girl—you have been too quiet at Court of late. The rumors can only serve to help us both in the future."

"I exist only to obey you, my love," she said with a charming little pout, and she licked her lips so that they glistened in the firelight. Immediately de Sayreville felt a throbbing response in his crotch. The lovers smiled at one another, and Maraline rose in a liquid, feline motion; taking him by the hand she tugged him to his feet and led him across the room until they stood by the bed. She was tired of waiting.

She undressed slowly, appreciating his lascivious gaze as it ran across her tiny body as she slowly removed his clothes, tantalizing him with a flick of her finger here and there. When they were both naked, she lay back down upon the bed, and smiled as she opened her white legs very wide and her lord mounted her.

PART V

1586

1

October of 1585 had brought heavy snows, and during the early winter months Aurora had not seen Blacklaw. The Court had moved back to Whitehall in November, and in December Constance and Aurora had returned to their London home.

When spring arrived at last, Aurora fled outdoors as if she had been shut away all her life. She could not get enough of fresh air and sunlight, and delighted in walking for long hours through the intimate gardens at Constance's home, or through the magnificent gardens and grounds at Whitehall.

It was in the garden of Constance's house that Richard found her one spring afternoon. Seated on a marble bench, she had been reading, the fragrance of the colorful flowers drifting to her with the soft chirps of the birds in the background. But the warm sunshine had proved too much temptation, and so she had closed her eyes and drifted off in a nap.

A shadow fell across her face, instantly cutting off the warmth; her eyes flickered open and she stared up at the person before her. She blinked, trying to bring her eyes in focus, and for a moment, she wildly hoped it was Blacklaw. Then she recognized her unexpected visitor.

"Richard!"

He smiled, and sat beside her. "I hope that I am not disturbing you," he said earnestly.

"In truth, I had been reading," she said, indicating the book lying across her lap, "but I believe I must have dozed off.'' He smiled, but looked so serious that she was moved to say, "Is something amiss, Richard?"

"Not . . . amiss, Aurora. But I must talk with you," he said.

"Yes?"

"I had thought to wait until your father had returned to this country, but it does not seem likely that he will be home for many more months."

She felt a little strange inside, almost afraid to speak. She didn't want to lie to Richard, but she had no other choice.

" 'Tis true, he won't be home for quite some time. Alas, bad weather has detained him. What is it you wish to discuss with me?"

"Aurora."

He turned around so that he could face her, and she saw that his expression was just as serious as his voice. Something inside her seemed to twist as she waited for him to speak.

"Aurora, I want you to marry me. I love you—and want to make you my wife."

Stunned, Aurora could only look at him. She hadn't expected this.

"Even though our acquaintance is of many months, I know this must be sudden, but please consider my suit. I love you, Aurora." Tentatively he took her hand and held it loosely, almost as if he were afraid that it would break.

Aurora didn't know what to say. She didn't love Richard, but how could she say that to him? He had lain his heart bare before her; she couldn't step on it, crushing it into the gravel. She liked him, and didn't want to lose him as a friend. But to consider him as a husband . . . she had never really believed his interest would lead to this, although she had thought about it.

"Richard . . . I don't know what to say. I'm speechless. Perhaps . . ." Words failed her, but he came to her rescue.

"I understand, Aurora, my love. You must think. Very well. I won't trouble you any longer today, but I do hope you will consider what I have said." He rose, still holding her hand, and then bent over it in a very courtly fashion. "Good day, Aurora."

"Good day, Richard."

She watched as he threaded his way along the roundabout

garden paths, and finally, when she could see him no longer, she blindly picked up her book and clasped it to her bosom.

Richard de Sayreville, the scion of a wealthy and influential family, had asked her to marry him. She could scarcely credit it. She loved Giles—but she hadn't seen him in months now; and she didn't even know for sure if he cared about her. He claimed that he did, yet he never stayed with her for more than a few hours at a time. Surely, if he truly loved her, he could declare his love and they could be together. Surely, he wasn't just using her, was he? That small suspicion spread coldly through her, and she wished she could dismiss it, but it wouldn't fade.

She had to talk to someone, and now. She jumped to her feet and rushed into the house. She found Constance in her parlor. The woman glanced up as Aurora ran into the room, out of breath, her cheeks flushed.

"Goodness, child, whatever is the matter?"

"Constance, I must speak with you at once. It's very important."

"Very well."

Aurora stood by the window overlooking the Thames and clasped her hands together. She did not even see the boats that sailed upon the broad river. She was shaking almost uncontrollably, and she didn't know why. She took a deep breath.

"Richard de Sayreville was here."

"Yes, I saw him from the window. He seemed very intent on something."

Constance's voice sounded neutral, almost cool, and Aurora wondered if she should proceed. But she had no one else to turn to.

"He asked me to marry him."

Constance's face relaxed into a smile. "That's wonderful, Aurora. I think Richard is a fine young man, and you—" She stopped, then frowned. "You didn't refuse him, did you?"

"I didn't refuse, but I didn't accept, either." She gave the older woman a pleading look. "I don't know what to do, Constance. I'm so confused."

The woman's tone was brisk. "What is there to be confused about?"

"I don't love Richard, but I do care for him."

"That's a very sound basis for a marriage. Love can always grow later under those circumstances; you at least do more than tolerate him, and certainly you don't despise him."

"Yes, I know, others have married with far less in common, but I love . . . another."

Constance arched an elegant eyebrow, yet remained silent.

"I still love Giles. I haven't been able to stop loving him."

The woman's breath hissed inward. "I see." She tapped her fingers, then looked at Aurora thoughtfully. "This does pose a problem. Particularly as you do not know the mind of Giles Blacklaw, do you?"

"No."

"Many women have loved Giles, as you may doubtless have guessed. None have had him." Constance shook her head. "I would counsel you, Aurora, to take Richard's offer. You could do far worse."

"I suppose you're right."

"I think it will be the best for you and Richard. Please, Aurora, forget Giles—I don't say this because we were once lovers; I say it because he has no room in his heart for love." She stood. "Now, I must see to our supper. It will soon be time to dine, and we have much to do tonight."

When Constance had left, Aurora stood for a few minutes more, then went upstairs to her bedroom and sat down on the bed. Instantly Lucye crawled into her lap. Aurora was no better off after talking with Constance than before. What would she do?

"Oh, Lucye, I'm so confused."

The cat raised its head, then rubbed against Aurora's hand as the girl stroked its fur. And yet she really knew what she had to do—she had to talk to Giles, and soon. This time they would not make love; they would talk. She shivered, suddenly afraid.

2

Aurora did not have long to wait, because Blacklaw made his next appearance within the week. When he arrived, he was surprised to find Aurora still up, sitting by the fireplace. She stood at once and crossed over to him. She was so happy to see him, and yet for so long had been dreading this confrontation.

"Giles, I'm so glad you're here!" She laid her head against his chest.

He kissed her forehead, then her lips, but she frowned slightly when he moved away to sit on the stool by the hearth.

"Are you tired, my love?"

He nodded. "I rode many miles today." He put one hand up to hide a yawn, then said, his voice filled with amusement, "I think tonight I might just fall asleep in bed."

"As long as you're by my side, nothing else matters, Giles."

Again he was silent, almost as if something troubled him. Weariness, she told herself. She went over to him, and laying her hands upon his shoulders, began to massage the tight muscles. They felt knotted, as if he had been exerting himself much, and once again she wondered what business it was that took him away from her so often. Business or woman? came the crafty question inside her, and she tried to push it away, but was not wholly successful.

She continued to rub his shoulders and back in silence. He

did not break the silence, but remained hunched over, as if in deep thought. Finally, she spoke.

"Is something wrong, Giles?"

"No."

"Are you sure? You're so quiet tonight."

"Can't a man be silent once? We needn't all be chattering magpies."

She pressed her lips together. Was he comparing her to a magpie now? She gave his shoulders an extra hard squeeze and was satisfied to hear him grunt. Magpie, indeed. Had she offended him? And yet how could that be? She had given him all her love. What more could he want of her? Did he worry about his . . . *business*? About another woman, suggested a small voice within her, and she trembled slightly.

She kneaded the muscles of his back, until finally he reached up and took her hands in his, then drew her around to sit on his lap. She nestled her head against his, and stared into the fireplace. Tonight she was a little uncomfortable with him, unsure of herself and of what she should say.

Usually he would ask her questions about Court and those she saw there, but tonight he didn't seem to care. She decided to tell him what had happened since she'd last seen him.

"I haven't heard any further rumors circulating from Maraline. Which is good," she added when Blacklaw didn't respond. "And Faith and I have been busy, going riding through the city. And I've had many visitors, now that the weather is fine."

"Umm?"

"Many of them were gentlemen." He said nothing. "Richard de Sayreville has been the most persistent."

"So it seems."

She might as well have said that the sun rose in the east and set in the west. He didn't seem to be paying attention at all, and not for the first time she wondered if he only came to her to relieve himself. As soon as she thought that, she found herself shocked, and the color rushed into her cheeks.

She remained silent for several minutes, and when Blacklaw still had not spoken, she took a deep breath and plunged forward.

"Yes, Constance is very happy to see Richard visiting so often, and as it happens, not a week ago he asked me to marry him.'' Blacklaw neither laughed nor looked angry. Disturbed, she sat up very straight and looked down at him. He was frowning deeply.

"Giles?''

He didn't even look at her.

"Giles, did you hear me?''

"Yes.''

"And?''

"And I think, Aurora, that you ought to accept his proposal.''

"What?'' She leaped up and spun around to face him, her hands planted on her hips. "What do you mean, I ought to accept his proposal?''

"Just what I said, Aurora.'' His eyes would not meet hers, though, and his frown had deepened. He did look tired, almost exhausted, but all pity for him had fled from her.

"But I would be married then . . . we wouldn't be able to see one another.''

"Yes.'' He stood and walked a few feet away from her. "I think that would be best.'' His expression was almost fierce.

"That we not see one another?'' She couldn't believe that she had heard aright. She loved Giles . . . and she had thought he loved her. Why was he sending her away from him? "What have I done, Giles? I must have done something wrong.''

"No, you've done nothing. Nothing at all.''

"Nothing? But why are you punishing me?'' she demanded, aware that her voice was rising. She didn't care; all she wanted from him was an explanation . . . an explanation that she could understand. . . .

He shrugged. "If you wish to see it in that light, Aurora.''

"How else am I to see it? I have loved you, and I thought you loved me. And now, you tell me to marry another man. I don't understand.'' Her voice was a child's plaintive one.

"It's very simple. You would have no future with me. You know that; you have known that for a long time. I never hid that fact from you. If you wish to live a happy life, you must marry Richard de Sayreville. I have little doubt that he loves you and would take care of you in the manner you wish.''

"I don't want to live a 'happy life' with him; I don't love him. However could I be happy?''

For the first time that evening a slight smile played about

his lips. "You do not have to love your husband to be happy."

"I would."

"You're very young yet, and very naive. You'll learn in time."

Her eyes filled with tears. "But, Giles, I don't want to marry him. I love you; I want to marry you." She went to him and slipped her arms around his neck. Firmly he removed them, then patted her hands, almost as if she were a child. She drew back as if she'd been burned.

"I must go now. I can't stay any longer, Aurora." He spoke almost mechanically, and once more his gaze would not meet hers.

"As you will, my lord." She spoke stiffly. She rubbed her hands across her eyes. The tears had stopped flowing, but she still felt like crying. Her chest ached, and she wanted nothing more than to fling herself into his arms. He would only push her away, she told herself bitterly.

He hesitated before crossing the room to the door. There he paused.

"I will see you again," he said.

She said nothing.

The door opened quietly, and he slipped outside. With the almost silent snick of the door's closing, her world crumbled.

"Go to hell!" she cried out to the closed door, then sank onto the floor and began sobbing. The tears flowed down her cheeks, and she pressed her fist against her mouth to muffle the sound.

He was gone from her, almost as quickly as he'd come into her life. Gone. Taking his love, her love. Gone forever. A new wave of weeping seized her, and her shoulders shook from the sobbing. Lucye crept over to her and licked her hand, then curled up on the hearth, one eye open and watching its mistress. Gradually, Aurora's sobs quieted; she was exhausted, and at last she could cry no longer. Yet she hurt so much inside that all she could do was keen in a low voice. She drew in a rasping breath and slowly heaved herself to her feet.

Momentarily she was dizzy, and she reached out to the mantel to steady herself; then, slowly picking her way, almost as though she had drunk too much, she crossed to the bed. She threw herself across it and, closing her eyes, told herself to go to sleep. But tonight, she knew, there would be no sleep for her.

3

Two days later Richard called on her. She had regained her composure the morning after Blacklaw had been to see her, but she was still quite pale.

"I've brought you a surprise," the young man said, handing her a small bouquet of red, pink, and white flowers, with delicate white lace wound carefully about the short stems.

She took the bouquet and exclaimed over it. "How beautiful, Richard. Are they from your mother's garden?" He nodded. She touched the fragile petals, taking care not to disturb them. Their odor was spicy, and she breathed deeply of the pleasant fragrance. "Thank you," and reaching up, she kissed him on the cheek. Blushing slightly, she turned away. "I must put them in water at once."

He nodded, and waited while she left the room. He was still in the same position when she returned a few minutes later, the flowers now in a glass vase. He smiled at her, and she returned the expression. For a few minutes he talked of inconsequential matters, then abruptly he cleared his throat.

"Aurora."

"Yes, Richard?"

"Have you thought over the matter I posed to you last time we met?"

She remembered Blacklaw's expressionless face, and the anger and pain which she still felt. She took a deep breath, aware that her hands were slightly trembling. "Yes, Richard, I have. I would dearly love to become your wife."

Instantly his face was transformed. Gone was the shy youth; in his place was a man whose every wish had just been granted. He took her hands in his and slowly raised them to his lips. "I will do everything in my power to make you happy, my love."

She smiled up at him, trying to act like the happiest woman alive. Yet all she really wanted to do was cry.

"Have you seen Lucye?"

"No, my dear. Isn't she in your room? Normally she's there most of the day."

"I've looked," Aurora said, "and called for her inside and out."

"She might have just wandered into the garden by mistake. She'll be back soon."

"I hope so." Aurora felt uneasy, and she wasn't sure why. Lucye never went outside, and it bothered her that the cat hadn't come to her call.

"I'd like to talk to you about your decision," Constance said, setting her needlework down. Aurora waited.

"I think you've made a good choice, dear. Perhaps your heart isn't yet with Richard, but it soon will be. He'll be a kind and good husband, and there is little more that you could ask for."

No, Aurora thought dully, there *was* much more that she could ask for than marriage to Richard. But she was beyond that now. She couldn't turn back now, not when she knew she could never have Giles Blacklaw, knew that he had not wanted her . . . ever. She drew in a deep breath, and it seemed that a ragged pain shot through her chest. She must have made a sound, for Constance peered at her closely.

"Are you all right, child?"

"Yes, thank you. I—I think it must be all the excitement. I'm a little tired."

"I've little doubt as to that, my dear. I know you're worried about Lucye too. I'm sure she'll return within the hour. And who knows—she might present you with a litter of kittens in a short time. Now, you must rest. There is so much for us to plan, and so little time in which to do it."

Chatting about the many things that needed to be done for the impending wedding, Constance led the girl upstairs to her bedroom and helped her undress, then tucked her into bed. Aurora's eyelids drifted downward as she fell asleep, but not before she had seen the expression of concern on Constance's face.

4

Richard told his parents at once of his plans. His mother rejoiced at the news, but Lord de Sayreville met his son's bold announcement with an indulgent smile and clapped him upon the back. Soon the announcement of the marriage was made at Court, with a date in October for the wedding day.

Richard's family gave many parties at Court for the young couple; friends of his family and those who wished to gain favor with the de Sayrevilles also celebrated. Constance threw a large party in honor of her young ward, inviting the many friends Aurora had made thus far at Court. Aurora supposed that Constance's party was a success; certainly Constance seemed to be happy with it. But during none of these events could she feel even remotely happy. She moved through all almost mechanically, hardly aware of what was going on around her.

It was at just such a party in July that the Queen requested to see Aurora. She felt the flutterings of nervousness stirring in her stomach, but forced herself to be calm. She mustn't act as if she'd just come to Court—or had done something to break the law.

"Your Highness," she said, curtseying.

"Rise, Lady Aurora," the Queen said, a frosty look on her heavily painted face. "I understand that you are to marry young Richard de Sayreville." She peered at the girl. "Is this correct?"

She nodded. "Yes, Your Majesty—but only with your kind permission, of course."

A smile slipped onto the Queen's lips. "Well-spoken, child. And, of course, I think the match is a good one. You will make young Richard a good bride, just as he will make you a good husband. Certainly he is handsome enough, is he not?"

"Yes, Your Highness."

"There is much ugliness here at Court, Aurora, all of it hidden behind pretty exteriors. You must always be on the guard against those men whose only desire in life is to deceive women."

Aurora nodded, thinking of Blacklaw.

"Richard is nothing like that, my dear, and I think you have made an excellent choice."

"Thank you, Your Majesty."

They talked for a few minutes, and were soon joined by others. When Aurora saw Faith that afternoon, she quickly told the other girl what had transpired with the Queen.

"It's good that she approves," Faith said. She studied her friend for a moment, then asked, "What's wrong, Aurora? You don't seem happy, not since the announcement of the marriage."

" 'Tis nothing," Aurora said lightly.

Faith did not respond.

"You have something to tell me, though," Aurora went on.

"What?" Her friend looked astonished.

"Who is this 'lost love' of yours?"

"He's not a lost love; that is, I mean, he's not my love." Faith blushed.

"I don't believe you. Who is he, Faith? You can trust me—I am your friend."

"Very well." Faith folded her hands in her lap and looked down at them, but as she did so, a smile spread across her face, painting it with a radiance that Aurora had never seen there. "His name is John."

"A promising name," Aurora teased. Quickly she subsided with a look from the other woman.

"I met him some time ago."

"At Court?"

"No. In the city. At a market. It was very crowded, and we were jostled up against one another. My basket was knocked from my hands, and he picked it up for me."

"And?"

"And we have met several other times since then." Faith kept her eyes lowered.

"But he's not at court?"

"No."

"Why not?" Faith seemed to hesitate, so Aurora put her hand on her friend's. "You *can* tell me, you know. I would never tell anyone else, if you asked me not to. Your secret is safe."

Faith nodded. "He is a scholar."

"That's very good."

"Yes, but he's poor. And," she drew in a deep breath, "he is Catholic."

"Ah." Aurora smiled slightly, then sat up. "Wait. You said his name is John; he's a scholar and poor?" Faith nodded. "His last name isn't Maxwell, is it?"

Faith looked astonished. "Yes, it is, but how did you know?"

Aurora laughed. "You won't believe this, Faith, but John was one of my tutors before I came to London."

"No!"

"Yes! Constance knew of him, and thought him excellent, and so he helped me learn . . ." Her words stumbled to a halt. She mustn't say too much, she realized.

But Faith seemed not to have heard her friend's last words. "You did like him then?"

"I thought he was a most handsome and gentle man, and I couldn't be happier for you." She hugged her friend, then smiled at her.

"And it doesn't . . . bother . . . you that he is Catholic?"

"No."

"Nor me," Faith confided. "I worry about my father, though."

"And so you've said nothing to him about John?" Faith nodded. "Perhaps we could go to Constance, and perhaps she could be persuaded to talk with your father. She might make him see reason."

"Do you think she might?" Faith asked, her voice eager.

"I do, indeed, for Constance is very fond of John, too."

"Oh thank you, Aurora. You're such a good friend." She hugged her friend. "And when you and Richard have a child, you must promise to allow me to be a godmother."

With a lump in her throat, Aurora nodded. Richard's children, not Giles'.

"But enough of me," Faith said. "I have been very selfish when we were talking of you. I know that this matter will work out for you, Aurora. If you don't love Richard now, you will come to love him afterward, because he is a good and gentle man. And who is to say that this way might not be the better one?"

"Who is to say," Aurora repeated slowly. "Yes, I think you must be right, Faith. I am quite sure that you are."

But all the while, in her heart, Aurora knew she was doing the wrong thing. Yet she had no choice now. Giles Blacklaw had left her with no alternative.

5

"However did you lure the cat away?" Roxanne demanded as she watched Maraline brush her hair. Alice and Mary sat on stools nearby but said nothing. Mary had been particularly quiet since her arrival, and Maraline wondered momentarily at that. She reminded herself that the stupid little girl never had anything to say.

"Oh, that."

The blonde glanced at the black cat crouching in the metal cage. The cat had meowed almost constantly since its arrival. When it was not pacing back and forth in the small confines of its cage, it gnawed continually at the bars, without success. Maraline would be glad when the damned nuisance was gone from her rooms. It made too much noise, and its shed hair clung to her clothing as well.

"I had one of my servants make friends with one of *hers,* and he was able to grab the cat one day when she was away."

"Brilliant!" Alice said admiringly.

"Yes."

Roxanne put a hand out to the cat, then snatched it back.

"Look at what this beast did!" She held out her hand so that Maraline could see the four long red scratches and the faint gleam of blood. Alice tsked over her friend's wounds and handed her a linen handkerchief.

"I know," Maraline said with a sigh. "It's so savage. She must have put a spell on it to keep it tame in her presence."

"Do you think that . . ." Roxanne's voice trailed away as

she slipped the handkerchief around her slightly bleeding hand.

"Do I think what?"

"That she and the cat . . . well, you know." Roxanne and Alice exchanged looks.

"No, I most certainly do not." Maraline turned around to face her friend. "Whatever do you mean, Roxanne? Do tell me, please."

"Do you think that she and the cat were lovers? I have heard that witches sleep with their familiars—and with the devil, too."

Maraline's perfect lips curved upward in a smile. "Of that I have no doubt. I'm sure that the most filthy practices went on between the two."

"Oh," breathed Roxanne.

"How terrible," Alice murmured, though she looked excited at the thought of such bestiality.

"What will you do with the cat?" Mary spoke for the first time.

"First, I want to show the filthy animal to someone, and then I'm afraid that this creature will lose one of its nine lives."

"You'll kill it?" Alice asked.

"Not me, silly."

"But what if it tries to put a spell on you, or something like that?"

Inwardly Maraline sighed and seriously wondered how Alice and Roxanne could be so superstitious. What utter nonsense. These girls would not go far at Court. They had absolutely no imagination.

"I won't do it, but someone else will dispose of it. Safely, too, so that it cannot harm me . . . or you"—she saw with approval that her friends shuddered—"and then *she* will be discovered as a witch."

"You're so clever," Alice said.

"That's why she's our leader," Roxanne said.

Maraline smiled. Mary said nothing.

Days passed, and still Aurora couldn't find Lucye. She searched through the grounds once more, looking everywhere, afraid that the cat was ill, or worse, dead. She went from house to house in the immediate neighborhood and asked if anyone had seen Lucye. But no one had. When she and Constance moved back to Court, Aurora began asking everyone she knew if they had seen her cat. Again, no one had.

From time to time she even sent a servant back to the house to check to see if Lucye had returned. Constance, knowing how hurt Aurora was, suggested that Lucye might have adopted someone else for a while, and that in a month or two she might return.

Aurora shook her head. She knew that her pet would never do that. Something was wrong. Dreadfully wrong—and between the disappearance of Lucye and the approaching marriage, she found little happiness.

6

Richard de Sayreville was now Aurora's constant companion, going everywhere that she went, coming to visit each day and staying late into the evenings. When she was feeling less than charitable—which was more often than she liked—Aurora wished that she had more time to herself, and less time with her intended. She felt as though she were being smothered by his love and attention.

These thoughts made her guilty. Richard loved her, and she should appreciate that. He fondly embraced her and stole a kiss or two; and all the while, as his arms were around her, Aurora felt removed from him, as if she actually stood apart from him.

Every time Richard kissed her, or stroked her hand, she could not help thinking of Giles Blacklaw and of the love that she had once had for him. But angry as she was, Aurora could not hate him. Not that she didn't try. She did, but the hatred would not come. Only the anger remained, and grew, as well as the despair. As the weeks slipped away the date of the wedding inched closer.

And still she had been unable to find Lucye. She feared that the cat was dead; every night she cried, alone in her bed. She missed the soft purring of her pet, the comforting warmth that curled up next to her, and she wondered what could have become of the cat. No one in the house would let the cat out; after all, they'd been instructed not to. And Lucye had never before been tempted to sneak out through an open window. How had she left?

In the meantime, to take her mind off her own miserable life, Aurora had decided that Faith, at least, should be happy. She had gone to Constance and told her how Faith had met and fallen in love with John Maxwell. The widow had been delighted with this unexpected news, and had readily agreed to talk to Faith's father. She claimed he was a tolerant man and would need little convincing on her part.

Aurora certainly hoped so. That, at least, was taken care of.

As the weeks of July passed, and the Queen began her processions, Constance and Aurora returned to Grey Wood to escape the heat of London. Here, Aurora thought, as she wandered through the corridors, here it had all begun, years ago. Years ago she had met Giles Blacklaw and fallen in love with him, as impetuously and quickly as Faith had fallen in love with John, but with far worse results. Sighing, she returned to her room and lay down on the bed. She stared up at the ceiling, seeing nothing, thinking of nothing, waiting until Constance called to her.

In August, while Elizabeth was traveling up north, the generally happy mood of the Court was marred by a scandal. One Anthony Babington was arrested, suspected of being involved in a plot to assassinate the Queen. The Court was shocked.

Subsequently, with the aid of the rack and other instruments of persuasion, Babington confessed to his part in the plot. But he was not the only one involved in it. He claimed that Elizabeth's Catholic cousin had been plotting to kill her.

No one at Court disbelieved it because it was well known that Mary had little love for Elizabeth—the opposite holding true, also. Elizabeth returned to London at once, and talk of the uncovered treason was on everyone's lips. Even Aurora, for the moment, forgot her own problems.

Babington's fellow plotters were arrested, and within a few weeks it was announced that they would be hanged at Tyburn. Most of the Court intended to watch the hangings, but Aurora declined. She had little stomach for that.

Babington and his friends were executed; Mary Stuart was

arrested, and meanwhile, the government began searching for others involved in the Babington plot. At once, everyone became suspect.

Constance told Aurora that she would wait until the anti-Catholic talk at Court died down before she talked with Faith's father. Faith told Aurora that she feared that John might be suspected, simply on the grounds of his religion, and Aurora urged her friend to tell John to leave London until the trouble had died down.

At that moment Aurora was sorely tempted to confide totally in her friend. She wanted to tell Faith about her imprisonment in Bridewell, about her release and her new life, about her love for Giles Blacklaw; but the words froze in her throat. She couldn't. Not yet, anyway; perhaps some day.

Thomas de Sayreville, who had proved instrumental in the discovery of Babington's treachery, was well rewarded by the Queen for his vigilance. He boasted of his accomplishment; and the even-tempered Lady de Sayreville was sickened, knowing that many men had gone to their deaths because of her husband.

Because of Thomas de Sayreville's involvement, Aurora wondered if Babington were really guilty. Was he simply a dupe, used by someone more cunning than himself? Yet she could not help remembering how Blacklaw had asked her to take note of what happened at Court. Of what consequence could that be to him? Unless . . .

No, she wouldn't allow herself to think that of anyone, not even Giles Blacklaw. She despised him and she despised his mysterious "business." But no—he could not be involved in this.

And yet the thought would not leave.

7

"Well, what do you think of my scheme?" Maraline asked her paramour.

Thomas de Sayreville said nothing but continued staring out the window.

"Well, Tom?"

"It won't work," he said finally.

Amazed, the blonde girl stared at him. "What? You must be mad, darling. Of course it will work—I've thought it through very carefully. You have the cat killed in some way that looks as though Aurora worked black magic; then someone we know discovers the cat's body, and shortly thereafter she is accused."

"No."

"Yes."

He shook his head.

"Why not?"

"Because you forget that she'll soon be a member of my family."

"You can still stop that."

"Maraline," he said, "I don't want to be tainted with witches and black magic. Think of what that could do to my own work. Think, Maraline."

She shrugged. "You can't have her marry into your family, though."

"I know, but there are other ways of stopping the marriage."

Clearly skeptical, she raised one thinly plucked eyebrow.
"Such as?"

He slipped a hand down her bodice and squeezed one of her
breasts, then kneaded it roughly with his fingers. She moaned
once and squirmed with desire. She licked her lips, and in the
candlelight they gleamed wetly.

"That you will find out in due time."

"Tom."

"No use in trying to coddle me, my dear. I won't tell you
yet."

"Tom." She kissed his mouth, running her tongue along
his lips.

"No."

She half-turned away, arms folded across her chest, her
face set in a pout. "You're so unfair to me. You don't love
me."

"Get into bed, and I'll show you how little I love you,
bitch."

She smiled and began to undress.

"Well, what do you want?" de Sayreville demanded of the
man facing him. He had left Maraline just a little over an
hour ago, and he was tired. He'd ridden the bitch hard
tonight, and he wanted to sleep. Now he had to cope with this
interruption.

"I have something interesting which you might like to
hear."

"Umm." Since Babington's arrest and subsequent execu-
tion, de Sayreville had kept his own special activities to a
minimum. He would wait out this new storm until the government was lulled, then he would begin again. Thus what his
spy had to say could be of little interest. Or so he believed.

"It's about the man visiting the young lady, my lord," the
man said with an ingratiating grin.

"Yes?" de Sayreville said impatiently. His prospective
daughter-in-law had not seen her late night visitor for some
time, and since then de Sayreville had lost interest in the
matter. Apparently this would lead nowhere. He set down his
quill and folded his hands. "Have you discovered the man's
name?" At least, he could hear that.

The man's grin widened, revealing the blackened stumps in his lower jaw.

"There is a price—of course, my lord."

"Of course. How foolish of me to forget." He reached into his pocket and withdrew a few coins. He tossed them to his spy, and the silver gleamed in the candlelight. "Now, the name. I don't have all night." God's blood, but he was tired.

The spy leaned close, and de Sayreville wrinkled his nose fastidiously, smelling the rotten odor of the other's decaying teeth.

"The name of the man who visits Aurora le Grey is . . . Giles Blacklaw."

De Sayreville paled. "Blacklaw," he whispered, his voice hoarse. He sat back in his chair and stared at the man. "You must be mistaken."

"No, sir, I'm not. I overheard him give his name one night. It's him all right. Giles Blacklaw. Yessir." The spy nodded with satisfaction. His patience had finally been rewarded.

"Here," said de Sayreville. He fumbled with the leather purse once more, withdrawing a gold sovereign, which he handed to the surprised man. "Forget that you ever heard that name."

The man grinned and nodded, pleased with his unexpected profit.

"Go on then. I have what I want, and you certainly have what you want."

The man bowed. "Any time, my lord."

The spy quietly closed the door behind him, and de Sayreville stared unwaveringly into the flame of the candle atop his desk.

Giles Blacklaw . . . he had not heard that name in years. He had thought . . . had hoped . . . the man was dead, had believed at best that the other was exiled and would never return to England. And yet here he was . . . and for some time now Blacklaw had been visiting Aurora, the very girl who was to marry his son in a few days' time.

De Sayreville stood abruptly, scraping the chair along the floor. Locking his hands behind his back, he began to pace, his fatigue forgotten. From time to time his fingers clenched and unclenched. The girl who was to marry his son. Was this not a coincidence? And a convenient one at that?

Could Blacklaw somehow have engineered the match? No, that was impossible. Or was it? Blacklaw hated him, and would do all in his power to destroy him. And the girl had been completely unknown until Constance Westcott had brought her to court. It was said the girl had a father traveling abroad, but no one had ever heard of him; no one had ever seen him. That was most curious, was it not?

So, perhaps, Blacklaw had seen a way to harm him. He had the girl come to court, and subsequently she met Richard, and from there things fell quickly into place; Richard, the fool, believed himself in love, and had proposed to her. Yet, how could the girl's entry into the family harm him? How, indeed?

He must do something, and he had little time now, not nearly as much time as he'd thought. He must act quickly if he were to rid himself of Giles Blacklaw once and for all. De Sayreville smiled, and the yellow candlelight gave his face a sinister look.

8

The eve of her wedding had arrived, and Aurora told herself she should be happy. But she wasn't. She had left Constance early, pleading exhaustion, and the widow had nodded and smiled, knowing how much there was to do upon the morrow. The past few months had been spent in preparation for the wedding, and Aurora had had few moments to herself.

Now, alone at last, she sat in her bedroom by the fire, her arms locked about her knees, and stared into the flames. Tomorrow it would be done. She would marry Richard de Sayreville, and be his bride. And that, finally, would be that. Only it wasn't a very happy solution for her, certainly not the one she had once looked forward to.

All she thought of was Giles Blacklaw, even though thinking of him still made her furious. Yet she could do nothing to prevent it. She lost sleep at night, wishing fervently that it was he whom she was marrying and not Richard, as gentle and worthy as that young man was. She closed her eyes. How she wished she could see Giles one last time . . . just once . . . that would be all that she needed to lay that last ghost of love to rest.

She felt a touch on her shoulder, and she looked up to see Blacklaw standing over her. Surely she had fallen asleep, and this was a dream. She rubbed her eyes, but he stood there still. No, 'twas real enough.

Giles had come to her, almost as if he had known what she was thinking this last night. Perhaps he felt the same way.

No, she told herself as she slowly rose to her feet, he didn't care for her. Didn't she understand that by now?

He had moved some feet distant from her now, and his expression was unreadable. Nervously she plucked at her sleeve. She waited for him to speak, and when he remained silent, she forced herself to look at him.

"What brings you here, my lord?" At least, she thought thankfully, her voice was steady.

So was his when he answered. "I wanted to see you one last time, Aurora."

"Indeed?" She raised an eyebrow, hoping it was a haughty gesture, but knew it was lost upon him. "I am surprised."

He said nothing.

"I have much to do yet tonight. I don't have time to talk."

"Then I won't keep you any longer."

"Very well."

"Shall I offer my congratulations?"

Her lower lip trembled ever so slightly. "If—if you wish to, my lord."

"What do you wish me to do?"

"I wish nothing from you."

"I see."

She swallowed heavily. "You should go now." She walked away from the fire, toward the window, and was aware that he stood no more than a few feet distant from her. Far away, and yet very close, too.

"Aurora."

She whirled around. He was by the door now, his hand by the latch. He had moved so quietly that she had not heard him. This might be the last time in her life that she saw him, one part of her said; she couldn't stand it any longer.

"Giles!"

His hand stayed.

She flew across the room and leaned against him. Almost as if he could not prevent himself, he raised his arms and put them around her; then he bent his head and kissed her lips.

How she had missed his kisses, his embraces! She almost wept with joy as she hugged him closer and returned his kisses with an ardor equal to his own. His breath was warm upon her cheek as he nuzzled her ear, and he murmured without words to her. Their kisses grew more frenzied and, without speaking, he picked her up and carried her to the bed, where he placed her gently. In the semi-darkness they undressed, and then he began making love to her—long, languorous, exquisite love.

They murmured words of love, and stroked one another, and when their passion rose, they cried out as one voice, then sank in a tangle of warm limbs, their passion spent. For a few minutes both man and woman slept, satisfied and wrapped in each other's arms, and when they awakened a shaft of silvery moonlight thrust through the window into the room. Aurora curled up along the length of Blacklaw's body and turned her face blindly to his. His lips sought, and found, hers, and once more they began to make love. After the second time, he stroked her hair slowly, twisting a curl or two around his finger. They did not speak, beyond murmuring the other's name, and she knew without his saying so that he would have to leave soon. She couldn't bear the thought. It was nearly morning, and she knew she should sleep, but she couldn't. She had been with Giles, her own true love, for one last time.

He kissed her again, his lips gentle, and she knew he was preparing to leave. He slipped out of the bed and began to dress. She followed him, standing by the bed and watching him. The moonlight bathed her body in a white light, and he came to her and took her hands in his. He pressed his lips against hers once more, then turned, and was gone.

For a few minutes she stared at the closed door, then became aware for the first time of the cold October night air. She shivered and returned to the bed, still warm from their lovemaking. She huddled beneath the covers, and the tears came, unbidden, to her eyes.

9

Early the next morning, Constance awakened Aurora, who had only fallen asleep when the first light of dawn had come through the windows, little more than an hour ago. Reluctantly, she rose, leaving the warming comfort of her bed to wash her face and hands in the cold water.

Constance returned after a few minutes and began talking briskly. "Your bath water is heated, if you're ready now, dear. Come, let's not dawdle. There's much to be done yet."

Aurora nodded, yawned, and followed Constance. She didn't linger in the bath, but scrubbed her body and washed her hair quickly. Afterward, as she combed her hair dry by the fire, she yawned, then closed her eyes. She was so tired. She wanted nothing more than to go back to bed and sleep away the day. Yet, in a few hours . . .

Aurora returned to her bedroom and pulled on her chemise and stockings just as Constance brought in her wedding gown.

"Everything else is taken care of, my dear. I'll help you dress, if you wish, and once I'm ready, we'll leave for the church, where the de Sayrevilles will meet us. Richard had mentioned something about coming to take us both with his family, but I thought it best if we waited. It isn't good luck for the bride to see the groom before the wedding."

Not good luck . . . Aurora almost laughed aloud. What could possibly happen? she wondered. Could the wedding be called off? For several minutes Constance tried valiantly to distract Aurora with tales of her own wedding day. The girl listened, without hearing. Dully she ran a brush through her hair, tangled it in a curl and jerked at it, only vaguely aware of the sharp pain in her scalp.

"Here, here," Constance said. She took the brush from the girl's numb fingers and began to brush her hair in long, firm strokes.

Finally, when her toilette was finished, Aurora began to dress. Constance helped with the elaborate collar and the fastenings. Once finished, Aurora took out a small enameled jewelry box and drew out the strand of tiny pearls Richard had given her some weeks earlier. She fastened the clasp and, taking the handmirror Constance offered her, stared at her reflection.

She was pale, almost as pale as death, she thought, and she pinched her cheeks to bring some color into them. She looked as though she wore the white makeup affected by some many ladies of the Court; today she would have no need of that cosmetic. Her eyes were red from crying, but she knew it was too late to do anything about them now. Anyone seeing her would doubtless attribute the red eyes to prenuptial nerves.

She set the mirror down, and brushed a fold of her skirt. Her stiff collar fanned out behind her neck, so that she could scarcely turn her head. Small pearls adorned the collar's lacy scalloped edges. Her bodice was gold brocade, rows of pearl buttons marching down the front; the sleeves were long and full, with silver buttons. The white brocade skirt was heavily embroidered with silver and gold thread, depicting fantastic creatures and scenes. She wore a wide, pink sash trimmed with gold braid around her waist, and upon her feet she wore gold slippers.

She supposed she looked quite pretty, but she really didn't care. "How do I look, Constance?" she asked mechanically.

Constance studied her for a moment, then a forced smile appeared on her face. "You look beautiful, my dear. A truly ravishing bride. Are you ready now?"

She took a deep breath. "As ready as I'll ever be, I think."

"Good. I'll see if the coach is ready. Wait here until I return."

Aurora nodded, then decided to sit until the widow came back. Her mind was blank; earlier, thoughts had roiled through it, snatches of conversation, scenes repeated as if in a play; now there was nothing. Nothing but pain and anguish.

10

The ride to the church was short. Too short, Aurora thought, as Constance guided her into the building. It was odd how Constance kept steering her, almost as if she feared that if she let go, Aurora would come to a standstill. As, perhaps, she might. Only vaguely was Aurora aware of the large number of people in the church. Tears had blurred her vision, and while she heard the murmuring of voices around her as she entered, she saw little beyond the tear-misted golden light of candles and indistinct, pale faces.

Aurora knew that many important people were among the guests today. Even the Queen had deigned to attend. She knew, from what Constance had been telling her for the past week, that the church was ablaze with hundreds of candles and that garlands of autumn flowers were wound around pillars. Yet she saw none of this.

She was aware only of her misery, and once more tears threatened to spill from her eyes. What an irony, she thought, that those who saw her tear-filled eyes probably thought that joy was the cause.

Constance escorted her to the altar, where masses of gold and russet flowers created a festive look, and left her there alone. A moment later someone touched her hand, and she looked up to see Richard smiling at her. His hand was warm, and involuntarily she clasped it. He was handsomely dressed in gold and blue.

The Anglican priest was a short, heavily built man with a

round face; he was dressed in a black cassock. As the priest stepped forward, he smiled broadly at both of them, then opened the Book of Common Prayer.

"Dearly Beloved," he began; something squeezed Aurora's heart. She repeated the words mechanically, all the while aware of Richard's looks of love.

"O Eternal God, Creator and Preserver of all mankind, Giver of all spiritual grace, the Author of everlasting life," the priest intoned. Suddenly the priest's voice faltered, and then stopped altogether, and she became aware of a distant shouting. She glanced at Richard, then slowly turned, and watched in astonishment as a man strode down the center aisle. She blinked rapidly, not believing what she saw.

The man was Giles Blacklaw.

11

What was Giles doing here? She stared, stunned, hoping desperately that he had come to stop the wedding. But she realized what danger he was in. How foolhardy he was to come here!

She caught a flicker of motion out of the corner of her eye and turned to see Lady de Sayreville with a shocked expression on her face. The woman looked near to fainting, and was being held upright by an equally surprised Constance. Richard stared at Aurora, bewildered.

Lord de Sayreville wore an expression of extreme hate; with no hesitation, he leaped forward and pointed toward the advancing Blacklaw.

"Guards! Guards!" he called to the Queen's Guard. "Stop him! Arrest that man!"

Involuntarily Aurora took a step toward Blacklaw, only vaguely aware of Richard's surprised stare. Blacklaw continued to approach her, brushing aside attempts to stop him with a minimum of effort, while de Sayreville insistently charged the Guards to stop the man.

Confused—for Blacklaw hadn't done anything yet—the Guards looked to the Queen for guidance. Elizabeth, one thin eyebrow arched, raised a hand slightly, indicating that they should wait. Aurora could tell that the Queen was confused, too. Richard was now staring at his father as if he had never seen him before: Philippa de Sayreville looked away from her husband.

The only sound in the church was de Sayreville's shouting. No one tried to quiet him, and he stood alone, hands clenched into fists at his sides, the knuckles white.

"Your Majesty," Blacklaw said, and he bowed in her direction. "My lords, ladies. I am sorry to interrupt such a solemn ceremony, but I must tell you something of the greatest import, and which could not wait any longer. It is only in this past hour that I have found proof of something which must be brought to your Majesty's immediate attention."

"Take him out of here!" de Sayreville shrieked, and he lunged at Blacklaw, who did not move. Several of de Sayreville's friends seized his arms and tried unsuccessfully to silence him. "Get that man out of here. Don't listen to anything he says! He is a traitor to the Crown!"

"I wish to hear what this man has to say," Elizabeth said. "Proceed, Lord Blacklaw."

He faced the Queen, and as he spoke his voice was clear and deep. "As the Queen's loyal subject, I must inform Your Majesty of high treachery."

Shouts and murmuring broke out among the gathered guests, and de Sayreville's voice could be heard above the crowd's as once more he ordered the Guards to seize Blacklaw. Blacklaw continued as if he hadn't heard the other man's outburst. "I am sorry to bear this news, but I must tell you that Thomas de Sayreville has plotted against Your Majesty."

Elizabeth turned her head and gave de Sayreville a cold look.

"It's a lie!" de Sayreville said hotly, his face flushing. "Would you listen to the word of a Catholic, of a man whose land was seized by the Crown, whose title reverted? No! What can we know?" With a visible effort, he forced himself to speak in a normal tone. "Your Majesty, I appeal to you . . . do not listen to this traitor."

"Your Majesty, Lord de Sayreville is the head of a small group of noblemen who feel that you have been too lenient in the past with Catholics and other religious dissenters." Blacklaw's voice was tinged with irony, but he continued, his eyes fixed on the Queen.

"They have met for some time now, and finally de Sayreville and his friends formed their ultimate plan—to assassinate you today, Your Majesty."

Again there was shouting, and somewhere in the back of the church someone screamed.

"In the interval after your death, Your Majesty, de Sayreville planned to set himself up as the Protector of England, a position not without precedence, as you know. He would then proceed to have Queen Mary of Scotland executed—supposedly for her previous treason, but actually because she is next in line for the throne—and then her young son, next in the royal succession, would come to the English throne as monarch. But he would be a boy-king, manipulated by de Sayreville and his friends."

"These are lies, terrible lies," de Sayreville said in a reasonable tone of voice. "Your Majesty." He smiled, but Aurora could see the sweat on his face. "Your Majesty, I would have no reason to do what this man accuses me of."

"I have proof of this," Blacklaw said, without a glance at de Sayreville, and he stepped forward and handed Elizabeth a document. She unrolled the parchment and studied it, her brow furrowed. She read it slowly, then reread it. When she was finished, she rolled it up and turned her intense gaze on Blacklaw.

"Further," and here Blacklaw first looked to Aurora, then to de Sayreville, "I can prove that many years ago Thomas de Sayreville worked against his good friend Giles Blacklaw, and cheated him of the woman he was to marry, as well as his family's lands, which de Sayreville subsequently received from the Crown."

Aurora stared at Blacklaw, then at the Queen, while Richard could not keep from looking at his mother, who kept her eyes lowered.

De Sayreville moved closer. "That man," he said, pointing with a trembling finger, "is a Catholic and a traitor. Blacklaw has never held the interests of the Crown close to his heart, Your Majesty—not as I have, always your obedient servant."

De Sayreville stepped closer to the Queen. "Even when we were mere boys, he cheated me, Your Majesty, and as we grew to manhood, he continued. It is a pattern of his life, and no one should listen to him. No one, Your Majesty. He lies."

As if sensing something, Richard called out to his father, but de Sayreville ignored him, and thrust his hand inside his jacket. Before anyone could react, he pulled out a pistol, which he cocked and aimed straight at the Queen.

Without pausing to think, Aurora launched herself against him, hitting de Sayreville's arm. He grabbed her and they struggled together, while the others around them froze. Then with a resounding crack that echoed throughout the church, the pistol fired, and Aurora slumped to the stone floor.

Everyone moved at that moment. Elizabeth leaped to her feet, while the Queen's Guard rushed forward, grasped the older de Sayreville, and snatched the pistol from his limp hand. Both Richard and Blacklaw moved quickly to the fallen girl. Philippa de Sayreville took one step forward, then sat down, a tortured look on her face. Constance rushed to where the two men knelt by Aurora. She could see that the girl was bleeding, but she didn't know how serious the wound might be, and the quicker they got the girl to a surgeon, the better.

Elizabeth, plainly irritated at the unexpected twists and turns of this story, which had begun so long ago, glared at the assembly.

"You are *all* under arrest," she announced, and she turned to leave.

"Please, Your Majesty," said Constance, going to the Queen. "It would not be kind to arrest young Aurora while she is wounded. Would you allow me to tend her at home?"

"Oh very well, Lady Westcott. We will allow this one leniency because we cannot believe the girl knew any of this. We believe she may have been an innocent dupe. But in the meantime, you and you and you"—a bony finger stabbed at Blacklaw and de Sayreville and the two members of his family—"are under arrest."

With an angry rustle and a frown for them all, the Queen left the church.

12

To Constance's relief, Aurora's wound proved to be only a flesh wound; the ball fired from de Sayreville's pistol had grazed her upper arm. After a few days of rest, she was up and walking around Constance's London house. Once in a while she felt faint; more than anything, she was anxious to know what had happened after she was shot.

"Where is Blacklaw?" Aurora asked Constance. Thus far, the widow had thought it prudent to say nothing of what Queen Elizabeth had said and done while the girl lay resting.

"He's in the Tower."

Aurora paled. "The Tower? But what has he done to deserve such treatment? What happened? I want to know everything."

Constance helped the girl to sit down, then said, "After you were shot, the Queen ordered all there—and the de Sayrevilles and Giles—to be locked up until matters can be sorted through."

"But Blacklaw has done nothing wrong—he only told her of Lord de Sayreville's treachery."

"I am sure she keeps them in comfortable enough quarters for now."

"But what if she doesn't?" Aurora realized that the others had been sent to the Tower as well, yet she had given no thought to Richard. But she was convinced of his innocence; she could not believe that he knew anything of his father's treachery. Neither could Lady de Sayreville be implicated in the plot, she felt sure. This plot could only have been the brainchild of Lord de Sayreville.

"What of my marriage?" she asked after a moment's hesitation.

"The Queen is disallowing it, so you should not worry upon that account."

That, Aurora thought ironically, was the only good news thus far. She wanted to go to the Queen and tell her of the pair's innocence. Yet how could she be completely sure of that? She had no proof. Yet, she *knew*. "What if Lord de Sayreville somehow implicates Giles? What if the Queen comes to believe him guilty of treachery? We must think of some way to help Giles escape from the Tower!"

Constance laughed, a skeptical sound. "I trow that's impossible, my dear. I know of no one who has ever escaped the Tower."

But Aurora refused to be defeated, and in that moment she realized what she must do.

Each day Aurora petitioned for an audience with Queen Elizabeth; finally, when she was about to give up hope, she was granted one. As she was ushered before the monarch, Aurora swept a low curtsey.

"Rise," said the woman on the throne. "I trust your wound is healing."

Aurora glanced down at the bandage still wrapped around her arm. The wound was hardly more than a deep scratch now, but Constance insisted that it be covered a little longer.

"Yes, thank you, Your Majesty. It pains me not at all."

"We are glad to hear of that, Mistress le Grey, for you incurred your grievous wound in saving our life." The heavy-lidded eyes stared at her, and light flickered off a diamond ring as Elizabeth moved her hand. Suddenly, Aurora realized why she'd been granted the audience.

"It is specifically because of that, that I am willing to listen to you today," Elizabeth continued. "Before we proceed, I must thank you for your service."

Aurora blushed a little and bobbed another curtsey, then looked expectantly to the monarch. The woman gazed at her shrewdly. "We come now to the purpose of your audience, for if I am not mistaken, you have a singular purpose in mind.''

"Yes, Your Majesty, I do." Aurora took a deep breath. She had rehearsed this in her mind a dozen times before she had come to see the Queen today, and still the words were difficult to speak. "I have come to speak in defense of Giles Blacklaw, Your Majesty."

"I see."

A faint smile seemed to be playing around the corners of the Queen's painted lips, but Aurora couldn't be sure. Perhaps it was simply a trick of the light that had softened her harsh expression.

"Your Majesty, I do not know what he's done in his past, for he hasn't spoken of it to me, but I do know that he would not be involved in treachery toward the Crown."

"Indeed?"

"Yes, Your Majesty. I think 'tis obvious how he wished to stop Lord de Sayreville, and I believe that you will see Giles Blacklaw's innocence."

"And what of the son? Do you think he was involved in his father's plot?"

Aurora shook her head adamantly. "No, Your Majesty. I think that Lord de Sayreville is the only villain of the family. Lady de Sayreville and her son are innocents, knowing nothing of Lord de Sayreville's treasonous activities."

The smile seemed to broaden. "You speak quite well of Blacklaw, and yet you were about to marry young Richard."

"Yes, Your Majesty." Aurora looked down at the floor.

"I see."

And no doubt the Queen did see the whole of the matter, Aurora thought. Elizabeth seemed to be one of the most perceptive people she'd ever met in her life. She blushed a little, then looked at the monarch and waited for her to speak.

"How did you come to know Blacklaw? For it is my understanding that he has not moved openly among society for some years."

"Several years ago, Your Majesty, Lord Blacklaw came to Bridewell, and purchased my freedom from that terrible place."

Briefly the girl explained to the Queen how she had come to be in the prison, and how she had come to be free once more. She also told how Blacklaw had had her educated as if she were a noblewoman.

"Extraordinary," Elizabeth murmured. "And do you know for what purpose he freed you?"

"No, Your Majesty, I do not."

"Ah, I see." Elizabeth's fingers drummed against the arm of her throne. "Well, Mistress le Grey, you mustn't worry now about them. But, too, neither can you expect for Blacklaw or your other friends to be released at once—if at all. This matter is far more complicated than you realize, and there is much to be investigated. That is all I have to say upon the matter today."

Aurora knew better than to argue further. "Very well, Your Majesty. Thank you for allowing me to speak with you."

Aurora returned home, but could report no progress to Constance. She went up to her bedroom and sat down to think over the audience. It hadn't been as productive as she'd hoped. Matters were more complicated than Aurora knew—or so the Queen said. Did this mean that Elizabeth knew that Blacklaw had acted the role of a highwayman? But that necessity had been forced upon him by poverty. And now she knew that his lands and title had been stolen by Lord de Sayreville—the father of the man she had almost married.

If Blacklaw were found guilty of highway robbery, he would be executed. If he were found guilty of treason against the crown, he would be executed. She had no choice, Aurora told herself. She would simply have to help him escape. No matter the consequences.

13

"I've had the most curious note," Constance said a few days later.

Aurora looked up from her book. She hadn't been reading, but had been thinking about how to get Blacklaw out of the Tower.

"Yes?"

"It's from someone at Court named Mary Prentice. Do you know her?"

Aurora frowned slightly in concentration. "I seem to remember a girl by that name. I think she was a good friend of Maraline."

"Hmm. Well, she wants to see both of us, and as soon as possible. What do you think I should do, Aurora?" Constance asked.

"Have her visit. It can't harm us, can it? Not after all we've been through."

" 'Tis true. I'll send a reply at once," and so saying, Constance pulled paper and quill to her, dipped the pen into the inkwell, and began writing.

Mary Prentice turned out to be the person Aurora had remembered, a quiet young woman who seemed far too nice to be associated with Maraline.

"I don't mean to intrude," Mary said, twisting her handkerchief through her hands.

"It's all right," Constance said with a reassuring smile. "What may we do for you?"

"I thought it was wrong, and that was the reason I had to come to you."

"I beg your pardon?" Constance asked, bewildered by Mary's flat pronouncement.

"I thought it was wrong, what they were doing, and so I sent the note to you."

"Thought what was wrong?" Aurora asked. "And who are 'they'?"

"Maraline and the others."

"Ah."

"And the wrong?" Constance prodded gently.

Mary turned her unblinking gaze to Aurora. "They took your cat."

"What? Lucye? How did they do it? Where is she? Is she all right?"

"Maraline paid a servant to take the cat, and she wanted to have it killed, to make it appear that you had used it in a black magic ceremony."

"A what?" Aurora looked blankly at the widow, then back at Mary.

"Maraline was going to have you accused of witchcraft."

Stunned, Aurora and Constance stared at one another, then looked at Mary for further explanation.

"I'm afraid it's all my fault, at least in the beginning. She wanted to do something to you, and because at the time I wanted to be her friend, I mentioned that I had heard you had a cat, and that you talked to the cat, as though it were human. She and the others began rumors, and Roxanne went to her father and said you were a witch. Then Maraline took the cat, and she kept it in a cage, and after some time she was going to have the cat killed, and then its death would be blamed on you."

Aurora struggled to speak calmly. "I see, Mary. And where is the cat now?"

"I hid it from Maraline. After Lord de Sayreville was jailed, she went mad, throwing everything in her rooms around and tearing things up. I was afraid she might hurt the cat. She didn't like it, and it didn't like her. I never wanted it to be hurt, nor you, Lady le Grey. Truly, I didn't."

"I believe you," Aurora said. "But now, can you tell me—or show me—where the cat is? I want her back very badly, Mary."

"Whenever you want."

Aurora glanced at Constance, who nodded. "I'll go with you now."

"Take the coach, Aurora, if you are returning to the palace," said Constance.

She nodded, and followed Mary out of the house to wait for the coach. Once they were inside, Aurora stared at Mary Prentice. Although she was glad Mary had stepped forward, she had nothing to say to her.

A short time later the coach brought them to Whitehall, and Mary led Aurora into the private compartments of those in attendance on the Queen, and cautioned, "Don't let anyone hear us now."

They walked quietly down a dusty, disused hall, and Mary pushed open a door. The room within was filled with discarded furniture, and was even more dusty than the corridor outside, and had only one window, through which the light came dimly.

"She's over there," Mary said, pointing to a far corner, dark with shadows.

Aurora felt a prickling along the back of her neck, and stepped forward cautiously. Suddenly, something, someone, lunged at her. A knife gleamed in the dim light. Aurora threw herself to one side, the knife just grazing the skirt of her gown. She whirled around and saw that her assailant was Maraline. The blonde wore a stained gown, and her long hair was disheveled. Her eyes gleamed as though from a fever.

"You," Aurora said evenly. She glanced to Mary, who was staring with shock at the blonde girl. "You thought you would lead me into a trap, didn't you?"

"No," Mary said, shaking her head. "I didn't know she would be here. Honestly, I didn't."

" 'Tis true," Maraline said with a giggle. "She didn't, but I watched her and saw what she did. I knew where she put that damned beast, and I knew she would go to you. So I waited. For you, Aurora, because you are the cause of all my trouble."

"I've done nothing."

"Because of you, Thomas is in prison, and now I may be implicated. All because of you."

"No," Aurora said, "because of your own greed, because of your own stupidity."

She saw the slight movement and so was ready when Maraline rushed at her again. The knife arched down toward her, and she ducked away from it. It was hard to move with the cumbersome furniture in the way, but she pushed a stool in front of the blonde, who stumbled. The knife fell from her hand. Aurora stooped at once and picked it up; holding it with the blade pointing toward Maraline, she said, "Now, the tables are turned, Maraline. Just stay there, so that you don't get hurt." She flicked a quick look at Mary. "Where's my cat? You said she was here? Is she?"

"Y—Yes. Over there."

Keeping her eyes on Maraline, Aurora slowly backed toward the corner Mary had indicated, and looked down. At her feet was a small metal cage. She stooped and opened it, and with a mild meow Lucye bounded into her arms.

With tears in her eyes, Aurora hugged the cat to her. The poor thing was pitifully thin. Hadn't Maraline ever fed the cat? Lucye was grateful to see her mistress and licked her chin. Aurora glared at the blonde, who was shuffling slowly toward her. "Get away from me, Maraline. I don't want to hurt you, but I will if I have to. I have recovered what is mine. Now let me pass."

"No."

"Yes." This last was from Mary, who reached out and put a hand around Maraline's wrist.

"Let her go. You've done enough to her, Maraline. Let her go home now."

"You bitch," the blonde spat. "Let go of me this instant."

"No."

Aurora inched past them. Maraline's attention was focused entirely on Mary. When Aurora reached the door to the room, she broke into a run, and didn't stop running until she reached the coach. She jumped in, told the driver to take her home and then, with Lucye pressed against her breast, she began to cry uncontrollably.

14

"I'll help you in your endeavor," John Maxwell had said. "Giles has helped me more than once."

"Thank you, John." She smiled at him, grateful for his assistance.

At her side Lucye lay curled up in sleep. She was a little heavier than when Aurora had returned home with her; no doubt because she and Constance had given Lucye saucer after saucer of milk, and some very select cuts of meat from their table. Aurora smiled and stroked the cat's side. Lucye purred in response and sleepily opened one eye.

"What do you want me to do?" asked John.

"It will be easier for you to do this than anyone else. Please, go to Tower Hill and study the fortress. Make sketches of it, if you can, so that we may know all of its features. And if possible, try to talk with someone who has been in the tower—a guard, or perhaps even a released prisoner. I need to know as much about it as possible."

"You set a high task, Aurora."

"I know that, but I know, too," she said, putting her hand on his, "that you won't fail me—or Giles. We both need you."

He grinned. "I'm away then."

He left with a wave, and afterward Aurora mentally checked his name on her list. She had only a few whom she could truly trust to help; John and Faith were uppermost on the list. She had already explained the situation to Faith, and had been about to ask for her assistance when her friend had made the request unnecessary by volunteering her help. Aurora, tears in her eyes, had thanked her with a hug, then asked Faith to learn about the Tower soldiers and when the guard was changed.

Constance might help, too, Aurora thought, although as yet she hadn't approached her. At that very moment the widow entered. "I have news for you, Aurora."

For a moment Aurora's heart seemed to twist inside her chest. What if it were bad news? "Giles is hurt?"

"No, nothing like that, my dear. But I did think you would be interested in this. Lady de Sayreville and her son have been released. They were held only under house arrest, while they were questioned about Lord de Sayreville's activities. It's said at Court that your audience with the Queen convinced her that they were innocent."

"Praise be to God," Aurora murmured. "I am glad to hear they are free. I think . . . perhaps . . . that I should see Richard."

"I think it would be only right."

"But not now. I think that when he's ready he'll come to me."

"There is more." Aurora waited. "Maraline Chambelet has been arrested and imprisoned."

"For what?" When she had returned with Lucye, Aurora had told the widow about her encounter with Maraline. She had resolved not to go to the authorities about the blonde; now it seemed she wouldn't have to worry about that.

"For her part in de Sayreville's plot," Constance said. "She was his mistress, and spied for him upon the Queen in her role as a Maid of Honor."

"How terrible for the Queen, and for her friends. How is Maraline faring?"

"I understand that she's professing her innocence most vocally to anyone who will listen, and has charged that it was you who were the instigator. I think you needn't fear anything she says about you. The Queen knows that she has nurtured an asp within her bosom these past years. Now, I must be away. I have errands to run."

"Oh, a moment, Constance."

"Yes?"

"You know that I want to somehow free Giles, do you not?"

"Yes."

"I have already enlisted the aid of John Maxwell and of Faith. Will you help us?"

The woman looked at her for a long moment, then nodded. "Yes, for you, and for Giles. Whatever you wish me to do, Aurora."

"Thank you."

When Aurora was once more alone, she stared out the window as snow began to fall, and she wondered whether she would be able to help Blacklaw. Was she just being a fool, thinking that she could actually help him escape from the Tower? Just her, and three others? She grinned.

She knew she would triumph. She had to—she loved him, after all. She remembered that night of love on the eve of her wedding, and she shivered, recalling the ecstasy of his kisses and caresses. She could not let him die.

15

In mid-November Richard de Sayreville finally paid a call upon Aurora, who welcomed him. It was apparent that he was ill-at-ease, and Aurora wished to soothe him, even though she felt a little uncomfortable as well.

"I had thought to visit you earlier than this . . . but did not."

"I understand."

"I must commend you on your bravery in saving the Queen's life. No one else moved but you. You were very courageous, Aurora."

"I did it without thinking, Richard. I wasn't even aware of what I was doing at the time—at least not until I was shot."

"Still, it was very brave. I hope your wound is better." She nodded.

He lifted his eyes to meet hers. "I don't know how to say this, and I'm not sure that you'll wish to hear it. But, I wanted to tell you that I still love you, Aurora."

Her face softened. "I know, Richard, and I care for you very much. I always have, and I think that I always will. But I have something to say, too, that you may not wish to hear. I am afraid that I do not love you. Not enough to marry you, you see." His expression was a little wistful, and she felt sorry for him—and for herself because she couldn't love this excellent man.

"I think I've always known that, Aurora. You were always good to me, and in a way I fooled myself into believing that after we were married, you would grow to love me in time. But, I didn't realize that you loved another man.'' He smiled at her surprise. ''Yes, I've been talking with Faith, and she told me. I'm glad she did, because it made my visit today easier.''

''I'm sorry, Richard.''

He shrugged slightly. ''Perhaps it's all for the best. After we were released from house arrest, my mother and I had some very long talks that we had postponed for too many years, and she told me of a man she loved when she was younger. His name was Giles Blacklaw, and she told me how my father betrayed both her and him. But she also told me something else, something that has raised me out of the despair I've felt since we were imprisoned. She revealed a secret to me, one that she's kept all these years. Thomas de Sayreville is not my father.''

''What?'' Astonished, Aurora stared at the young man standing before her.

''Yes. My true father is Giles Blacklaw. She and Blacklaw were engaged to marry, when my fa—Lord de Sayreville— betrayed his good friend. As soon as that was done, de Sayreville married my mother, totally ignorant of her condition. When she presented her husband with an heir a few weeks early, he thought nothing of it. And all these years I thought him my father, even though I hated him.'' Richard took a deep breath and ran a hand through his hair. The past few weeks had seemed to age him, and he now looked far older than his twenty years.

''I am sorry, Richard.''

He flashed a brief smile at her, giving her a glimpse of the Richard-who-had-been. ''I'm not sorry, Aurora, not in the slightest. I'd far rather be the son of Giles Blacklaw than of Thomas de Sayreville. Blacklaw is an honorable man; de Sayreville has lived a life of deceit and treason. No one could be proud of a father like that.''

And so, she thought, Philippa de Sayreville was the woman Giles had once loved—the only woman who remained in his heart, Constance had once said.

''Has your mother been to see Blacklaw?'' she asked casually.

''No, she hasn't, and I don't think she will. I think that

whatever they felt for one another is gone now. Too much has happened over twenty years. Perhaps that's for the best, too.'' He paused and smiled gently. ''I also came to see you for another reason, Aurora. As you might imagine, I feel somewhat uncomfortable, as well as dishonest, in the role of the de Sayreville heir, and have decided that I must leave England. I shall go to the continent to seek my own fortune, my own name, perhaps even my own title. My mother will leave soon after I do. She has no wish to remain here. And I do not think Lord de Sayreville will live much longer.''

''I will miss you, Richard, when you leave, truly I will.''

''And I you. The man you love is a very lucky man, Aurora. I am sorry that it couldn't have been me, after all.''

''Please, Richard, I want us to remain friends. Is that all right?''

''Yes. I will cherish your friendship forever. Thank you, Aurora. I don't want to take any more of your time; I must leave now.'' He took her hand in his and kissed it lightly, then turned and was gone.

Tears came to Aurora's eyes and spilled over onto her cheeks. She wept for this poor lost young man, denied so much by Lord de Sayreville.

''I have studied the Tower from Tower Hill, and this is what I've found,'' John Maxwell said the night he met with Aurora, Faith, and Constance. He set the sketch he had made down in front of them. ''We must pass over the Outer Moat on a stone causeway—the only way in by land—to the Lion Tower (so named because the Royal Menagerie is maintained there).'' He pointed to it on the sketch. ''Here, too, are the Lion Gate and a drawbridge. From there we move across another short causeway to the Middle Tower, then by drawbridge across the Inner Moat to the Bywater Tower.

''This tower is the gatehouse of the Outer Ward and the main entrance through the outer circuit of walls. At this point we have reached the portcullis, which should be raised at this time of the day. On either side of the archway are guardrooms, but you needn't worry about those. From there we pass through the Bell Tower, and then we are inside the fortress proper.'' He looked up. ''Any questions?''

''Not yet,'' Aurora said.

"To our immediate right will be St. Thomas's Tower, under which is Traitor's Gate. If Lord de Sayreville is sentenced as a traitor at Westminster, he will be brought in by boat through Traitor's Gate. Right next to it is the Garden Tower, where Giles is being kept," John concluded.

"Good work, John," Aurora said. "And what have you learned, Faith, about the sentinels?"

Faith carefully recounted what she had observed about the movements of the guards. When she was finished with her report, Aurora leaned back and looked at her three friends.

"I have a plan," she said slowly, "and I want to discuss it with you now."

They listened as she outlined her ideas. Constance asked a few questions, and they all discussed the plan to see if it could be improved.

"When?" Faith asked.

"We will go to the Tower on the last day of the year," Aurora said quietly. "A fitting end to this terrible year, wouldn't you say?"

16

The driver brought the cart to a stop on the stone causeway just outside the Lion Gate.

"What's your business?" a Tower guardsman called out as the man strolled toward the cart.

"I come with supplies."

The guardsman peered at the driver through the gloom. It had been overcast all day, and now fog was beginning to rise from the river. "I don't remember seeing you before. Are you a new 'un?"

John, disguised in rough clothing, with a woolen cap pulled over his forehead, nodded. "Aye, the old one—he run off with a girl what could be his granddaughter."

While the guard laughed, John glanced down at his hands, now dirty and rough with callouses. Aurora had insisted that he rub dirt into his hands and to allow them to roughen so they would look more like a carter's. He held his breath, waiting for the guard to respond; the man finally grinned and waved him through. "Go on."

John nodded to him, lifted the reins and clicked to the pair of draft horses, and the cart rumbled over the causeway through the Lion Tower, then across to the Middle Tower, and then he was stopped at the Byward Tower, where he was challenged again. He explained why he was there, and was waved through, once more. As he passed the raised portcullis, he breathed a deep sigh of relief. So far, so good. As he passed through into the Tower itself, he could not help looking around, even though it was getting increasingly difficult to see in the fog. This was the first time he had ever been this close to the fortress, and he prayed it would also be the last.

The wooden wheels rumbled along the cobbled street, past the Garden Tower where Blacklaw was held. John smiled at some of the guards, as if he were an old hand at this sort of thing, then guided the cart a short distance away to the stores, where supplies were kept. Slowly and carefully he maneuvered the vehicle against a wall. Other carts, half-unloaded, waited nearby for their drivers to resume their work. He glanced around and saw no one along the street.

"Ssst," he called softly, and something stirred under the bales and bags of supplies.

Within seconds Faith and Aurora slipped out of the cart. Both were dressed in men's clothing, with their hair pinned up under caps, and had rubbed their faces with dirt. John glanced at them and nodded, and Aurora tried in vain to smile. Faith lingered by the cart, helping John unload some of the supplies into the stores. They stacked the bales of hay and straw and bags of grain neatly, arranging them so that the supplies took up a great deal more space than they required, thus blocking the path of the other carts.

Apparently unnoticed, Aurora slipped away, moving purposefully toward the Garden Tower. She looked up at the building of grey stone and thanked God that Blacklaw hadn't been put in the huge, fortresslike White Tower.

She had a story prepared, should anyone stop her, but she doubted that she would arouse suspicion. Why should she, when she blended in so well with the carters and workmen in the enclosure? She ascended the narrow stone steps outside the Tower; once she reached the wall, she caught a momentary glimpse of the foggy river before she slipped inside. There were few rooms here, and she knew which one held her beloved.

She glanced in through the grate on the door. The room had white-washed walls and dark beams overhead, and she could see several pieces of furniture—a low chair and a stool, several small tables, and a narrow bed along the far wall. Candles in pewter bases dispelled the gloom, and clean, fragrant rushes lay on the floor. These weren't luxurious quarters, by any means, but they were surprisingly more comfortable than Aurora had imagined. Giles was sitting on the bed, reading, and had not yet noticed her presence.

Suddenly from outside the Tower, she heard cries of "Fire! Fire!"

She pressed against the doorway as a guard ran down the stairs from the guardroom at the top past her and outside. She knew what he and the other guards would find: the cart John had driven was ablaze, as planned. She heard men shouting in the resulting confusion, and she grinned. Now was the time.

She glanced back through the grate and met Giles' curious eyes. She smiled at him, but he didn't for the moment recognize her.

"Good afternoon, my lord," said Aurora.

"What? Who is that? Aurora? Is that you? Good God, whatever are you doing?"

"Stand clear of the door, Giles," she whispered as she took a small pistol from the fold of her coat.

"Stand back," she commanded again, and when he moved away, she pulled the hammer. The pistol discharged, the sound loud within the stone walls, but its noise was swallowed by the cries of those outside. The ball blew the lock away, and she pushed open the door.

Before Blacklaw could do anything more than stare at her, she seized his hand and led him quickly out of the Tower and along the wall until they reached a stairway. There they stopped and she handed him a cloak and hat.

"Pull the hat low over your face," Aurora ordered, and they descended to the courtyard.

Guardsmen and soldiers were frantically trying to put out the blaze before it spread to the nearby rooftops; only a disinterested bystander could possibly have seen that it was a rather confined blaze, after all, and probably of little danger. In London, no fire was insignificant.

At that moment a shepherdess, in whom Blacklaw saw a striking resemblance to Constance, managed to turn her herd of frightened, bleating sheep into the courtyard. The sheep, panicked by the fire and the shouts of the men, jumped and baaed desperately, milling about and adding more confusion as they managed to trip up one guard after another. The smoke and fog made a blinding combination, and it was difficult to see clearly more than a distance of a few feet. The shepherdess quietly disappeared, leaving the guards to try to push the sheep out of the courtyard.

Aurora glanced at Blacklaw. "Follow me."

"Of course," he said, with a touch of irony.

They pressed through the milling sheep and men, and the bales of hay that spread across the cobbled streets, past squealing pigs that had somehow found a way out of their pens, back through the Lion Tower.

"We're going for help!" Aurora called and jerked her thumb back toward the mêlée.

A guard, distracted by the flames that from time to time shot above the walls, merely nodded. Several guardsmen ran toward the fire to see what they could do. Aurora and Blacklaw walked quickly away from the Tower up Tower Hill along the old city wall, only pausing when they could no longer see the Tower. Out of the shadows of a doorway, three ruffians slunk forward.

Blacklaw grew rigid, but Aurora put her hand on his and laughed softly.

"Easy, Giles. These are friends."

He peered closely at them, and saw that they were indeed friends—or at least resembled them. If he were not mistaken, he was staring into the dirty, smiling faces of John Maxwell, Faith Hopewell, and Constance.

"Constance?" he asked.

"Hello, Giles," she grinned; and, rubbing some grime off onto her apron, she extended her hand.

"Come on, we don't have much time," Aurora said. "I have little doubt they will discover soon enough that their bird has flown."

In silence, the group pushed through the crowded streets, listening to the excited talk about the fire at the Tower. When finally the light began to fade from the sky, they reached their haven, an abandoned house close to the gates of the city. Once inside, Aurora lit a candle and, in the faint light, she grinned at Blacklaw. The others, weary after a long day, threw themselves down on chairs. Blacklaw said nothing, but merely stared at them, a half-smile on his lips.

"Well," Aurora said finally, her tone a little brusque as Blacklaw's silence lengthened, "aren't you going to thank us? After all, my friends and I engineered your rescue."

"You did?" he asked, as though surprised.

She nodded, and to her complete bewilderment, he burst out laughing. She stared at him, incredulous. She glanced at her friends, who were also staring at him.

"I am sorry, Aurora," Blacklaw said, aware that the silent group was looking at him as if he had lost his wits. "I truly am. I know that you went to a great deal of trouble and must have spent many hours planning this escape"—and here he had difficulty in not laughing once more—"but first, I must take you somewhere, and then all will be explained."

"Where?" she demanded. "What do you mean?"

"I cannot tell you—not yet."

She shrugged, aware suddenly of just how weary she had become. And now he wanted her to go someplace else, for whatever reason. "Very well, Giles. If you insist."

He nodded. "I do."

She turned to the others. "Constance, please return home, I will see you later."

"Will you be all right, Aurora? Should one of us go with you?" John asked. He was looking at Blacklaw as if he had never seen the man before in his life. With a frown on her sooty face, Faith stood by John's side. Only Constance did not seem completely surprised by Blacklaw's unusual behavior and request.

"Good God, John, I'm not taking her back to the Tower."

"Oh, very well, then."

As they headed toward the door, Blacklaw called to them again.

"For God's sake, all of you—wash your faces," and once more he broke into a perplexing paroxysm of laughter.

When she was at last alone with him, Aurora gave him a sober look. Had his wits been somehow addled during his stay in the Tower? He did not seem grateful, and was regarding this entire matter rather too lightly.

"Well, now, where will you be taking me, Lord Blacklaw?"

He grinned at her formality. "Come."

Under the cover of the darkness and the fog which crept silently around them, they left the house. The fog muffled their footsteps as they walked through the twisting alleys and streets. Just when she was about to ask him how much farther they had to go, Blacklaw, in an undertone, told her to stop.

He led her down into a cellar beneath what appeared to be another abandoned house. At the far corner, he pushed through some rubbish, then came to a heavy cupboard, which he touched at the top.

To her great surprise the cupboard swung silently open and revealed a door where the back should have been. Blacklaw inserted a key in the lock and opened the door. Once they were in the darkness beyond, Blacklaw paused to bring the cupboard back into place and then to lock the door once more.

As they walked through the darkness, Aurora realized that they were now under the streets of London. Faintly she could hear the rumble of carts above, and occasionally the shrill cry of a passing hawker, but for the most part they moved in silence. The only immediate sounds were the whisper of their shoes along the rough passageway and a dripping of water nearby.

She was lost, and she didn't understand where he was taking her, and why. Aurora wanted nothing more than to sit down and to rest. She was very tired after the day's activity. Why hadn't he thanked her for what she'd done? Why wasn't he grateful? She frowned. She should have known better than to expect thanks from him. Doubtless, he thought he could have done it all himself, without their help. She should have left him to it, she thought bitterly. She tried to make conversation with him, but he quietly hushed her, which only served to further irritate her.

Finally—after what seemed hours but couldn't have been much more than thirty minutes—Giles and Aurora saw the faint light of a lantern ahead. Their pace slowed, and when they reached the source of the light, Aurora saw a flight of stone stairs beyond. They ascended the stairs and Blacklaw also had a key for the door at the top. He opened it and pushed aside a tapestry.

Aurora stared around at the simply furnished room, dimly lit by a handful of candles, and thought she recognized it. It was a room she'd seen once in Whitehall. Bewildered, she turned to him.

"I don't understand, Lord Blacklaw."

"Don't you?"

"But, it looks as if—but how this can be, I don't know—as if we're in one of the rooms within Whitehall Palace."

"That is quite so," said a woman, stepping out from behind a screen across the room.

Panicked, Aurora recognized Queen Elizabeth. Now all was lost.

17

Aurora took a step backward. Terror washed through the girl as the monarch moved toward her and Blacklaw. She had labored so hard to free him . . . and now this! All gone for naught! Blacklaw saw her expression of doom and, reaching over, caressed her cheek reassuringly. "I see that I have much to explain."

Elizabeth's lips broke into what looked suspiciously like a smile. Suddenly anger and frustration grew within the girl, displacing the fear of a few minutes before. Aurora glared at Blacklaw.

"Yes," she responded tartly, "I think it is high time, Lord Blacklaw, that you are honest with me—something you have not been from the very beginning of this escapade. And the quicker you begin your explanation the better." She crossed her arms, and stepped backward, so that he could not touch her.

"Trouble, as always," the Queen said with a gusty sigh. In response he grinned.

" 'Tis true, Aurora, that I have much to explain, much of it extremely convoluted, I fear. However, I will start now," Blacklaw added hastily, seeing the angry glint in Aurora's eyes. He took a deep breath. "My love, I have been working for the Crown all along."

She stared at him, shocked by his words, then looked to Elizabeth for confirmation. With a faint smile on her thin lips, the Queen nodded.

"Indeed, I have worked for Her Majesty since I returned from Europe and found that my estates had been seized. I was furious at what I saw—rightly—as a betrayal, and at once I went to the Queen to protest. Graciously Her Majesty listened to me, and eventually found that I was right. However, because of the strictness of the law, the decision affecting the seizure of my land could not be reversed—no matter how wrong it was—and thus Her Majesty suggested as a partial restitution this service to my country, for which I would be amply rewarded. And I agreed, for I had little other choice, as you might guess."

"But then you were never in any danger in the Tower."

"That is correct," said Elizabeth, smiling at the girl, then at the man. "No harm would have come to him there. Indeed, he was there for his own safety. Mistress le Grey, I must commend you, though, on the excellent plan that enabled you to leave with my prize prisoner here. The escape was absolutely brilliant. Did you devise it?"

Aurora nodded numbly.

"Good. You have a keen mind; I like that. You see, child, I had kept Blacklaw in a cell—a comfortable one, not unlike a room in a modest inn—to keep him safe while the last of those involved in the plot were rounded up. Further, Lord Blacklaw's name has subsequently been cleared although, for obvious reasons, I still cannot publicly acknowledge him. That would prove an embarrassment to the Crown, something the Crown does not need in these troubled times."

Aurora glanced at Blacklaw, then back at Elizabeth, then once more at the man. She felt as though the room were spinning crazily around her. She reached out, blindly feeling the reassuring hardness of a chair's back, and clutched it, as if the furniture were the only thing that kept her on her feet.

"What is to be done then?" she asked weakly. "What will happen to us?"

Elizabeth was smiling widely now, a most crafty look in her blue eyes.

"I have suggested that Lord Blacklaw, who is a veritable scoundrel by nature, try his hand at something new to him. I recommend buccaneering. The waters along the faraway shores of Peru and Brazil are particularly rich in bounty, and I know that our old enemy Spain dispatches many ships there to haul away the wealth of their newly acquired territories. Lord Blacklaw's venture would, of course, be subsidized by the Crown—with a certain percentage going to the Crown's coffers.''

"Of course,'' Blacklaw said, with a gallant bow toward his monarch. "Your offer is most generous.''

"Yes, it is.'' Elizabeth looked at Aurora. "You have other questions to ask, child? You looked puzzled.''

She nodded, still confused by what she was hearing. In an hour, her world had changed. "What of the de Sayreville plot then? That was real, was it not?'' She didn't know anymore if she could tell the difference between the true and the false. The lines between them had grown faint, almost to the point of disappearing.

"Yes, it was real,'' Blacklaw said. "I had long suspected that my former friend harbored ill feelings toward Her Majesty for various reasons, and I went to her with my suspicions. And when I continued to watch de Sayreville, I found that he plotted Her Majesty's death, and that he planned to kill you, too, after the wedding.

"To my dismay I found I couldn't gather all my proof before the wedding commenced, and so with little time to lose, I rushed to the church to publicly denounce de Sayreville in order to force him to confess or to be pushed into action. The document I presented to Her Majesty was not real. It was simply a piece of parchment with names written upon it. All this was to force de Sayreville's hand,'' he concluded cheerfully.

"You almost lost me,'' Aurora said slowly.

At that moment Elizabeth winked slyly at the girl, and murmured that she would leave the couple for now. When the Queen had gone behind the screen—no doubt it concealed a door, Aurora thought—and they were alone once more in the room, the girl whirled on Blacklaw. If he had thought she looked angry before, he was dismayed by her expression now.

"I demand to know why you took me from Bridewell. Answer me now!''

"Aurora, my love.'' Giles stepped forward and tried to embrace her, but she pushed him away, and he sighed. "In the beginning,'' he admitted, "I *did* use you. I had planned

for you to marry Richard de Sayreville so that, as a member
of the family, you could act as an unwitting spy for me.

"For some time I had suspected Thomas de Sayreville, but
I could never find any evidence to implicate him. I needed a
spy at Court—you, my love—and a spy in the de Sayreville
family would be even better. At the time I did not know that
Richard was my own son. As I said, this was at the beginning
. . . my plan in theory. Sad theory," he said ruefully.

"But as the months passed, and you turned from a rough
child into a beautiful and refined young lady, I knew that I
couldn't use you in that manner, and thus many times delayed
your introduction to Court. Yet I seemed to have no other
choice. Finally, when I realized that my feelings for you were
growing deeper, I tried to turn you against me, for I thought it
was best that you forget me and what might have been
between us. After all, I was—am still—a fugitive from the
law, and in disgrace, with no name nor land. What future
could I possibly offer you? None at all."

Aurora's glare intensified. "That's the stupidest excuse I
have ever heard." Surprised, he stared at her. "I loved you
with my entire heart from the day you took me from that
prison, and I would have followed you anywhere, outlaw or
not. It didn't matter to me that you had no lands or title—I've
little use for riches I have never known. You showed me
tenderness and love; you gave me hope."

Momentarily Aurora's expression softened; then she seemed
to recover herself and said sarcastically, "And I might remind
you that I did rescue you from prison today. It would be nice
if you thanked me, Lord Blacklaw."

Immediately Blacklaw looked chastened, although she suspected that she saw a slight smile playing about his lips.

"You are most correct to remind me that I've neglected my
manners," he said, putting a hand to his breast. "I have
much to thank you for this day, Lady Aurora. You have
rescued me from the Tower and saved my life."

"Saved your life? The Queen said you were never in
danger!"

"There are other ways to be saved," he replied cryptically.
He took a step forward. This time she did not move away.
"You know, I think that we must now consider ourselves
evenly acquitted of our debts."

Unmollified, Aurora continued to glare at him. "What of Lady de Sayreville, the great love of your life?" she demanded.

"I have not loved her for many years."

"That is not what I heard."

"You must have been listening to Constance, then, my love." She nodded. "Constance acted as a jealous woman might. She could not know what lay in my heart. Only I know."

Quickly Blacklaw slipped his arms around her. She tried to shrug him away, but could not, and even then, she wasn't sure that she wanted to. He pulled her closer to him.

"I love you," he whispered.

"Lies," Aurora declared, trying hard to frown fiercely and ignore the fluttering of her heart. She wanted to harden her heart against him; wanted to, but was unable to do it.

"No lies, not this time," he said softly. "Never again, my love."

They embraced passionately, and kissed, almost as if for the first time. Their breath mingled, and deep within her Aurora felt joy spreading throughout her body. How she loved him! She responded fervently to his kisses and embraces; when they finally drew apart, somewhat shakily and very much out of breath, Blacklaw smiled tenderly at her.

"I do love you."

Aurora looked at him. "I love you with all my heart, Giles."

They kissed again, and for some time he held her and stroked her hair, which had come unpinned and now tumbled down her back.

"You know, my love, that I cannot stay in England now. I will soon have to leave. Will you come with me to share unknown and unforeseen adventures—and hardships on the far-off shores of Peru, or will you go on your own way? I will abide by the decision you make."

For a long time Aurora stared at him. Blacklaw began to feel uncomfortable, gripped by the fear that she might even now refuse him.

"It depends."

A coldness went through him. "Upon what?"

"If I can take Lucye with me."

Blacklaw stared at her, not believing he'd heard correctly, and he saw that she was quite serious.

"I am very attached to my cat," she said. "I lost her for many months, then found her, and had to fight Maraline to get her back."

"Did you, my love? Of course we will take her with us."

Suddenly Aurora smiled up at him and said softly: "The choice, I think, is quite obvious. I'll go with you, Giles. Anywhere you go."

As Aurora and Blacklaw embraced, Elizabeth, who had been shamelessly eavesdropping outside the room all this time, entered once more—this time a little more noisily. The couple sprang apart, but Elizabeth waved for them to continue, and then cheerfully called out for a minister to come and marry them at once.

"Because," she said in response to their startled expressions, "I cannot allow an unmarried—and unchaperoned—woman to travel with this rogue. Do you know, it will soon be New Year's Day. What presents will you give me?"

"We have only our loyalty, Your Majesty," Blacklaw said.

"That is quite good enough, my lord—your loyalty to me and love for each other will be my New Year's present. In this one special instance, I shall give you a present first." From one finger she pulled a heavy gold ring, set with a single ruby, and handed it to Giles. "Let this trinket do as the wedding band."

"You are most gracious," Blacklaw said, bowing and kissing her hand.

"Watch out for this rogue," the monarch said with a smile to the girl.

At that moment a somber-faced priest entered, so quickly that Aurora began to suspect that he, too, had been lingering outside the room.

The priest opened the missal and began intoning the marriage ceremony. Hearing it for the second time now, Aurora gazed up at Giles; this time, she thought, it is the right man.

And thus, with the Virgin Queen of England as their witness and as the church bells across London began ringing in the first minutes of the new year of 1587, Giles Blacklaw and Lady Aurora became husband and wife.

Highly Acclaimed
Historical Romances From Berkley

_____ 0-425-10006-5 **Roses of Glory**
$3.95 by Mary Pershall
From the author of <u>A Triumph of Roses</u> comes a new novel about
a knight and his lady whose love defied England's destiny.

_____ 0-425-09472-3 **Let No Man Divide**
$4.50 by Elizabeth Kary
An alluring belle and a handsome, wealthy shipbuilder are drawn
together amidst the turbulence of the Civil War's western front.

_____ 0-441-05384-X **Savage Surrender**
$3.95 by Cassie Edwards
When forced to live in the savage wilderness, a beautiful
pioneer woman must seek the help—and passion—of a fierce
Indian warrior.

_____ 0-515-09260-6 **Aurora**
$3.95 by Kathryn Atwood
A charming favorite of Queen Elizabeth's court, Lady Aurora
must act as a spy for the dashing nobleman who saved her life—
and stole her heart.

Sweeping Stories of Captivating Romance